THE KNOT IMPOSSIBLE

A TALE OF FONTANIA

Books in the Tales of Fontania series
The Travelling Restaurant
The Queen and the Nobody Boy
The Volume of Possible Endings
The Knot Impossible

www.TalesOfFontania.com

First published in 2015 by Gecko Press
PO Box 9335, Marion Square, Wellington 6141, New Zealand
info@geckopress.com

Text © 2015 Barbara Else
Cover and illustrations © 2015 Sam Broad

© Gecko Press Ltd

First American edition published in 2016 by Gecko Press USA,
an imprint of Gecko Press Ltd.

Distributed in the United States and Canada by Lerner Publishing Group,
www.lernerbooks.com

Distributed in the United Kingdom by Bounce Sales and Marketing,
www.bouncemarketing.co.uk

Distributed in Australia by Scholastic Australia,
www.scholastic.com.au

Distributed in New Zealand by Upstart Distribution,
www.upstartpress.co.nz

A catalogue record for this book is available from the
National Library of New Zealand

The author and Gecko Press acknowledge the generous support of
Creative New Zealand

Design by Luke Kelly, Wellington, New Zealand
Printed in China by Everbest Printing Co Ltd,
an accredited ISO 14001 & FSC certified printer

ISBN hardback (USA): 978-1-776570-03-4
ISBN paperback: 978-1-776570-04-1
Ebook available

For more curiously good books, visit www.geckopress.com

The Knot Impossible

A Tale of Fontania

RUFKIN'S TRAVELS IN FOUR ACTS

by BARBARA ELSE

~ WITH ILLUSTRATIONS BY SAM BROAD ~

GECKO PRESS

DEDICATION

Once upon a time, the world was rich in magic. It was used wisely, not wasted on anything selfish or mean-spirited. It was saved for important things like making sure babies slept safe in their cots, that people had enough to eat, and that the world was peaceful. There were dangers, as there always is with magic. But there was also common sense. Some people began to experiment with science and machines, and that was all right. You see, everyone thought somebody was in charge.

— Polly, *The Travelling Restaurant*

CONTENTS

ACT THE FIRST
A PLAGUE OF CAVE-LIZARDS

ACT THE SECOND
THE END-OF-DAYS

ACT THE THIRD
RESTLESS ADVENTURERS

ACT THE FOURTH
THE NECESSARY CHILD

ACT THE FIRST

A PLAGUE OF CAVE-LIZARDS

SALVAGE AHEAD

The luggage had red and gold stickers: *Family Summer Tour, Drama and Song.* The driver had already stowed some in the limousine. Rufkin let his parents hug him as they said goodbye, but he couldn't smile. His older brother, Oscar, promised to send postcards. His sister, Ahria, said she'd miss him. Rufkin managed to speak at last in a wobble-free voice. "Amaze them as usual. Go break a leg." His father locked the front door, then Rufkin's family drove away to the wharves and the *Lordly Sword* without him.

Rufkin had to wait on the steps for twenty-five minutes. But at last the steam-taxi hooted. Here it was to cart him and his old canvas bag off to the salvage yard.

Traffic was heavy through the city. The taxi passed Brilliant Academy, but he didn't look at it. All he could think of was a line from *The Jailbird of Battle Island*: "This is the bitter summer of discontent." He kicked the empty passenger seat in front of him.

The taxi driver eyed Rufkin in the mirror. "I should've asked for your parents' autographs. D'you have the family talent?" He put on the brakes. "Uh-oh, what's happening?"

A steam-bus sat lop-sided in the road with a broken axle.

A traffic policeman was waving like a stout ballet dancer as he tried to shift steam-cars and bicycles, steam-trucks, a tram.

The taxi moved ahead in hiccup-hops but had to stop again near City Square.

The driver gave a sour whistle. "Something's going on up by the bridge. We'll be stuck here for ages."

Rufkin sat fiddling with the hero figurine in his jacket pocket. He also had a letter from his father to the people at the salvage yard, and a twenty-dollero note in case he had a chance to spend anything in the next six weeks. It felt crisp and tough. He felt the opposite. But a treat might help. He flung open the taxi door.

"I'll be back." He raced into the square, found the zine-seller's booth, and slapped down his money.

"Latest issue of *Heroic Hodie*, please."

The seller shook his head. "Sold out."

"It was only published yesterday," said Rufkin.

"So you've still got your money." The zine-seller grinned. "How about five fanzines of *Major Murgott the Resolute*? Bargain price."

"He's old and retired," said Rufkin. "That's why they're cheap."

The man held other magazines up in a fan. "*Old Adventurers Special? Famous Inventors of Fontania...Royal Recipes for Picnics...Spies of the Nation?*"

By now Rufkin was grinning as well. "The one about spies is all guess-work."

A newsboy chanted, "Cave-lizard plague reaches City of Spires!"

"Spare an old soldier a single penny!" a beggar called.

Rufkin took back the twenty, tossed a friendly salute at the zine-seller and ran to the beggar. "Here." He stuffed the twenty dolleros in the old man's hand.

The beggar blinked. "Thanks, boy, but...are you crazy?"

Rufkin laughed, stood in the Attitude-respectful and gave a bow.

"Latest on the pla-ague," chanted the newsboy. "Public hopes Queen can resolve it with magic."

—

DONKEY AHEAD

The taxi reached the bridge at last and Rufkin's moment of good humour guttered out.

"Foundations undermined," shouted a scraggy policeman. "Foot traffic only."

Workers were struggling away with picks and shovels. Men peered into the excavations. Women young and old shook their heads, scribbled notes, and exchanged remarks.

"Scientists," the driver said. "Each with their own pet theory. Who knows why the bridge can't stand on its own two feet? Pour more cement—that should fix it."

He handed back some of the fare Rufkin's parents had pre-paid.

"That'll get you where you're going on the other side. I wouldn't cheat a son of Tobias and Maria Robiasson. That performance of *Dragon Lord and Gifted Girl* still gives me chills."

Rufkin slammed the taxi door harder than he'd meant. He had a glimpse of small craters in the roadway, even a flick of what might be a tail and a flash of blue.

A street vendor tried to sell him coffee. Another newsboy flapped a paper and cried, "Cave-lizard plague. Price of metal up again. Little duke gone missing."

The policeman shunted Rufkin through a barrier onto the walkway with other grumpy people who'd rather be having a ride. His bag grew heavy as he lugged it up the curve of the bridge. In it was a purple knitted beanie with a pom-pom. There were also patched shirts and thick pants that would last through six weeks of hard work in the salvage yard.

He reached the top. Back in the City of Spires, banners flew from the highest towers and most of the low ones. In the port, masts and funnels of the ships shone in the sun. Beneath the bridge, Lazy River flowed in its muscly way, twisting with currents. The view of the other side of the estuary stretched way down past mangrove swamps. Beyond those, Rufkin could just make out a cluster of small wharves and a roof or two. That would be the engineering yard and the marina where rich folk kept their pleasure boats. He couldn't see the salvage yard yet. His spirits sank into his boots.

He'd missed lunch. But once he was off the bridge he had to pay every last dollero of the taxi refund to a man with a donkey-cart. The animal plodded past the mangroves on a raised road edged with scrub, wooden wheels jolting and squeaking. As the cart rolled on, the donkey sped up now and then—it took Rufkin a while to notice that it happened when little craters pock-marked the roadside.

The donkey-cart man didn't talk much. He only yelled at the troubled donkey. Rufkin didn't blame it for being jumpy. He was jittery too. And annoyed. At himself. At his parents. But mostly—to be honest—he was disappointed in himself.

His mother had sighed the way she did when she played the frazzled Queen of Monkey River. "My lovely boy, I will pine for you. But we must all accept that you'll never conquer your terrible stage-fright. Mister and Mistress Mucclack will keep an eye on you. They'll make sure you are quite safe."

Did *quite* mean *very* or no more than *slightly*? He wanted to boot the side of the cart but it would upset the donkey.

The cart lurched past a new chain-link fence that glinted blue. Then came a big double gate to the marina and engineering yard, where a house was attached to a group of big sheds.

Further on they came to the gate saying *Salvage Yard, Skully and Wanda Mucclack*. The donkey-cart man tossed down Rufkin's bag. The donkey staggered a couple of steps, then galloped off the way it had come.

Rufkin followed a path to a cottage, took the steps to the veranda and used the knocker. Some flurrying sounded inside and the door was flung wide. He opened his mouth to explain who he was…

"Boots," whispered the sturdy but stooped old man who must be Mister Skully Mucclack.

"Off," mouthed Mistress Wanda Mucclack, skinny, hair streaked with gray in an untidy knot. "Put them on the rack with all of ours."

In the half-minute he'd been out of the cart, Rufkin's boots had become rimmed with black mud.

"The cave-lizards are not too bad," Mister Mucclack whispered. "You're fine in your socks up here on the veranda. Just remember, when you put your boots on again, double-knot the laces. Whatever you do, tuck your pants' cuffs into your socks."

~

Rufkin's stomach rumbled. From the Mucclacks' kitchen table, the City of Spires was a blurred backdrop of towers far over the water. Up close the view was the walkways and workings of the salvage yard, then the muddy edge of the river mouth.

Rufkin heard the far-off clang of a warning buoy. Barges of all kinds waited at anchor in the estuary to be summoned when a wharf had an empty berth for them to load or unload. A ferry cruised down from Lazy River. A steamship steamed off from the city into the haze of the horizon. A cruise ship headed out too: the *Duchess of Dogjaw*, the biggest and newest. Rufkin had read about it in a paper last week when he should have been doing last-minute study for his exams.

Mistress Mucclack sat at the head of the table, chin in her skinny hand. Mister Mucclack, gray-speckled beard, clattered a spoon against an iron pot on the stove.

"Cockles and carrots." Mister Mucclack heaved the pot onto the table. It made a sizzling sound on the wood.

"Careful, you old dolt," whispered his wife.

Mister Mucclack grinned at Rufkin and a gap showed in his teeth. "We have our rules. No loud words unless the house is on fire."

"So if cockles and carrots are not your favourite supper, merely murmur your dislike," said Mistress Mucclack. "Mind you, neither whispers nor shouts will change the menu." She served herself a bowl of pale carrots and gray cockles still in their shells.

"There might have been sea kale to add a scrap of green," said Mister Mucclack. "But I've had no time to scavenge about. Tomorrow will be my dear wife's turn to cook. Wanda, you might have time to scavenge sea kale now we have a boy to lend a hand."

"And what a boy! Tobias and Maria's youngest son." Mistress Mucclack smiled. Her wrinkles fanned out like feathers so for a moment she looked pretty, like a grandmother heron. "It's a long few years since we worked with your parents. Now they're rich and famous, and we're just busy and happy."

"So we're to teach you to manage salvage in only six weeks," said Mister Mucclack. "To save and rescue after shipwreck. To fix and mend. To use and use again. How to sort out."

"Thank you, it sounds exciting." Rufkin did his best to act the part of Truthful John Who Never Said Wrong.

"It does." Mistress Mucclack removed a woody piece of carrot from her mouth and dropped it back in her bowl. "Skully and I will have to learn it ourselves speedily if we're to teach you." The two of them shook with silent amusement. "Don't mind my tease," she said. "Salvage is the same principles as making scenery and fixing costumes, which we did for a decade or two."

Mister Mucclack opened a bottle and poured half a glass of red wine for himself and two sips' worth for his wife. The crimson label read *Bloodberry Wine, Adventurers' Rest,*

Coast of Beaks. Rufkin supposed he ought to know where that coast lay. Another school project he'd failed. Maybe dinner would lift his mood.

He gathered nerve for his first bite. The carrot—hmm, very nice. He forked a cockle from its shell and tried it. More spongy than rubbery.

Something knocked under the floor near his foot. Another bump came nearer the kitchen bench. Mister Mucclack kicked the floor with his heel.

"They're coming further up the yard every day," whispered his wife.

"You silly old chump," whispered her husband. "We didn't expect a boy, but now we've got one, don't scare him or he'll be no use."

Rufkin had a piece of cockle stuck in his back teeth but he spoke up anyway. "How big are the cave-lizards here?" The Mucclacks looked at him. "Well—if I see one, what should I do?"

Mistress Mucclack shuddered and took one sip of her wine. "Stand still. As soon as it glances away, take a careful step to higher ground. The main thing is never, whatever you do, cut off one's tail. It is said to grow instantly into a new lizard."

"We doubt it's true. We also share the thought that it's best not to find out by personal experiment." Mister Mucclack swigged his wine in one go. "The other thing is to be thankful they're not fire-lizards."

"Fire-lizards?" asked Rufkin. "Around here?"

"It's another tease," Mistress Mucclack whispered.

"We've heard that children benefit from a tease or two."

"There's no pudding, and that's no joke or trick," said Mister Mucclack. "Cockles usually call for an implement. If you've eaten your fill, take a toothpick from the jar on the windowsill."

Mistress Mucclack had her second sip of wine, pushed back her chair and gathered the bowls. "You're not a big eater for a boy. Hard work will fix that."

Mister Mucclack held up a finger. "But how strong is this boy? Teaching him is one thing. Did Tobias really expect him to be actual help?"

"He tried to explain yesterday evening over the phone, but it was all buzzing and hiss." Mistress Mucclack picked the letter from Rufkin's dad off the dresser and read it again. "If and how the boy helps is up to us. He is here because he can't succeed on stage. And at school…" She let out a low whistle and folded the letter. "I'll just say woeful."

"I made the C Team in slogball. That's an improvement," said Rufkin. "I nearly made the debating team."

His father had waved the paper headed *Brilliant Academy— End of Year Statement of Success*. "My boy, in every subject, the teachers say you could be good but you never try. For Mathematics it says, 'must learn to try harder,' then you've got unending dittos. Geography. Science. Even in Physical Exploits. Cross-country— slogball—gymnastics. It's saying fairly nicely that our son is lazy."

His mother had held his ears so he had to look at her. "It can be good for a child to have early struggles. It makes them resilient. Rufkin, you are a bobbing cork. You float through each day as if nothing matters but having fun. If the stage is not an option, you must try elsewhere. That means, first of all, improving at school. And learning about hard work!"

Mistress Mucclack, oven dish in her hands, peered at him. "The boy's turned peaky. The remedy is an evening stroll around the yard."

Mister Mucclack winked. "What every old man needs at his side is a clever and kind old woman."

Mistress Mucclack went pink in the cheeks. "A sweet old man deserves no more."

"That can be your second lesson on happy marriage, Rufkin. A compliment each morning, a second one every night." Mister Mucclack gave a satisfied grumble. "Now, back in your boots. Don't worry too much. At dusk the cave-lizards tend to be sluggish."

—

STORM AHEAD?

Rufkin knotted his boots as tight as he could and tucked in his pants' cuffs. He took a wary step from the veranda, then trod over planks that bridged channels of mud. He was thankful when they reached a solid path. In front of him, the Mucclacks walked arm in arm through the salvage yard. It was full of junk but still so tidy his eyes hurt. The boats were lined up neat as cutlery on cradles and at two small jetties.

Another chain-link fence separated the yard from the engineering business and marina. That looked even tidier: huge square workshops, rows of boatsheds, slipways and ramps, locked gates to walkways where vessels were moored in a fishbone pattern. Clean concrete paving led right to a high wooden fence at the far side. Rufkin couldn't see over it, but beyond must be the mangrove swamp.

"We stay on our own side of the chain-link. No going over, that's the rule," Mister Mucclack said in a low voice as Rufkin joined them.

The light was going faster now, the sky a purple-gray sheet behind funnels and masts. Lights started to twinkle in the port and in city towers. It was so pretty it made

Rufkin's heart ache. He dropped back. Twinkles showed on the estuary too: blue port lights of boats making their way to the wharves, red sparkles of starboard lights from ships steaming out on the tide. By now his own family would be well over the horizon aboard the *Lordly Sword*. Oscar might be writing the first postcards he'd promised. Then again, probably not. He'd be rehearsing the violin, trumpet, and drums. His sister Ahria would be singing along. They'd have six weeks of summer on stage with his mother and dad. Rufkin's throat ached too with missing them.

A private yacht with a glowing blue B on its funnel came swiftly from the city to pass Tiny Isle. It belonged to Madam Butterly, the richest person in Fontania. Rufkin's parents knew her. She'd had that super-yacht for ages but it still made every other ship look second-rate.

The breeze gusted sharp. The warning buoy clanged. How brave and lonely it sounded. He heard another sound, like a high voice calling once. *Help!*

A shiver went down Rufkin's spine and through his stomach. He ran to the Mucclacks. "Did you hear that?"

The wind blew another gust. A goose flew overhead—*ornk.*

"Birds," said Mister Mucclack. "Finding a roost."

"Or an early night bird waking up," said Mistress Mucclack. "Mind your footing."

Six more geese flew in a V-shape, calling against the gray sky. Rufkin shook off the scary moment.

Mister Mucclack started to point here and there: ships with their sides peeled off, ships with their bows staved in, other ships merely ancient and past it.

"Over there are the hulks we're saving for scrap," said Mister Mucclack. "They'll be stripped of their innards. Those ones are due to be towed away to be restored. That lot over there, they're new but they're leaking—no idea why. But they'll be dumped. It all needs guarding and sorting, so this is where you'll be till your parents send someone for you."

He sounded as if Rufkin would be here forever.

The wind whistled through holes in the sides of a sailboat.

Mistress Mucclack put her hands over her ears. "No storm was predicted, was it?"

Skully Mucclack hunched his shoulders. "We can't deny it seems set for a top-notch hurricane."

"It won't get worse than this," Rufkin said. "The Queen would manage it. She'd never let a storm damage the City of Spires."

"She's busy with the Council of Wisdom and the cave-lizards," said Mistress Mucclack. "The royal riverboat set off two days ago crammed with scientists and advisers, all banners flying."

The Mucclacks moved on. Rufkin didn't like the idea of his family on Old Ocean if there was going to be a hurricane. Nor did he like the idea of being in a cottage on the edge of the estuary, with Queen Sibilla out of town. This summer King Jasper was on vacation for the first time in eighteen years. He was at the far end of Lake Riversea with his wife Queen Beatrix and their children. For the first time his sister, Queen Sibilla, was in charge on her own. *It is a challenge for which I am eager*, she'd said in all the papers. *Now I am grown up it is time to be fully responsible*. Rufkin didn't call it being fully in charge or responsible if she had help from the Council of Wisdom and one of the dukes had gone missing. Which one might it be? He thought there were dozens.

The wind gusted again and shoved Rufkin off balance. He pretended he was ducking about on purpose and ran past the Mucclacks and down a jetty.

"Boy!" hissed Mister Mucclack.

Rufkin walked more slowly, past ghostlike boats. The estuary had an oily gleam.

Something in the water caught his eye. It was a bit of wood with one end that looked chewed. There was an H and an E on it, but any other letters were awash. He fished in his pocket for something to throw. There was only his Lord Hodie figurine.

He heard Mister Mucclack's boots behind him, a fierce whisper, "Come back." His jacket was gripped at the waist by a strong hand.

Rufkin was glad to go. The wind was thumping at him now. They returned to Mistress Mucclack, hands to her head as if the breeze would unravel her knot of gray hair.

"Back inside," she said, "before this wind whisks under our coats and balloons us over the sea to Little Skirmish."

"There was lettering on a board," said Rufkin. "H and E, something."

"The name of ship, maybe," said Mister Mucclack. "The *Helfrida*, or the *Hello Peter*. Water chews words away."

Rufkin ran ahead over the walkways. He'd thought for

a moment the word on the board could have been HELP, in awkward capitals like a child uses when it starts to learn. And the chewing seemed done by jaws rather than water. He shivered again at that moment of fright that had gripped him.

Boots off, inside, Rufkin peered through the curtains into the dusk. In the channel, shipping lights floated as if everything was calm. But masts in the marina glinted as they tossed to and fro. Scraps of paper, dead leaves, and empty cans whirled in the salvage yard. The storm was so wild that the roof began thrumming like a pot on the boil.

HARD WORK AHEAD, BLAST IT

All night the roof thrummed. All night wind battered the windows. The sheets felt damp. Rufkin dozed, woke, and listened; dozed again. Weeks to go—of this and the Mucclacks. For goodness' sake, it wasn't as if he'd never tried at Brilliant Academy. He'd come twenty-fifth out of thirty-five in the cross-country. That meant ten in the class were slower than him. Not everyone could come top in Mathematics or Geography. Oscar and Ahria did in their classes, but they were outstanding at most things. And they never had stage-fright so bad it froze them to the spot like it did Rufkin, blinded, deafened, blood hammering in his ears.

"Life isn't fair," he heard himself say aloud. Then he must have slept deeply. He seemed to be in his own bedroom. It was crammed with the latest and best toys and gadgets. That bit was true, though he knew he was dreaming.

Next thing, sunshine glowed through the spare-room curtains at the Mucclacks' house. The wind lay quiet. He hoped breakfast wouldn't be a repeat of cockles and carrots.

A mumble began through the wall—the Mucclacks' voices, low but still clear. He pulled the blanket over his head. It grew stuffy and prickly. He pushed it down for air.

"…six whole weeks," Mistress Mucclack said in a carrying whisper. "A child."

"If we'd wanted a child, we would have found one of our own," said Mister Mucclack.

"You have to feed a child. Find clothes that fit it. Keep it away from dangerous things," said Mistress Mucclack. "Entertain it."

"We'll make hard work fun," said her husband. "He can watch me drive the bulldozer while he picks up rubbish. He can gather scrap, load it in the metal crusher, then watch me crush it."

"After that bad night, I can't face taking care of a child," said Mistress Mucclack.

"Go back to sleep," said her husband. "I'll lie and think till I hear the boy up and about."

Work ahead. Hard work and boring. Rufkin slid out of bed. It was lucky his clothes had no noisy fastenings. He crept to the kitchen but didn't dare grab any food in case he alerted the Mucclacks. The door closed behind him with a faint click and he tied on his boots. Cave-lizards—he'd heard them under the kitchen floor but he'd seen no sign of them. Just teasing, those Mucclacks.

Sun struck the highest spires over in the city. The estuary flickered with points of light. The summit of the bridge was in view, gleaming as if the storm had polished it. It was hard to believe last night had been so terrible. The wind had scoured the salvage yard clean as well, or at least packed litter away into corners and nooks.

The walkways looked slippery. Rufkin didn't want to tread on patches of gravel in case they made a crunch, so he set off for a solid path that led toward the fence. He'd be able to see the engineering yard through the chain-link.

He tripped over a sudden bulge beneath his feet and landed flat. *Ow!* The bulge burst like a blister and spurted out gravel. Down the hole that was left, Rufkin saw a tail, a gleam of luminous blue—the tail vanished. Rufkin crouched, holding his breath.

Another flick—then a cave-lizard's snout appeared at the rim of the hole and sniffed. The creature was no bigger than a kitten but its teeth were rows of little needles. Rufkin had forgotten to tuck his pants into his socks. Where was Mister Mucclack with a shovel to give it a wallop? Where was Mistress Mucclack with her boots to give it a kick?

Another cave-lizard put its claws on the rim beside the first. Its black eyes flashed. It spotted Rufkin, stiffened and stared. Rufkin's breath seemed stuck in his lungs. The cave-lizard darted right at him—his hand brushed an old red bucket, something touched his ankle, he snatched the bucket and swung it down. The lizards fled underground.

Shuddering, Rufkin brushed his pants' leg to make sure nothing was up it. He stuffed the cuffs tightly into his socks. Then he dropped a rock down the hole and glanced back at the cottage. Nobody was stirring. He'd go on to the fence, but very carefully.

It was a fair trudge past the row of cranes, the bulldozer, and the metal crusher. At last Rufkin came to the fence. It was strong old wire-link, except for one section that had the bluish gleam of that new metal, what was it called? It began with a Z. Zirbonium.

He didn't want the Mucclacks to catch him climbing over. But the tide was low and the fence ended at a rocky outcrop. He could climb around there. All he wanted was one quick look.

Rufkin gripped the wire and edged for the rocks. Bubbles swelled in a patch of mud and made glistening circles. A bigger bubble burst near his feet and he smelled something foul. He laced his fingers into the wire links and braced himself. This had been a bad choice. He'd gone a bit sweaty. The outcrop looked slimy. He'd probably slip.

A seagull cried overhead. Another cry came from somewhere along the shore. In the marina? It sounded like a cry for help again but must only be a wading-goose. He craned to see any signs of life. Not even a feather.

He should trudge back to the cottage for what might be a terrible breakfast.

Rufkin thought about it for a heartbeat, then the cry came again. It sounded like a lonely child much younger than he was.

—

RESCUE AHEAD

Would the cry come a third time? All Rufkin heard was a musical jangle of ropes on the masts in the marina. He thought of calling out himself. Why wasn't anyone else around yet?

He struggled on around the slippery outcrop, climbed carefully over some collapsed tangles of security wire, and clung to the other side of the fence while he edged up to the concrete paving. The doors of the engineering sheds looked bolted shut.

By being here at all he was trespassing. But anyone would expect a boy to be curious. If someone came, he'd just say he heard someone cry out. If he'd been misled by a bird call, he'd promise not to do it again and give a smile. He'd have missed an hour or two of gathering trash anyway. Besides, the concrete paving was totally safe.

He ran over the engineering yard into the marina. The private sailboats and steamboats, even a small red paddle steamer, all seemed deserted. Last night's storm had been so strong, heaps of boats should have slipped their moorings. But only two were swinging about. Rufkin hurried to the very last mooring and checked whether something, perhaps a cabin boat, was bobbing out of sight on the low tide. No. Just a few sticks and the back end of a toy elephant.

The storm had wrenched some boards off the wooden fence. Through the gaps he saw a stone reinforcing wall. It led down to the swamp, where branches had been torn off some big mangroves. Further into the swamp, something of a fair size lay at an angle. It could be a vessel blown there by the storm.

Another faint cry sounded. Rufkin couldn't tell if it was a gull or a *help* or imagination.

What would Lord Hodie do? Check it out.

The broken boards could make good footing. He picked one up, poked it through the gap and tossed it so it fell flat. Yes, it might do. He'd be able to carry maybe two boards at a time. Would they reach as far as the thing he could see?

It took a while, clambering up and down the sloping stone wall, heaving and dragging. He used broken mangrove to make extra footing. He slithered only once and landed with one hand and one foot down in the mud. Something moved under his palm. He leaped up so fast he surprised himself. He'd gone very sweaty.

As he neared, he saw that it really was a ship lying there, one with a flat bottom and a small upper deck. A riverboat, scooched deep into mangroves and mud. It must have been here for months. At high tide it would be underwater. The metal sides were blisters of rust. There was a funnel, and two short masts, one of which had broken near the base and hung over the side. Parts of the wooden railing were shattered. There was nobody up on its deck.

Rufkin had run out of boards. He nearly turned back. But a hero like Lord Hodie would keep going. Was there was any way onto the boat? Not up the dangling mast. Its snarl of wire looked very tricky. But maybe there was a ladder bolted to the side. Or a length of chain he might be able to use—ah, there was a rope. He could step close enough to give it a yank and find out if it was firmly attached to something on board. But he'd have to stand in a stretch of mud. His skin prickled all over.

Even if I came third to last in gymnastics, he told himself, *nobody's here to laugh if I give it a go.* He made three leaps, three more, and grabbed the rope. He kicked up, the rope swung him, and he bashed his shoulder. He swore and kicked again. In five more kicks he reached the railing and toppled aboard. He sat up and grinned.

This would have been a wonderful ship when it was new. He could see how cheerful the brasswork must have been; could almost smell pies keeping hot in the galley, taste an ice-cream-on-a-stick from the chiller-cupboard.

"Help," said a small voice. It came from the cabin.

~

Rufkin had acted frightened many times in rehearsals for the family tours. But he'd never been truly frightened before today, when the cave-lizard nearly went up his pants' leg and when he'd felt that live thing in the mud under his hand. This third fright, right now, made his mouth go dry. He crept along ready to leap back over the rail in the next second.

A sheltered porch was set in the overhang of the upper

deck. There he found a sliding door, open the breadth of a hand. He dared to look in.

At first all he made out was a dull brass fretwork of ducks on an overhead beam. He eased into the cabin. There was a counter, stairs to the upper deck, and padded benches around the walls. One of the long cushions lay on the floor—and there was something on it.

Rufkin's mouth went drier. After a moment he edged closer…

It was just a puppet, grown-up size, with a purple and red coverlet up to its shoulders. Its eyes were closed, its face and frizzy hair thick with a rusty dust tinged with blue.

Something clattered. Rufkin jumped. From behind the counter crawled a child. Boy or girl, he couldn't tell.

"Help," it said.

—

HELLO AND HELP

"Hello," said Rufkin. It was the only word he could think of and seemed good enough.

The child had round gray eyes. Its face was smeared with—at a guess—previous meals, old tears as well as fresh ones, the smudges of playing in sandpits and with play dough, and some of that rusty-blue that was on the puppet. Its clothes were what Rufkin saw on most kids that age: a sort of waistcoat, a striped long-sleeved top, and soft trousers, all smeared like its face. No shoes, just a pair of gray socks.

"Who are you?" asked Rufkin.

The child blinked. "Help."

"I've got that," said Rufkin slowly. "Are you a boy or a girl?" It wasn't the sort of question he'd ask of anyone older than three or four.

The child looked at Rufkin's work pants, then patted its own legs.

"A boy like me?"

The child didn't shake its head. Rufkin supposed that meant a yes.

"I'm Rufkin," he said. "What's your name?"

The boy said nothing.

"Nobody else here? Nobody but you?"

The boy frowned. He still said nothing.

"How old are you?" Rufkin asked.

The boy held up two fingers on each hand and twisted his skinny wrists to check from both sides.

"Four," said Rufkin. "Help. That's what you want."

This time the boy gave a grin.

Rufkin had better take the kid back to the Mucclacks. They could call the police or whatever. He reached out a hand, but the boy slipped back behind the counter. Well— that was probably okay. He'd be safer staying here than following Rufkin down the side of the boat and into the mud and over the boards and around the slippery rocks at the end of the Mucclacks' fence.

"Wait, then," said Rufkin. "I'll be back as soon as I can." Silence.

"By the way, did you write the word on the bit of board? Was it 'help'?" Silence, but somehow a different sort of silence.

"It was a good 'help'," said Rufkin. "Good letters."

The silence was pleased.

~

Rufkin slid back down the rope and jumped at once to reach a board and balance on it. He didn't know how he'd managed. He didn't know how the board stayed on top of the mud either. But it did, so he wouldn't question it.

Sun made a sheen on the mud. It was so bright that he shaded his eyes with one hand above them, the other below to make a portal to see through. He tried hard not to think of cave-lizards and sprang from one board to another, then up through the gap in the fence to the concrete paving.

The wavelets on the estuary were starting to creep higher. He'd better hurry. But somebody was moving around on the other side of the fence that marked the road he'd come along in the donkey-cart only yesterday.

"Ahoy!" he called, then felt stupid. It might sound as if he was pretending to be a sailor. It was what his father would shout in similar circumstances, but people expected it from the famous actor, Tobias Robiasson. They also forgave him most things because of his being a celebrity.

The person straightened up and peered at him through the chain-link. It was a girl with her hair in braids. She was oddly dainty yet dressed for dirty work, completely covered in a pink boilersuit. She wore pink-spotted rubber boots, and carried a stout basket. She also wore green rubber gloves.

Rufkin hurried over the paving. "Listen…" he began.

"You don't look rich or famous but you're the Robiasson," she said.

It wasn't easy but Rufkin smiled. His dad always said that a smile costs nothing but can win plenty. "There's a little boy. He's lost. He needs help."

The girl glanced around. "Where?"

From here, because of the raised area and the fence, Rufkin couldn't see any sign of the riverboat. "There's a boat stuck in the mangroves. We need to fetch someone."

The girl tilted her head as if he was an item in an exhibition. "You're trespassing."

"I know," said Rufkin. "But because I'm doing it, I also know we really need to find someone. A couple of men from the engineering shed. Or at least the Mucclacks. But their phone's been acting up. Can you use yours and call the police?"

The girl frowned as if she didn't believe him and walked away. She bent down to the muddy strip between the fence and the road, and put something into the basket. Rufkin followed on his side of the fence.

"There's no absolute hurry," he said. "But he's a very little boy and the tide's turned. So in the next half-hour, help would be good. It's more important than collecting whatever you're after."

The girl glanced at the foot of the fence where the edge of the paving looked nibbled. "There's a good one. I can't reach it. Toss it through to me."

The only thing he saw was a small mud-filled crater in the paving. It had circles where a bubble had burst. Then, in the centre, a sort of solid curve emerged. No way was he going to touch that.

"Go on," she said. "I saw it first. It's worth part of a penny."

She was so bossy that Rufkin wanted to march off. But she would think he was scared. Which he was.

He looked again. She'd been gathering the things herself from the edge of the road. Her basket was full of them.

He snatched it up as fast as he could, a small circle like a ring, dull blue metal, warm on his fingers. He stuck his hand through the fence and lobbed it at her. She clanked it into her basket with the others.

"What is it?"

She gave another scornful look. "It's a cast from the lizards."

A jolt went through him. "They make casts? You mean it's their droppings!"

"Only sort of. It's mostly metal. Wipe your hands on your pants, you'll be all right." She held the basket against herself and smiled.

He wiped his hands on his backside as hard as he could.

"I'm Nissy Symore." It wasn't a smile, it was a grin. There was an important difference. "You're Rufkin Robiasson, son of Maria and Tobias Robiasson. You're to stay with the Mucclacks. I heard them whispering. They'll be paid for having you and they'll be nice to you. They don't like me. My mam's not rich like your parents. But I will be." She shook the basket. The lizard casts rattled. "This is how I'm starting out."

Why should he care about any of her plans? He glanced at the engineering sheds. Still no one in sight. "If you're not going to help, I'll run to the Mucclacks."

"Help? Of course not. You're only acting some game." Nissy took a spotted notebook from her pocket and began jotting in it.

What a useless girl.

Nissy put the notebook away and kept scanning the verge of the road for more rings.

"Listen. The boat's been in trouble since last night, I think," said Rufkin. "It looks ancient but it must have come ashore in the storm. How else would the kid get there?"

But no. He'd heard the boy call and seen the board with the H and the E right at the beginning of the storm. So the boat must have got there earlier.

"The little kid is all on his own. Honestly. If you don't believe me, stand on something so you can see better."

Nissy put the basket aside, stood on a patch of shingle, then set a toe of her boot into the chain-link. She climbed partway. "Nothing." She jumped down again.

Rufkin set his own boot into the fence and struggled up. He couldn't see anything either. Some of those mangroves were huge. Which meant the tide would come in deep, he knew that much.

He clambered to the top, swung over, and landed on hands and knees beside her. "Please—the Mucclacks are pretty hopeless and so is their phone. I'll pay to use yours." He had that twenty dolleros. No, he didn't. The old soldier had it.

For a moment Nissy looked interested. "How much pocket money do you get when you're rich? Do you still have to do chores for it?"

It was none of her business. "Please let me use your phone."

"Mam would ask why. I can't let her know I've been out," said Nissy. "For one, Mam's not keen on the lizards. They've grown bad round here and they're much worse this morning. For two, she didn't like that storm either. She said it was only over this part of the estuary." Her forehead crinkled. "Mam's been working too hard. So have all our mechanics now ordinary metal's so expensive. And the customer complaints! There's more each day. You rich people don't have a clue."

"My parents give millions to charity," said Rufkin. "They earn every cent."

She picked up another cast, then tossed it away. "Not worth it. Broken."

Rufkin's hands clenched. "There's a little boy in trouble."

Nissy shot him a sideways glance and walked off.

—

A SLICE OF THE BLACK STUFF

At least Rufkin was on the road now. He ran for the salvage yard gate, down the path to the Mucclacks' veranda—oops, tugged off his boots and flung them at the rack—then was into the kitchen.

They were in matching brown robes and striped nightshirts. She was stirring what smelled like porridge. He was burning what smelled like toast.

"You've not been out already?" Mistress Mucclack said in her whisper.

"Don't let Tobias and Maria know you slipped out while we were snoring," added Mister Mucclack.

"Phone!" Rufkin gasped. "Where's the phone?"

Wanda Mucclack pointed the porridge ladle towards a stack of brooms and a floor mop.

Skully Mucclack guided his wife's hand with the dripping ladle back to the pot. "Why do you want a phone before breakfast, Rufkin?"

In sentences as short and clear as possible, he told the Mucclacks what he'd seen. "And the tide's coming in," he finished.

Both Mucclacks stared at him, then at each other.

"It must be one of his games," murmured Mistress Mucclack.

Rufkin bunched his fists. "But it's true. A little boy. That girl didn't believe me either."

"Girl." Mistress Mucclack's face went even more skinny with disapproval. "That Nissy, I suppose. She's a stubborn one. Oh, Skully, my dear, here is another problem with having a child. Other children torment and oppress them."

Mister Mucclack scratched peanut butter on the blackest piece of toast and started crunching. He seemed to say something while he chewed, unless it was only untidy chewing.

"Swallow," whispered his wife. "Now try again."

He did. "It would be even worse if you were the parent of a tormentor and bully. Imagine how ashamed you would be, how disappointed in your ability as a young one's upbringer. You might disguise your sadness with rage and thus turn into a bully yourself. Did you bully the girl first, before she harassed you?"

Grown-ups were meant to help. "This is abysmal," muttered Rufkin.

"He said the most difficult word when all he means is 'very bad'," Mistress Mucclack said, and smiled.

Rufkin spotted the phone at last, on the wall near the stack of brooms. Most of the wall looked rickety.

"May I?"

Before they could say no, he picked up the handset. There was only a breathy snarl. He pressed O for Operator. It gave a fizz and two hisses.

"Reception's very bad the last few days," Mistress Mucclack murmured. "It is *abysmal*. Something could be nibbling the wires. Water rats. Maybe those lizards. If it is cave-lizards and the Council of Wisdom doesn't do something, we could hold a demonstration and carry placards."

Rufkin looked out at the estuary. The tide hadn't started rushing yet. But it would.

"Dear boy?" Mister Mucclack held up the toast rack. "A slice of the black stuff?" A spark flew from the toaster and there was a bang. "Curtains for that," said Mister Mucclack.

"Three new toasters in the last three months," breathed his wife. "And the cost keeps rising."

Rufkin began to think he'd imagined the riverboat, the puppet on the mattress, the strange little boy. Had he even been outside? Could it have been just a waking dream?

~

Rufkin sat down, remembered touching the lizard cast, jumped up, rushed to the bathroom, and scrubbed his hands with a nail-brush.

Of course he hadn't imagined it. He was used to illusion. The son of great actors was familiar with make-believe, stage tricks, and so on. There really was a deserted or lost child there in the swamp.

Rufkin had been sent here in the first place to learn to try hard. So he sat at the table, chose the least burnt slice of toast, and spread it with honey. He chewed fast. Then he jumped up and bowed to the Mucclacks as if he were a prince and they were equally important aristocrats. "Thank you for a substantial breakfast."

They chuckled and nudged each other.

"Now I'll make myself familiar with the salvage yard. I'll walk about with care." He bowed again and left the kitchen.

Behind him Mistress Mucclack chuckled. "He talks like a serious book, the little dear. And he does so poorly at school?"

Rufkin felt his face redden. Lucky no one could see. He jammed his feet back into his boots. The sun and a light breeze had dried off the walkways. Up in the engineering yard there was still no sign of any mechanics. And no sign of Nissy, thank goodness.

He hopped up on the biggest bulldozer to see past the marina into the mangroves. At first there was no glimpse of the broken boat. Then a glint of sun showed what might be the tip of a mast.

Something splashed near the shore behind him. He jumped and stung all over with fright. But it was a pair of fishermen rowing a large old dinghy. He clambered down and picked his way to the water's edge, trying to stand on stones that might protect him from any cave-lizard. His boots were solid. He checked that he'd tucked in his pants' legs.

"Ahoy!" he called.

"Ahoy, boy!" a fisherman called back. They didn't stop rowing.

Rufkin smiled to show he was friendly, and pointed upriver. "Do you see that boat in the mangroves?"

The men stopped now and shaded their eyes.

"You might not," said Rufkin. "It must have got stuck there before last night's storm. There's only a little boy on board."

One of the fishermen laughed. "You're convincing, lad. You should be on stage. Last night was calmer than custard."

They started rowing again.

"Please, tell the coastguard! Get the police launch!" shouted Rufkin.

They rowed harder, as Rufkin would himself if he had to get some distance from a crazy boy.

"There was a storm," he said aloud. "I felt it. I heard it. So did the Mucclacks and Nissy."

All right. He must persuade the kid to come with him to the Mucclacks. They could hardly say a four-year-old didn't exist if one stood in front of them.

~

Rufkin struggled around the outcrop again. Waves splashed there now. He slipped and soaked one of his boots. He hauled himself along the other side of the fence and back into the engineering yard. The fishermen's dinghy was motionless in the estuary, like a boat in a painting. A tanker was heading for port in the City of Spires. He hoped its wake would chuck the fishermen out.

By the time he'd crossed to the stone wall, more and more bubbles were bursting down in the mud. There were plenty of lizard rings too, hard with a blue rainbow-ish sheen which might have sounded nice if he'd tried to describe it but really was nasty.

Somehow the boards he'd laid were still in place. And here he was at last, back at the riverboat. This time it took only six kicks to reach the deck.

"It's me again," he called. "Hello!" He looked into the cabin.

The puppet still lay on the long cushion but the boy had moved it. Now it had an arm up beside its head. The kid sat on the floor next to it. He held a jar with half a cookie in it and had crumbs on his chin.

"What's your name?" asked Rufkin again. "Call me Rufkin, because that's mine."

He expected it to be too tricky a joke for a four-year-old, but the boy's mouth twitched in a smile. He didn't give his own name in return though.

"Do you like toast?" asked Rufkin.

The boy fished the half-cookie out of the jar.

There wouldn't be toast, anyway, because of the exploded toaster. "What about porridge?"

No reaction.

"Fried banana? Eggs?" asked Rufkin. "Eggs with peanut butter on? Let's go and find some. Come on."

"Help," said the boy, but he didn't move except to tug the coverlet over the puppet's blue face.

"Look. You say you want help. I'm trying to give it." Rufkin noticed he was standing with his hands on his hips, like his father. That might look bossy and bullying, though his dad was mostly neither unless he was acting.

Rufkin had seen frazzled parents at parties and in shopping malls, so he knew there'd be screams if he tried to pick the boy up and haul him along. So he scratched his head, gave his best smile, and held up his hands like little plates in the gesture that said *What shall we do?* Without a smile the boy copied.

Someone outside called, "Hello?"

Rufkin darted onto the deck and looked over the side. "Nissy!"

She peered up. Her basket was full to the brim with cave-lizard casts. "So you weren't lying. Not about the ship at any rate."

Rufkin didn't bother to dignify that with a reply. "Hurry back and tell your mother."

But Nissy set the basket down on the end of the last board and took off the green gloves. She jumped a couple of strides and put her hands on the rope. In only four kicks of her pink spotted boots, she was on deck.

He moved his right arm in a welcoming gesture towards the door, then followed her in.

"Oh, my stars," she said. "I should have believed you."

⁓

REVERSE AHEAD

Nissy wiggled her fingers. "You're meant to pinch yourself to see if you're dreaming. I could pinch him to see if he's real."

"Don't be mean," said Rufkin. "He was eating cookies. Just feel the crumbs."

Nissy crouched so she was on the same level as the little boy. For the first time Rufkin liked her—a tad.

"What's your name?" she asked.

The boy widened his eyes then blinked. Maybe the only word he knew was *help*. But he was clever enough to write it as well, or at least write an H and an E.

A screech sounded outside in the mud. Not a nice sound.

"The Mucclacks' phone still isn't working," said Rufkin. "Now you know I'm not joking, can I use yours? Oh— that is..." Poor people sometimes didn't have phones, or mechanical message-birds unless they were second- or even third-hand and, therefore, likely to lose a wing or tail feathers and disappear without delivering anything.

Nissy stood up. "We won't tell Mam I was out here. She might guess, but I'll say you bossed me. The phone will be working by now, with any luck."

"Your phone wasn't working either?" asked Rufkin.

She shrugged. "It's off, then it's on again, then it's off. Now, kid," she said to the boy, "you have to come with us."

The boy stayed at the foot of the mattress.

"Suit yourself." Nissy bent to look at the puppet. "What a mess." She straightened up. "Come on. We'd better hurry."

What had Rufkin been saying since he'd first seen her? She was very annoying. "Hang on a tick and don't worry. We'll be back," he told the boy.

"Race you," he said to Nissy. He swung down the side of the boat and waited to make sure she didn't slip into the mud.

"*Ew*, look, bone and bloody bits." She pointed at a spare leg with no lizard attached. "Part of a dead one. It's fresh, in the last minute. Do you suppose they eat each other?"

She stopped to grab her basket, but by the time Rufkin had reached the sloping stone wall she was right behind him. She hurried across the marina, up past the engineering sheds to the house.

"Mam!" Nissy led Rufkin in.

What an odd sort of front hall. It had benches around the sides. Notices were pinned on a corkboard. There was a big green board, too, for chalking instructions. Like: *Tidy tools save tempers, time and dolleros.* His own home had a separate coat room, a circular rug with silver fringing, and a carved hall table with a silver tray for all the fan mail.

A very tall woman wearing thick socks and holding a screwdriver hurried in from another door. "Nissy! Why aren't you at school? Oh, it's the weekend—no, it's vacation—who is this?"

Nissy hesitated. Rufkin stepped forward and held out

his hand. "Rufkin, ma'am. Pleased to meet you."

"You're a Robiasson." The woman looked testy. Rufkin kept his hand out because normal politeness meant she would have to give it a shake. She made it a quick one with only her fingertips. "I'm Mistress Symore. I hope you won't try giving my girl the wrong ideas."

Ideas about what? He gave the Smile-disarming: it needed a medium-fast blink.

"Mam," said Nissy. "We need some workmen."

Her mother gave the screwdriver an irritated waggle. "They're late, the lot of them."

"Mam, then we need the phone." Nissy set her chin and began to stride past.

Mistress Symore tugged one of Nissy's pigtails to stop her. Once again she waved the screwdriver. "The wretched thing still isn't working. I've had a tinker myself. I managed to get the operator, then it cut out again. Blasted technology. We were better off with message-birds and written letters."

"The Mucclacks have the same problem," said Rufkin.

"The steam-car won't start either. Every time I think I've fixed it, something else goes *phutt*." Mistress Symore tapped the screwdriver on her chin as if that might help her think. "Just run off and play, but not near any mud. No wrong ideas," she said again to Rufkin, then disappeared back where she'd come from.

"The tide," said Rufkin. "How fast does it come in? How long have we got?"

"Tablecloths," said Nissy. "Wait here."

In half a minute she was back with red and blue checked

cloths folded under her arm. She ran out the door, Rufkin behind her. "Come on!" She tore across the engineering yard to one of its jetties. Rufkin dashed after her.

"Here." She handed him a tablecloth, flapped one open herself and started to wave it.

~

A police launch was steaming in mid-channel now. Rufkin and Nissy flapped the tablecloths high and hard but the launch steamed on.

The fishing dinghy was still fairly close. "Hey!" Rufkin yelled. "Over here! Help!"

There was a slight wind. If it was stronger out on the estuary, it would be too hard for anyone to hear.

Nissy's arms dropped. The tablecloth fell round her feet like a puddle. "Why won't anyone notice? Either they're all blind or you're not waving hard enough."

Behind him Rufkin heard a series of pops from a patch of mud beside the jetty. Cave-lizard circles—dozens, hundreds—made a carpet pattern.

"When are the lizards most active?" he asked.

"Night. That's why the best casts are there in the morning." She followed his gaze. "They're not meant…" Rufkin could see in her face she was very alarmed.

"Go home if you like," he said. "I'd better run back to the riverboat. It's awful to leave the boy on his own. I'll just have to drag him. I'll tie him up like a parcel if I have to."

He hurried off the jetty. Foul whiffs rose from the mud in the bursting of bubbles.

Nissy was behind him, both tablecloths bundled under

her arm. "We'll wave again from the boat," she panted. "We'll be higher. The police will see."

"There might be something on the boat to signal with," said Rufkin. "A megaphone. A whistle."

"I can whistle." She stopped, stuck two fingers in her mouth, and she was right. Quite shrill, the *quite* that meant very.

The fishermen glanced this way, still with their rods out, but stayed hunched as if they were telling long lies about how many they'd caught on previous trips.

"They're not interested because we're only kids." Nissy shaded her eyes to see the police launch. "Look. It's going backwards."

She was right about that too. The tide, or a current, had turned the launch around and was taking it stern-first upriver. It was heading—or rather, backing—in the direction of the bridge. Miniature figures walked up and down its deck, peering over the side, over the stern at the rudder, clearly puzzled. Other shipping—steamboats, barges, freighters—had started to drift without direction as well. Behind Rufkin and Nissy came a loud twang. The road fence had sprung a hole. As Rufkin looked at it, more wires twanged apart.

Something else caught his attention—something appalling. It looked as if the Great Bridge of Size, only a year old and the pride of the city, had tilted a bit.

"The Queen's in charge," said Rufkin. "And the Council of Wisdom's taking care of things too. King Jasper wouldn't have left his sister in charge if she wasn't ready."

Nissy's voice was not nearly as brash as it had been. "Let's hurry and fetch that boy."

—

HELP AHEAD—SQUELCH

Rufkin was truly scared and dismayed. It was especially awful trying to run carefully so he didn't slip off his boardwalk into clusters of cave-lizard bubbles. His jacket was clammy. Had any grown-up seen something going terribly wrong all over the estuary? Those boats drifting strangely, the lop-sided bridge?

He and Nissy reached the riverboat. He was fed up with scrambling but this time did it in three kicks.

As soon as Rufkin was aboard, the little boy ran to his side and grabbed the knees of his work pants. "Help."

"I agree you need it," Rufkin gasped. "I'd say we all do."

Nissy leaned on the railing and began flapping a tablecloth. Rufkin snatched the other up from near her foot.

"*Ow!*" She stumbled.

"I didn't touch you," said Rufkin.

"It's not always about you." She grabbed something off the deck. "It flew into my cloth."

It was a message-bird, brown with age, still whirring. Its wings were shiny where the owner must have held it time and again to wind it up.

"It's a piece of junk." Rufkin tried to take it.

She pushed him away. "Listen."

Rufkin strained his ears. The bird was speaking.

"Communication break-*squawk* ... engineering fail-*squawk*." It paused for a moment. "Queen *squawk-squark whirr*."

Rufkin tried to take the bird again but it began another message. This one was deeper and clearer. "Police launch *Lady Helen* calling City of Spires Coastguard. Emergency. Engine failure..." After another set of squawks the voice came through again. "Can only go backwards and now it's in circles...*squawk*...communications out of...*whirr*...very embarrassing for police to...*squark*..."

"Weird," said Rufkin. "The police have up-to-date equipment."

Nissy pointed to the dinghy. "At last." It looked as if the fishermen were coming to shore. She dropped the bird and flapped the tablecloth again.

But the fishermen were only tying up alongside a larger dinghy with three men in it. There was a moment when they all seemed to be having a chat. It also looked to Rufkin as if actual things were handed from the bigger boat to the smaller. A box. Several boxes. The bigger boat pulled away towards Tiny Isle.

At last, an oar each, the fishermen started rowing for the marina.

"Help," the little boy whispered at Rufkin's side.

"Any minute." Rufkin put a hand on the kid's shoulder.

On the launch, a policeman waved in the direction of the dinghy. Rufkin could tell he was yelling. The fishermen might not have heard, but they must have seen him. After all, they were facing the launch. But they took turns to glance at the shore, then at the launch, and kept going full tilt for the marina. At the slipway, the men tumbled out, put a small box under each arm—decided on rather larger boxes instead—and left the rest.

Because of the rising tide, Rufkin was high enough now to see into the dinghy, still packed with boxes. Strange. Anyway, a pair of strong grown-ups headed up to the marina forecourt.

Out on the water the police launch still circled backwards, drifting nearer the city. A cargo steamer that Rufkin had noticed leaving earlier was coming backwards now in the tide, shoved sideways as well by the flow of the river. A long barge was in real trouble—the tough little tug that should have been pushing seemed to be shoved by it, both going nowhere. All over the water, shipping was caught in a slow sort of stirring, like a giant washing machine in the process of breakdown.

The fishermen were running for the gap in the fence. They peered through, slid down the wall and crept onto Rufkin's boardway. All he could see were blurs of fisherman-jacket through the mangroves, but he could hear them clearly enough.

"…a bit of luck. Maybe we can store the stuff up high on the wreck and go back for more," one of the men was saying.

"Luck's holding these boards in place," said the other.

"*Argh.*" It looked as if the first man was trying to kick mud off his boots. "Horrible place."

"You're not scared of a few lizards," said the second. "It's just kids' stories."

"I don't tell those tales to my kid," said the first. "If he's scared, he won't sleep. If he doesn't sleep, he whines and moans."

The other man laughed. "I bet you don't tell him you're a smuggler, either. *Argh*, these toasters are awkward."

Smugglers. They'd still help three kids in trouble, wouldn't they?

Bigger circles than ever had appeared in the mud beside the riverboat. Rufkin grabbed Nissy's arm and made sure he had hold of the little boy too.

Now someone else—a woman—was coming into sight on the road, wheeling a bicycle. She hopped on and started towards the bridge.

"Mam!" screamed Nissy.

Mistress Symore put one foot down to stop the bike and tilted her head.

"Mam!" Nissy waved.

"Help," the little boy whispered. "Help."

Mistress Symore shaded her eyes. "Nissy? Is that a boat? What's it doing there? More to the point, what are you doing on it? Get home at once. Stay inside." She gripped the handlebars and sped off.

"She must have gone to fetch a new part for the phone," said Nissy. "Or to see why the mechanics haven't arrived. Where are the Mucclacks? They're no good at keeping an eye on you, are they?"

"They're really old so I don't blame them," said Rufkin.

"I did tell them I'd be careful. If they trust me, they won't even think of starting to look yet, and they won't look here."

The smugglers had stopped when they heard Mistress Symore and Nissy—*blast*, they might run off. One of the men let out a yell. Now all Rufkin could see was their legs through the mangroves. It looked as if they were in a terrible kind of dance. It would have been funny, but a dozen cave-lizards might burst from the mud any moment.

"How dangerous are the lizards, for true?" he asked Nissy.

"The bite's tickly at first. Later it's painful," she said. "But those rings are worth money."

"Over here," Rufkin cried to the men. "Over here!" Then he filled his lungs even more than before. In the line used by Admiral Brinkwater in the hit play *Blood and Gore on the Deck*, he bellowed from deep in his belly. "For your country, Queen, and decency! All honest souls, this way!"

The smugglers sprang along the rest of the boards. They swore when the footing stopped a couple of smuggler-lengths short. Rufkin pointed to the rope. They set their boxes in the mangroves, like presents in a tree, then leapt for the rope one at a time. Faces freckled with mud, pants splashed with mud, boots thick with mud, they collapsed on deck.

"Help," said the little boy in a downcast tone. His head drooped on his skinny neck.

The men blinked at Rufkin, Nissy and the boy. Then they blinked at the riverboat, out at the estuary and up at the road where the distant figure of Mistress Symore was biking hard.

"What is this?" The smaller smuggler started into the cabin.

The other one followed. So Rufkin went too.

Inside, all five of them stared at the dusty puppet lying on the long cushion, both arms under the red and purple coverlet. The light made it look cross.

The smaller man stared at the fretwork above the counter, then back at the little boy at Rufkin's side. "Ah," he said. "Um."

"No," muttered the larger man. "This is more than we can handle. Let's brave the lizards."

They backed out of the cabin.

"Please, we need to get the boy to safety!" Rufkin ran after them. "The tide's coming…"

"Just go to the Mucclacks." The smaller man swung his legs over the rail. "That's the house at the salvage yard."

"You can't leave us," said Nissy.

"Sorry, we're doing it." He dropped from sight.

The second smuggler hung on the rail a moment longer, knuckles white with the effort. "We're not going to get done for the price of a few imported toasters and irons. Whoever that kid is, his clothes are posh. Don't you know there's a missing royal? We're not getting mixed up with police or publicity. Remember this—you never saw us."

He let go the rail. There was a squelch in the mud below.

—

SLED AHEAD

Rufkin stared at Nissy. They both stared at the boy. Missing royal? Posh clothes? They just looked grubby to Rufkin.

A scream came from down in the mud. Rufkin peered over the rail. Bubbles were popping around the men's feet. They danced away through the mangroves like spots of water skipping on a skillet.

"Go to the Mucclacks!" he shouted to them. "Send help!"

But now their heads bobbed in the scrub. He saw the boxes being tossed onto the raised road, then the smugglers were away.

"Help." The little boy shook his head and stuck his finger in his mouth.

"None at all," agreed Rufkin.

"If he is royal, he's very young." Nissy squinted at him. "He could be the son of Lord Trump and Lady Polly. They had six children and didn't expect any more. He could be the one they call the royal surprise. If so, his name's Vosco."

The boy took his finger out of his mouth and smiled.

"So you are Vosco." Rufkin tipped his head at the child. "Did you get lost? How?"

The little boy frowned.

This wasn't good progress. Rufkin reckoned that if he and Nissy were the only ones available to look after the youngest Duke of Fontania, it was bad progress. There was maybe only another hour before the tide reached here and floated little Duke Vosco to goodness knew where.

~

"Help me get him over the side," Rufkin began.

But Nissy was already climbing down and heading off.

"Fetch the Mucclacks," he called.

She hopped over the boards. Then he saw her scoot up the wall and across the concrete for her own home. He shouted again, but she took no notice. For a moment he hated her.

Then he discovered he could be even more frightened than he'd already been. He knelt down and tried to speak calmly, but this moment was too big for good acting. His voice shook.

"Listen. I'm going over the side. Then you must climb over too. I'll catch you. I'll piggy-back you. We have to go there." He pointed in the direction of the salvage yard. "They have huge cookies." It might be a lie. There were times for lies, weren't there? Rufkin made his face as trustworthy as possible.

Vosco blinked.

Rufkin swung over the side. "Your turn," he called. "Climb over."

The boy didn't even peep over the rail.

Rufkin climbed back and explained again. In the end, the only way to manage was to persuade Vosco to climb onto his back up there on deck.

He clambered down the side of the riverboat, the little boy clutching around his neck. It was a painful strangle. His boots nearly sucked off before he reached the first board, and he was scared the whole walkway would sink as he trod along. But somehow it held. He managed to stumble and jump the rest of the way. He gasped out a few remarks about the funny circles in the mud and kept telling Vosco to cling tight. He had to step over another dead cave-lizard. The creatures could die—that, in its way, was reassuring.

He struggled up the stone wall and crouched for a breath in the marina. "Walk for a bit," he gasped to Vosco. But Vosco clung tight.

The tide was creeping up the slipways. The end of the fence was far too dangerous now, no footing at all. But the new section of chain-link near the bulldozer had somehow sprung a hole. He wriggled through that.

Finally Rufkin reached the Mucclacks' veranda. He collapsed, levered Vosco's fingers free at last and thumped on the door.

It opened a crack. Then it opened wide.

"What are you doing with that child?" whispered Mistress Mucclack. Rufkin wasn't sure if she was talking to Vosco or him.

Mister Mucclack peered over her head. His big hand reached for Rufkin and helped him up. "You're red in the face and red round the throat," he said softly. "Where did you find this little choker of a chap? And look at your boots."

But now everyone was inside, Mistress Mucclack hauling off Rufkin's boots and finding him a glass of water, Mister

Mucclack sitting Vosco on a chair and rubbing his hands.

"Where are his shoes?" asked Mistress Mucclack. "Just look at that, little socks with a hole in the toe."

So Rufkin had proof in the form of the child that something very strange was going on. But the Mucclacks still took ages to grasp the rest of it.

Mister Mucclack thumped his big hands together like two rocks in a quiet collision. "The little duke alone on a broken rusty riverboat. In the midst of the mangroves and mud? Communications are damaged. Ships with engines can only go backwards or drift?" His thought-wrinkles deepened. "Is evil astray in the land?" he whispered. "Have enemies of the nation…"

"Shut up," breathed Mistress Mucclack. "This is no time for dramatic questions. You were never more than a stage manager, and for good reason. Oh, my dear Skully, taking care of one child is almost beyond me. Taking care of two? I am ashamed but I can't do it." She put her skinny fingers over her eyes for a moment. Then she stood straight. "I will never more live a quiet half-second if I don't restore the little duke at once to his mother and father."

That sounded even more dramatic to Rufkin.

Mister Mucclack smiled. "What an old man needs is a clever and kind-hearted old woman to urge him on. We'll use our truck."

"It broke down four days ago," his wife reminded him. "It's at the workshop and still twenty-seventh on their worksheet."

"An old man also needs various old vessels in his salvage

yard, and oodles of know-how." Mister Mucclack showed the gap in his teeth with a grin. It was a grin that proved how brave the old man was despite being sometimes doddery. Rufkin noted it for later, if he ever came to try the stage again.

~

"What about the puppet?" asked Rufkin. "The tide might ruin it."

"Then the tide ruins it," said Mister Mucclack.

"It must be brilliant onstage," said Rufkin. "I'd love to save it."

Vosco looked up at him, gray eyes brimming with trust and panic. It was a good look—Rufkin smiled at him and tried to copy.

"Our priority is to find the picnic basket." Mister Mucclack scratched his head and stared at the wall that Rufkin had noticed looked rickety.

Mistress Mucclack pushed the wall and it slid open. A well-disguised door. The brooms toppled like pick-up-sticks. She stepped over them and down into what turned out to be a garage large enough for their truck. It also stored an adult-sized tricycle, fishing gear, and a sled that looked more like a boat and had rollers rather than runners. It had a ledge behind the back to stand and push. There in the sled was the picnic basket. She grabbed it and jumped back to the kitchen.

"That's my sprightly Wanda," whispered Skully Mucclack.

"We could fetch the puppet in that sled," said Rufkin. "I think Vosco wants it."

"If you can do it, then do it," said Skully Mucclack. "That's my own invention, our all-purpose, all-weather floatable sled. It's invaluable along the littoral. That means, the edge between land and sea."

Mistress Mucclack didn't shout but she whispered fiercely. "No child should use your contraption without supervision. And we can't waste a minute."

Vosco's hand grabbed hard at the side of Rufkin's pants, nearly dragging them down. "Quit that," said Rufkin.

Mister Mucclack mumbled on. "There's still a good hour before high tide. I'm a believer in letting children try things for themselves with no interference."

"Rufkin's done enough without supervision already," said Mistress Mucclack. "Now, should we take pie? A thermos of last night's carrot and cockle?"

The little duke's eyes were the saddest, most desperate and begging Rufkin had seen in all his life. "Don't look at me like that," he said.

—

PULLEYS
AND PUSHING

Rufkin glanced around the shed. Plenty of rope. Tools. A large pulley. An even larger one. He grabbed a small one. Inside his own head was his own know-how.

He put on his boots again, saluted Mister Mucclack, and set a foot on the back of the sled.

The all-purpose all-weather contraption was excellent. He steered it out of the shed, shoved it round the bulldozer, and barged for the hole in the blue metal new bit of fence. Before he even touched it, the wire seemed to part even further with a musical twang. Weird but terrific. The rollers of the sled made mild thunder over the concrete.

The estuary and sea were strangely still. The tanker nestled against Tiny Isle like a huge puppy with a miniature mother. The police launch? Rufkin would have liked to know where it was in case it could help now. But there was no sign of it.

He had to heave the contraption through the gap in the wooden fence, but it rolled down the stone wall sweet as magic. The boards were steady under the rollers, though incoming waves had started to chew at the muddy ground.

Soon the stranded riverboat was in view. Maybe it had once ferried monarchs and their families to events of all kinds. It would have been as lovely as the new one he'd glimpsed two days ago from the top floor of Brilliant Academy. It had sailed upriver with Queen Sibilla and her advisers to sort out the plague, a-glitter with brass, a glory of fresh paint and banners.

He had no idea if he could manage to get the sled into the right position but it almost glided in the now-watery mud to lie alongside amidships (nice phrase, he felt pleased with it). He slung the rope and grooved wheel over his back. Quick as a circus performer, he scaled the blistered side of the old riverboat. For a moment he frowned at the puppet and the cushion, then set to work.

Rufkin knew about pulleys. He'd helped a hundred times (maybe just fifty but it felt like more), setting up scenery and all kinds of props. First he had to balance on the railing to attach a swivel to the overhang of the top deck above his head. If the rail didn't hold his weight, he was in trouble. If the swivel wasn't fixed right, the puppet would end in the mud. He'd lose it and that would be that.

A scary thought came into his head—the royal family were known to experiment with clockwork figures, ones that mixed elements of magic with machinery. King Jasper himself had invented the first message-birds. He'd made a clockwork boy with a magical heart. The puppet might be very special indeed.

He had another look at it. For goodness' sake, he was scaring himself for no reason. Vosco was having a bad time and the kid only wanted the puppet. After all, when Rufkin was that age, he'd refused to go anywhere without a mechanical bear called Gingery Bill.

Anyway, whether the puppet was clockwork, valuable, or just precious to Vosco, it should be protected. He rigged the rope under the cushion it lay on, once in the middle and once at each end so it made a safe packet. That made it easy enough to haul out to the deck and arrange lengthwise beside the rail. Rufkin heaved on the rope that ran over the pulley and drew the packet of puppet up—not quite as heavy as he'd expected—and pushed a bit to balance it on the railing. It teetered. Lizard circles below popped and stank.

Rufkin was certain he'd lose it but tried one more gentle heave. The cushion swayed up and out so he could lower it slowly down towards the sled, where it settled as sweetly as magic again. Seagulls screamed like a delighted audience. Rufkin whooped too, put a hand on his heart and took a bow.

Okay—enough—he was down over the side to the sled. He slipped the ropes off the cushion and left them dangling. He could fetch the pulley and everything later.

He took half a moment to look at the puppet's face again. The rust and blue was some sort of crackled old paint, patchy, perhaps even sticky. Someone should give it a good scrub and a repaint. Then a wave slapped the mud far too close to waste more time.

~

Rufkin shoved off on the side of the riverboat, and the sled glided on top of the mud to the board walkway. Again it went far more easily than he'd expected, which made him feel guilty for being a worryguts. It floated and rolled on through the mangroves, and he sort-of tingled the way he had when he'd rehearsed in the flying-harness for his part as Birdling in *Dragon Lord and Gifted Girl*. The worst struggle was shoving the sled back up the wall.

At the house at last, he left the sled by the veranda and rushed to the phone. It still wasn't working. *Hiss, splutter,* and *buzz.*

The Mucclacks had filled the picnic basket. They'd also arranged the table for lunch. Mister Mucclack set Vosco on a cushion so he'd be high enough to see his plate. Mistress Mucclack had washed his face and hands.

"Thin little arms and legs," she whispered, "big hands and feet like a puppy. Oh, I can see the man this child will be."

Rufkin grinned. *Got it,* he mouthed to Vosco and gave a thumbs-up. Vosco grinned back but he stayed at the table.

Mistress Mucclack fetched a pot of honey in one hand, peanut butter in the other. This looked better than carrot stew or blackened toast. What's more, there was cheese. She set sliced bread on an oval plate.

Rufkin took a piece for Vosco and cut it into triangles the way his mother had done for him when he was small. Vosco watched, eyes bigger than ever. He sat on his hands as if he'd been trained, so he wouldn't be tempted to grab early. Royal manners? In fact, the same manners as at Rufkin's home.

"As soon as we've eaten we'll take this little sir home," said Mistress Mucclack only just loud enough for Rufkin to hear.

"How?" He had seen no steam-car. They couldn't phone for a taxi or obliging friend. "You've only got the sled and the tricycle. We can't go in the bulldozer—can we?" That would be brilliant.

Mister Mucclack shook his head and his large nostrils whiffled.

"Skully has ideas," whispered Mistress Mucclack. "Lunch feeds the brain. So he might have more."

Vosco ate one triangle of bread. He broke the others into strips and laid them on the table so they read: H E L I. Then he frowned and dabbed a blob of peanut butter next to the top of the I. Rufkin tore a corner off his own slice and handed it over. Vosco set it on top of the blob. It made a better P, though rather pointy.

"The little chap's what I'd call a silent partner," said Mister Mucclack. "He's right, right? 'Help.' That's what we need, that's what we're doing. A useful word. Now, to sum up. Engines appear to be out. But wind isn't out. Muscles aren't out. Rowing or sail is how we'll get to the city, the police, and the Little Palace for this chap's parents."

—

THE KNOT IMPOSSIBLE

DISASTER AHEAD

From the veranda Rufkin saw the tide almost at its height. The mangroves would be just about covered. He shivered and looked at the estuary.

Rowing or sail in Mister Mucclack's quiet voice had sounded easy. But it was a fair distance from here to the city. Rufkin was still exhausted from piggy-backing Vosco. He was exhausted on top of that by rigging the pulley and shoving the sled. He fastened his jacket and pulled on his purple beanie.

The Mucclacks came out arm in arm and Vosco scrambled on the sled next to the puppet. He looked much happier. Mister Mucclack gave Rufkin a wink that made him feel he might have energy for the trip after all. He nearly asked if Mister Mucclack thought his dad would be proud of him, but that would be wet.

Mister Mucclack fetched a pair of oars out of the garage, frowned, and dropped one deliberately. It made a soft thump, fell apart like flaky chocolate and sent up dust.

Mistress Mucclack murmured through tight lips. "That's how long since we've had to use them and that's the only oars we have at the moment, my dear. We'll have to rummage for sails and hope for wind."

By now Rufkin knew what she'd find. Any patches on the sails not spotted with mildew would be full of holes. Even a sniff of wind would tear them like tissue. He found it hard to clamp down on a whine. It was mid-afternoon! High tide! Couldn't they give up for today? Did all of them have to go anyway? He could stay here with Mistress Mucclack. She might have some old magazines he could cut up. He could make his own Lord Hodie fanzine.

Mister Mucclack held a piece of sail and tugged at it. "They'll hold up enough to cross to the city, with any luck."

"We could just walk down to the end of a jetty," Rufkin suggested. "Someone might row past. We can give them a shout. They might take a message to the city. Or even simply take Vosco."

The little boy looked reproachful. Rufkin felt bad.

"Come along, we'll try it," said Mistress Mucclack. "It will give the little dear a ride in the sled." She set the picnic basket at the puppet's feet.

Mister Mucclack pushed the sled to the jetties. He began wandering up and down by himself to choose a suitable small vessel. The sky was overcast with purple-gray clouds again. There was no wind.

Vosco refused to get out of the sled. Rufkin peered upriver to the Bridge of Size. He was sure it had settled lower at the city end. Those foundations can't have been anything like deep enough. He glanced out to sea. A couple of small ships still drifted. There was no sign of a boat of any sort moving with purpose under the power of engine, sail, or muscle. A barge nestled with the tanker against Tiny Isle.

Mistress Mucclack had joined her husband beside an old rusty launch with a short mast. They were mumbling to each other.

Rufkin heard a jangle and a cry of annoyance. Nissy, wearing a pink coat now, was near the fence into the engineering yard. She'd dropped her basket. She kicked it. Then she shaded her eyes and peered around.

He turned away. The Mucclacks were coming back.

Vosco tugged at Rufkin and pointed behind him. Nissy was climbing over the old chain-link fence. Tough luck for her—she hadn't noticed the hole he'd used through the new patch. She picked her way to a path, then hurried towards them. A pair of binoculars hung round her neck.

"That girl," muttered Mistress Mucclack in Rufkin's ear, making him jump. "Always wants something for nothing. Usually gets it."

The Mucclacks waited, faces grim, till she arrived.

Nissy was tear-stained and red-faced too, with what Rufkin hoped was embarrassment at running off when he'd asked for help. "I thought I might be able to use the fishermen's dinghy," she said. "But it's floated away."

"Hello, Mister and Mistress Mucclack, how are you both?" Mistress Mucclack whispered. "Oh, hello, Nissy, and how are you? What do you want from us this time?"

Nissy blushed a deeper red. "I'm worried about Mam. She biked over the bridge ages ago. And look." She gave Mister Mucclack the binoculars.

Rufkin squinted. Had the bridge just given a judder on this side?

"No traffic at all now, not even on foot. I'm beginning to worry about everything," said Skully Mucclack. "Including the bridge and your mother."

The whole bridge sank a bit more, unless Rufkin was having a dizzy spell. He hoped he was. A bridge as big and new as that, collapsing?

Nissy used the binoculars herself and let out a cry.

Rufkin stood on his toes and put his hands around his eyes to help him focus. This end of the bridge had sunk even lower. It made him very dizzy.

"It's those lizards," whispered Wanda Mucclack. "They've undermined the very foundations."

"Why the cave-lizards should be so bad, I've no idea," said Mister Mucclack. "Before, there were crabs and tiny cave-lizards in equal measure, and all was well."

"Because there were enough gulls to eat them both," added his wife. "I blame the dredging."

"I blame the steamships," said her husband. "It's because of the steamships that we needed so many dredges."

"But most of all I blame the mining," said Mistress Mucclack. "The mining upriver that has driven clouds of dust into the air so down it comes all over my washing line and into my kitchen. The mining that has drilled far too deep and far too quickly, with no thought of the upshot. There used to be wonders deep underground and undersea. Wonders that were friends and companions with the wonders that lived in the sky. There are stories about caverns and networks so deep they should never be opened."

Rufkin didn't care what they blamed. All he wanted was

to be safe away from here, having the summer he'd expected. On the *Lordly Sword* with his parents, and Oscar and Ahria, all of them laughing at one of his jokes. Even with the Mucclacks and Nissy around, he ached with loneliness.

Vosco's hand brushed against his. He glanced down. The kid must be feeling pretty churned up too.

Rufkin scanned for a sailboat on the estuary, a rowboat. Nothing. He eyed the derelict launch beside the jetty. He supposed its short mast might hold a mildewed sail.

Mister Mucclack spoke in a hoarse tremble. "If the river's running hard, which it is, and the tide is high, which it is, the usual current should drive the launch from here to near the city shore. All we have to do is untie it and get on, then manage the sails for some extra help."

"Actually, it would be best to get on first," said Rufkin. "Untie it second."

Mister Mucclack gave him a look that said even though Rufkin was the son of old friends, he was in danger of pushing his luck.

~

Skully Mucclack hauled a small gangplank into position. Mistress Mucclack carried the picnic hamper and blanket onto the launch and set it all inside the doorway of the rusty cabin. Nissy and Rufkin hopped aboard too, but Vosco stood and whimpered next to the sled.

"He wants the puppet," said Rufkin.

"Let him want," said Nissy. "Mam says it's good for children not to get everything they ask for."

Mistress Mucclack's skinny nose gave a twitch. Mister

Mucclack, on the wharf stooping over the ropes, let out a snort.

Mist hung over the city now. Soon it would cover the whole estuary. Damp would seep everywhere. The puppet could be totally ruined left out in the weather. If Vosco really was Duke Vosco, not just a kid whose name was Vosco-Bob Smith or something ordinary, the puppet might be important to the royal family. Rufkin's parents would be impressed to hear that he had salvaged it.

He jumped back over the gangplank and toppled Mister Mucclack just as he knelt to the last rope. "Watch it," old Skully whispered.

"Sorry," said Rufkin. "Scoot aboard," he told Vosco.

The kid scurried on. The mist flowed steadily closer.

Rufkin grabbed the sled.

"We can't take the whole thing," whispered Mister Mucclack. "If you insist on the puppet, I'll lift it. Give me a moment."

"Don't worry, I've got it." Rufkin shoved hard. The sled stuck on the gangplank. He shunted again. The darn thing wouldn't budge.

"Drat the boy, pardon me for bad language. Wait." Mister Mucclack worked at the rope. "Who did this half-hitch?"

"You!" snapped his wife in her whisper. "Unless it was me." She clambered right over the sled and back onto the jetty. "Old duffer. Let my fingers do it."

Mister Mucclack stood up.

"Something's stuck this knot tight," hissed Mistress Mucclack. "It is impossible!"

With a final shove, Rufkin bumped the sled onto the launch far harder than he had meant. It banged against the cabin. There was a cry. Vosco? A bird?

A gust made the launch jerk—and the rope flew loose.

Rufkin stumbled and grabbed the rail. Nissy yelled. There was a *splash!*—gangplank, goodbye. The launch bobbed free on the waves, but the Mucclacks were still on the jetty.

Mister Mucclack fell to his knees again. "No!" he bellowed.

Mistress Mucclack flapped her arms and screamed her lungs out. "The children! We've lost the children!"

They kept shrieking and shouting.

The strength of the river swung the launch further and further from shore. Nissy had her jaw set, gazing at the collapsed bridge and the mist sliding over it. She wouldn't look at Rufkin.

Foam whisked and blew at the mouth of the estuary. But surely old Skully was right. The launch would be pushed to the middle, then the current would carry them safe to the city side. Surely.

Rufkin felt something beside him. It was Vosco. The little boy's hand brushed against his again, then slid right in and clung tight.

—

THE
END-OF-DAYS

SOME SORT
OF SHADOW

Rufkin couldn't really blame the Mucclacks for this. But his parents would feel seriously let down. After all, the Mucclacks had sworn to take care of him. And they were the grown-ups.

Spray blew over the rail. "You'd better stand back," he told Vosco.

Even with a fitful breeze from upriver, the launch stank of rust and old toad-oil. The current already had them crossing in front of Tiny Isle. On the ships stuck against its little cliffs and beaches, figures waved and probably hollered. If they thought Rufkin and Nissy could help, they were out of their minds. Rufkin stood to attention with a salute like a monarch reviewing his troops. Nissy rolled her eyes.

"Oh, come on, it is a bit funny." He stopped anyway.

The wind wasn't cold but Rufkin crouched down beside Vosco. Nissy poked her nose into the cabin. There was no door, nor anything inside like a bench to rest on. She made a face and sat on deck, as far as she could from the sled. The puppet's hair had gone frizzier. It must be from the salt in the air.

The launch reached the middle of the channel where

choppy waves tossed it about. Any minute it should start a swerve for the city and someone would come to help. Hardly any vessels lined the wharves there—a freighter, a ferry, another freighter. The mist had bunched back like fat fingers clutching the hills. He could make out the silver glint of the Grand Palace, a blue that would be the B of Butterly Ventures.

In a sudden blast of wind, Rufkin only just grabbed his beanie before it flew off forever. He ducked down.

After a few minutes he raised his head again. The city was further away—the launch was heading out to the wide horizon.

"No!" he cried. "Wrong! This can't be happening!"

Nissy jumped to her feet and screamed, "It's your fault. You're so thoughtless! Full of yourself!"

"You're the stupid one," he shouted back. "Someone will have seen us by now. They'll be coming any minute."

"How?" she cried. "Who?"

"I don't know. Someone. Like…Lord Hodie, maybe. I nearly met him once." Now he felt stupid. Why had he said that?

For a moment the wind came from all directions, moaning and arguing. Vosco's eyes grew huge and worried. He curled up on the sled beside the puppet.

"Nobody will save us." Nissy set her chin but it wobbled at once. "Certainly not your dumb hero." She swung into the cabin after all and rolled herself up on the floor in the Mucclacks' blanket.

By now the wind and current were definitely heading the launch out to Old Ocean.

"Stop!" Rufkin roared. If it kept going like this, they could end up at Battle Island. Or they could keep going for weeks right out to the Eastern Isle, even past that…

Rufkin told himself not to be dramatic. They'd be rescued before long. If not, Battle Island was where they'd end up. It usually took steamships two days to go that distance. In a sailing ship, it took maybe five or six. So how long would it take to drift there in a small rusty launch with no engine or sail? Too long for comfort, he knew that, and he wasn't comfortable now. How long could the rusty launch last?

~

The wind pushed the launch on till Tiny Isle was a dot far behind. Even further behind, the City of Spires was a scrawl on the shore. Now and then waves came at the launch sideways and slapped the hull like watery hiccups. Each time, Rufkin's insides gave a lurch too. He'd been seasick on large vessels before. It was terrible. He guessed that you didn't actually compare times you were seasick, it was just always far more awful than you wanted.

Nissy stuck her head out of the cabin, then drew back, sick or scared: he didn't know and couldn't care. He saw her scribbling in that spotted notebook from her pocket. At least they had Mistress Mucclack's picnic hamper for when they felt better. If they ever felt better.

Late-afternoon sun beamed down. The wind whoo-ed in a playful way. Vosco lay curled asleep, toe peeping out of his sock. Rufkin lay on the deck, arm under his head. He tried to doze. It was impossible.

When he sat up, there was no sight of the city at all, no

sight of land on either side and none ahead. Pure terror stopped him breathing for a moment. But he'd better take charge. He didn't know if Nissy was older than him, but drat if he'd be ordered around by her. Vosco might be a duke, but drat again if he'd be ordered about by a four-year-old with one word to speak of. *Ha*, he'd made a joke, even though it was by accident.

But did he want to be in charge of the three of them drowning when the hull filled up like a sieve in a kitchen sink? Did he want to be in charge of them starving to death after they'd eaten whatever was in the hamper? Did he want to be in charge of them bashing into rocks and then drowning? No to all questions.

The line of the horizon blurred into silvery dazzle; the lid of night was coming down over the sea. Rufkin stood up. He had to see the little kid didn't freeze to death. He thought about rolling the puppet out of the sled and onto the deck, but Vosco seemed happy enough next to it. In the end, he eased the coverlet down, then tucked it back properly over Vosco as well as the puppet. He thought for a moment, then settled his own purple beanie on the little kid's head.

In the empty shell of the cabin Nissy was sleeping. She'd snap at him if he woke her and asked to share the blanket. He didn't want to share anyway. She was drooling, onto the notebook.

He sat on the end of the sled and looked at the darkening sea. Bubbles gleamed on the tops of small gray waves.

A long shadow passed under the launch. Though it was

moving fast it seemed to take ages. His throat closed in terror—but of course it would only be the shadow of a cloud. He glanced up. The sky was overcast with no actual clouds. When he dared look back at the sea, the shadow had gone.

The feeling of terror stayed with him and turned to vast loneliness. He climbed into the foot of the sled, loosened a red corner of the coverlet, and tucked himself there. It would help keep Vosco's feet warm.

—

OAT-BARS
AND TIDDLERS

The lid of night closed entirely. No stars. No moon. Just the slurp of water, the creak of the hull, the snuffle of Vosco snoring, the approach and fading away of seabirds nattering.

Rufkin's head filled with images and impressions the way it did when he had the flu: odd noises, flashes of light, even echoing voices. Some nights were like this when he was ill, as if several days rolled into one difficult package. At one point he felt his head was somehow hanging over the end of the sled. His neck ached. His skull and brain together must weigh more than a pair of steel-tipped work boots.

At last his eyes opened properly. The clouds were dirty, like used cotton wool. He struggled upright.

The good thing was he no longer felt sick. He was hungry. How long had it been with no meals?

After a moment Nissy opened her eyes and blinked at him from the cabin floor. Her hair had come out of its braids and an elastic band dangled behind her left ear. She was pale, with smudges of dirt. He was surprised to feel sorry for her, though somehow knew it was easier than feeling sorry for himself.

But she shot a look at him and he knew she would come out with something mean. She pressed her lips together for a moment but only a moment. "I haven't seen Lord Hodie yet. Have we been saved?"

The boat slewed in a gust of wind. Vosco stirred. Though Rufkin couldn't see his face, the kid muttered something and threw an arm over the puppet. His little fingers patted its shoulder.

"Anyway, I'm starving." Nissy rummaged in Mistress Mucclack's hamper and brought out a banana. "It's gone spotty. I hate that." She peered into the basket again. "There's a knife. Also a corkscrew and can-opener. A flashlight, a packet of oat-bars—yuck, they know I don't like that sort."

Rufkin didn't like any sort of oat-bars.

Nissy rummaged some more. "There's a clock and a sun hat with strings. It's yellow. The clock's not going. We may as well share," she continued, "even though I don't like you and why should I? You don't like me."

She looked so annoyed that it was funny. He let out a laugh. Her chin jutted out.

Vosco awoke. He tugged off the beanie, stared at it, then glanced at Rufkin.

"Keep it," said Rufkin.

Vosco looked pleased and pulled it back on.

Nissy started to peel the banana. Luckily it was a large one. She broke off the first third for Vosco. He didn't take it but kept his hand out.

"He wants a piece still in the skin," said Rufkin. "That makes a good holder. Go on, give it."

"Don't spoil him." Nissy's chin jutted again.

"A third of a banana is hardly spoiling." Rufkin grabbed the two-thirds from her, took the middle part and passed the bit in the skin to Vosco.

He wasn't fond of spotty bananas either. But it turned out to be the finest he'd ever tasted, firm and sweet as if it was the very first and therefore best found on Old Ocean. The trouble with bananas was they never took long to eat, especially if it was only a third of even a huge one.

Vosco, beanie over his ears, knelt on the cushion and stared at the water. It was empty of anything but waves, swirls of foam and under-flashes that were probably fish, maybe eels. Or perhaps it was trash, like bags or bottles, or maybe only dead fish or eels. There was no sign of the long shape that had made Rufkin so achingly lonely. Even to think of it made him break out in another sweat.

Two lines of small waves furled out behind them, so he could tell the launch was moving. He supposed it was because of the soft wind, though it dropped away then blew again. The lines became more like a zigzag. A deep current must be pulling in another direction.

The sky was that purple-gray by now. Ahead was a thick line of mist. No—part of it was darker, a sort of lump. Land? Maybe the beginning of a storm cloud. The wind became a feeble whisper full of effort. But the current kept circling them towards the dark lump, whatever it was. The launch even seemed to speed up.

Vosco muttered to himself. It was his only word again. Nissy rolled her eyes. Rufkin decided not to roll his, even though the little kid could become boring.

The lump on the horizon had grown bigger. He kept watching, Nissy beside him at the rail. The patch grew bigger—bigger—

It looked like a jumble of trash, something to be swept into a giant dustpan.

The launch was definitely moving faster. Now the patch looked like a clutter of buildings. Nissy used the binoculars.

"It's ships." She let Rufkin see.

So it was. Ships in a huddle so close they looked tied together. Dozens, maybe a hundred. A cargo ship, a few yachts (large and expensive, medium and moderate, small and cheap). He saw several barges, the masts of old sailing ships, smart funnels of steam vessels, a tug. There was a super-yacht that might be the *Sea Honey*. A warship with the blue gleam of new turrets and swivel guns. And there, more or less in the middle, loomed the superstructure of the cruise ship he'd seen leaving the city wharves, the *Princess of Dogjaw*. As the launch closed in on the huddle, he saw that gangways, rope walkways and planks really did tie the ships together into a floating town.

Nissy took the binoculars back.

In the pock and slap of waves against the hull, Rufkin's ears picked up another sound—a drone, a moan as if someone had bellyache. Vosco put his hands over his ears.

"I hope that's not an animal." Nissy screwed her face up. "No—it's a trumpet."

The sound sorted out in Rufkin's head as well. A trumpet. Its wheeze was a rumptipaze, family code for *off-key, ear-hurting and jarring.* He loved saying it with an admiring smile to a terrible musician. Nobody ever admitted they didn't know the word; they had to take it as a compliment. A stab of missing his family went right through him.

Out-of-tune voices joined the trumpet's rumptipaze. So did the twang of a banjo, the deeper plunk of a guitar, the rhythm of someone banging a makeshift drum.

Now the launch was swerving to the nearest boat in the tangle, a long red barge. Its deck looked empty of freight. But a small crowd was gathered near the cabin where the noise was coming from. On ships jumbled along on the other side of the barge, Rufkin spied sailors, officers in uniforms, tourists in casual gear, fishermen, various all-sorts. Even at this distance they had the rumpled air of people at the end of a rowdy party who longed to go home but were stuck there waiting for taxis.

"The cruise ship left the night of the storm," he said. "They've been jammed together because of the breakdown—and by the current." Or something else, a shadow, swirling and circling? But how would he know? He shouldn't pretend.

"It must have taken days," Nissy replied in a shaky voice. "Will it be safe to get close?"

"Of course, stupid!" Rufkin felt guilty for biting her head off. It was just because he was relieved. "There are grown-ups now. They'll look after us."

She still looked worried. So did Vosco. By now they were so close that Rufkin couldn't see anything except the long red side of the barge. The sea had worn away some paint, but there were traces of a blue B. It could even be a barge he had spotted from the salvage yard on that first morning.

The rusty launch nudged it with a scraping sound.

"Ahoy! Permission to come aboard," Rufkin cried.

After a few moments a man in a captain's hat peered down at them. His face had been pickled red and brown by sea salt.

"Tiddlers," he growled. "Blast me eyes."

—

A MEDICAL OATH

"Any grown-ups with you?" the man shouted.

"Just us!" called Rufkin.

A less weather-beaten face, leaf-green with the blue spots of an ogre, appeared at the rail next to the man's. It wore a deerstalker hat. "Children. On their own. I must be dreaming."

"It beats me how that hulk they're in has floated this far, Doctor Goodabod," said the man. "Climb down and fetch 'em at once."

"Me?" The ogre's voice growled like a motor. "Captain Thunderhead, if this is the end-of-days, my desire is not to fall and drown. I would thereby miss the very last moment. It is scientific interest."

The end-of-days? The end of the world?

Nissy hissed at Rufkin. "Do they think we're all going to—"

Rufkin jabbed her. "Never say 'die,'" he muttered. "It might upset Vosco."

Thunderhead wiggled an eyebrow at the ogre doctor. "What about your oath as a medical person? You've sworn to help them who need it."

"Captain Thunderhead, that is correct," said Doctor Goodabod. "But my medical oath says, first do no harm.

If I climb down, I risk breaking a limb. Thereby I would break that oath."

The captain shouted with laughter. "And if you break one of your great thick legs, you also end your employment with Madam Butterly."

"We understand each other, Captain Thunderhead," said Doctor Goodabod. They slapped hands, chanting *dollero dollero*.

"I understand too," Rufkin called. "But if you don't hurry, we might drift off. Can you let down a ladder? We'll climb up by ourselves."

He felt a tug at his jacket. Vosco, pom-pom beanie still over his ears.

"Blast me eyes," said Captain Thunderhead. "Better and better. I thought there were only two tiddlers. I've just set eyes on a third. It's even smaller." He looked about. "Where's a grappling iron—very tidy, right here on a hook." He tossed it down. "That'll hold your bucket of rust for long enough."

Next a rope ladder bumped down the red side.

All the time the blurts of the trumpet sounded up on the barge, as well as chaotic song from the watching crowd. Rufkin heard plenty of shouts that the music was terrible. They needed his brother Oscar on his violin, his sister Ahria with her beautiful voice. Rufkin wished at once that he hadn't thought of them again. It upset his insides.

"Hurry up!" He pushed at Nissy and grabbed for Vosco. The kid ducked away and sat back on the sled. "Vosco, we have to leave. It's dangerous here. The grown-ups will help." He tried to loosen Vosco's fingers from the coverlet.

A silent tussle—but at last Rufkin managed to drag the

kid to the ladder. Nissy was already at the top. When her pink rubber boots disappeared from view, he made Vosco start climbing, himself right behind. It was a struggle to keep the kid moving one rung at a time...

Lord Hodie would manage without dropping him, Rufkin kept telling himself.

The doctor's knuckly hand reached down and whisked Vosco the last few rungs by the scruff of his neck.

Rufkin followed, tumbling over the rail to the deck of the barge. It was a long wide space like an open-air bowling alley. The air was chill. He was glad of his jacket.

Doctor Goodabod helped Rufkin stand up. Even for an ogre, he was enormous. His chest was so big he could probably take a breath and not let it out till late tomorrow.

"Thank you—" started Rufkin.

But the rumptipaze rumped up again. The trumpet player and a few others were on the cabin roof. A group on the deck was trying to dance. Vosco did a stamping shuffle as if he wanted to join in. Then he pounded off along the deck towards the music. Rufkin raced after him. As the kid neared the group, the music stopped. So did Vosco. Rufkin caught up.

"Trumpets, that's what they play at the Grand Palace," he heard somebody say. "Much better than this, though. They start teaching them young. If you're a royal it's all parties with music of the very best sort."

Vosco was scanning the people on top of the cabin and everyone standing about. His eyes were brimming. Maybe he'd thought the trumpet meant family would be here. He was shivering. Even through the waistcoat his shoulder blades stuck out like sharp little wing buds. Rufkin put an arm round him and rubbed. Then he slid his own jacket off. He managed to stuff Vosco's arms in and fastened a button.

Nissy had caught up too and was busy listening.

"Being royal's not always fun," one of the women was saying. "The brave young Queen, having to sort out the plague? That's hardly party frocks and a glittery handbag."

"Who cares," said a gloomy voice. "What matters at the end-of-days? Nothing at all."

"Why couldn't we have had the end-of-days on dry land?" said somebody else. "I'm fed up. Five days on the ocean."

"Good heavens. Children." A young woman hurried over. She wore leggings with a sparkly side-seam and a tunic with clattering dangles. Her beaded bag matched her scarlet canvas boots, the latest fashion. Rufkin knew, from having a stylish celebrity mother and older sister.

"Hello! I'm Calleena Beagle. Who might you all belong to?" She smiled at Nissy and Rufkin, and batted her eyelashes at Vosco. "Aren't you a little mystery under that grub and grime and that cute hat."

Vosco's tears overflowed at last and dripped to make cleaner pathways in all his smudge. The trumpet had started a new set of bathroom noises. The ear-hurting chorus began again in patches from the crowd, not only here but on the decks of ships crammed alongside.

Rufkin couldn't stand it any longer. "Even I can play the trumpet better than that."

—

RUMPTIPAZE

Calleena Beagle squeezed her hands into a ball to indicate happiness. It looked ridiculous. Rufkin would love to use the gesture on stage, though of course he never could.

"Harry! Stop!" she shouted to the top of the cabin.

The trumpet player shook spit out of the instrument. He was so tall and with such wide shoulders that he should really be bashing the drums. He wore casual pants and a plain sweater. His dark hair tangled over his ears and eyes. It was the curliest and glossiest Rufkin had ever seen not on a poodle.

Calleena smiled up at him. "Here's a boy who says he can play. He's just arrived."

"Yeah, get rid of Harry. Wrong hobby!" came a voice in the crowd.

"Why does he even try?" cried a laughing man with a Riversea accent.

Harry swung the trumpet on its crimson cord, swaggered and grinned. "It makes me look like a million dolleros."

Rufkin could see the man was acting. To keep people laughing? At least with that he was doing a good job. The trumpet probably just gave him an excuse to wander about.

"All right, where's the junior musician?" Harry called.

Calleena pointed to Rufkin and chuckled.

Rufkin stung with nerves. He hadn't meant he would actually play! He'd throw up, freeze and faint, several times, in various orders.

"Don't keep them waiting. Up you go," said Calleena.

He couldn't move. He knew this was all to keep the crowd's minds off the end-of-days. They really needed Oscar and Ahria. Nobody needed him. He'd just disappoint them.

But Vosco's eyes were on him, so big and trusting they made him feel sick. He already felt sick—his ears buzzed, brain buzzed, even his eyes buzzed. But it would be awful to disappoint the little kid.

Captain Thunderhead gave him a shove.

Rufkin put Vosco's hand into Nissy's. "Keep hold of him."

He didn't know how he got up the ladder—Thunderhead shoved him again probably—but here he was on the cabin roof.

Harry presented the trumpet with a sporty flourish. Rufkin was so nervous he could hardly feel it in his hands. But it looked well cared for. That red cord made it handsome. It had a fairly big mouthpiece and easy finger stops. It might have seemed rude, but to give himself more time Rufkin shook the instrument again and wiped the mouthpiece on his sleeve. Stage-fright squeezed him from belly to throat. He looked up.

Another mistake.

~

The knot of ships was even bigger than Rufkin had thought, two hundred ships or even more. In the distance thin gray clouds had begun to thicken into a bank. The gathering of grown-ups thickened also at the railings of the cargo ships jammed next to the barge. They were all watching him. His own eyes sort of went blind.

Harry nudged him. "Do something. Anything. Make it up as you go along. I had to."

Yes, that had been obvious. Harry might be a spy. If this really was the end-of-days, he'd be out of work soon. So would everyone. But maybe because Harry was right beside him, Rufkin felt a shred better.

"I...don't know many tunes. Stop me as soon as you've had enough." He gave a trembly grin down to the ogre. "The first one's for you, for saving us."

He put the trumpet to his lips. His nerves twanged and fizzed, but his breath started to play "The Song of the Ogre."

Goodabod reared back with a hand on his deerstalker cap, smiled and started to sing.

I'm green and I'm blue and I'm happy...

The audience joined in. Rufkin came to the end and began a new tune. All he could play was a march, a hornpipe, a nursery rhyme, and the death music from *The Wicked Baby*. He didn't expect any audience would let him get that far.

But they did. By then, though sweat dripped into his eyes, he was almost enjoying himself. He tipped his head back and with extra emphasis played the final *waa-waa* of the evil child's triumph when it overcame its enemies.

The people on the barge and all the other ships, Calleena,

the doctor and captain were full-throated with melody too, heads thrown back, loud as anything. *Waa-aa! Waa-aa!*

Rufkin ended, out of breath. He couldn't help but notice Royal Navy of Fontania uniforms, officers from the warship, moving around on the various ships, writing on clipboards. Taking down names, perhaps. Rufkin knew someone would have taken charge. Way over on the highest deck of the *Princess of Dogjaw*, a woman stood watching on her own. She was too far away to see clearly but her long coat looked like fur.

"Thank you, parentless boy!" roared Doctor Goodabod. "Now I can die happy. I owe you much."

Nissy grinned at him from the deck as well. Vosco's eyes shone. The stage-fright was almost worth it. No it wasn't. Never again.

Rufkin shook his own spit from the trumpet. He hoped the warship didn't have a naval band of its own all snickering at him. He fumbled the trumpet back to Harry and slid down the ladder. Then he leaned against the cabin and sucked air into his lungs.

Harry landed on deck beside him. The people around, as well as the crowds on the cargo ships, were still laughing and crying *Waa!* to each other.

Way down the far end of the barge something yellow popped up over the rail. It looked like Mistress Mucclack's sun hat. Someone must be checking the launch. They were welcome to the hat, the day had grown hot. Whoever it was gazed around at the *Princess of Dogjaw*—the warship—the freighters—then ducked out of view again.

Another captain appeared. "I didn't want a party on my barge. Clear off."

"Your barge?" Captain Thunderhead thundered. "You work for Butterly Ventures. As I do." He stuck out a thumb at Calleena and Harry. "And as they do."

"We do," said Calleena. "Trust me. I was on my way to find Harry, and here he was."

The barge captain spat on the deck. "Then why didn't he tell me? Suddenly here was this fellow who can't play the trumpet hanging about and trying to look at my manifest."

"Your what?" asked Rufkin.

"A bill of lading," said Nissy. She had her notebook out and was scribbling in it.

"Manifest means 'obvious,'" said Rufkin, "or 'reveal' or—"

"The girl's correct," said Thunderhead. "It also means bill of lading. A list of what's on the barge." He scowled at Harry. "What were you after?"

Harry grinned through the mass of curls and waved the trumpet. "A stage, that's all. An excuse to show off. Great party and there's no clearing up to do afterwards." He nodded at Rufkin. "Thanks, boy."

Rufkin felt the strength of that stare. He knew for sure Harry was acting. Perhaps he really was a spy.

As for a great party? With the sky so gray, Rufkin couldn't tell what time it was. But *party* implied there'd be food, whether it was pancakes for a late breakfast, a sandwich for lunch, or pie for early dinner. Or a snack like sausage rolls, maybe, or pretzels and dip. He'd had only a third of a banana in several days.

"Any chance of a peanut butter sandwich?" he asked Captain Thunderhead. He tapped Vosco's shoulder. Vosco nodded and made a small slurp. "He'd like some juice, too," said Rufkin.

"Too much sweet stuff will rot the teeth of any child," rumbled Doctor Goodabod.

"Blast me eyes, that's worth a thought at the end-of-days." Captain Thunderhead's weathered face creased with amusement.

"I'll take them along to the *Princess of Dogjaw*," said Calleena. "Peanut butter should be the least of it."

Great. Rufkin knew cruise-ship food. He gave his most charming smile.

That woman was still watching everything from the upper deck of the *Princess*. Rufkin felt he ought to know her somehow—from society magazines probably.

Calleena grabbed Nissy's hand and marched off. Harry seized Rufkin's hand, so Rufkin clutched Vosco. The little boy, bundled up in the too-big jacket and still in the beanie, looked as scruffy as a kid in a comic book.

In moments they were all teetering up a gangplank lashed between the barge and a freighter. It was exciting—creaks and squeaks of rope, a glimpse of ocean far below.

People called out, "Well done. Totally good tooting," and other cheery comments about his trumpet playing.

Rufkin shrugged and smiled and muttered thanks. This part of having an audience was all right.

"It was only luck they liked it," he said to Harry as they rushed on. "My older brother's heaps better."

Harry glanced down. What thick black eyebrows he had, piratical ones. "Just stay out of trouble."

Rufkin used his own eyebrows to show he was puzzled by the remark, and would never in a million years seek any trouble.

A naval officer waved at them with one of those clipboards, but Harry whizzed Rufkin and Vosco over another gangplank. For a few minutes he lost sight of Nissy.

"Lucky the navy's here," Rufkin said. "They'll sort things out."

Harry pulled them to a stop and peered round a lifeboat up on its davits. "All clear. Come on."

If Harry was avoiding the navy, it didn't work. They walked straight into a naval captain. The officer looked startled and snapped to attention.

Harry saluted him back. "Mistaken identity, whoever you thought I was. As you were."

Then he hurried Rufkin and Vosco over yet another walkway to another freighter, where another end-of-days party was frantic with hijinks, then onto a container ship. From there, the blue B of Butterfly Ventures was in clear sight again. Yes it was on the funnel of Madam Butterly's own super-yacht crammed way down among the hundreds of ships.

"Is Madam Butterly here? That would be…" Rufkin was going to say *brilliant* but Harry's face had gone stiff behind his dark curls.

"Yes, she is. And she's not pleased about any of this. None of us are pleased. We are all in bad moods." Now it sounded as if Harry was his true self, solemn and determined like a detective.

Of course. Madam Butterly was the woman Rufkin had seen up on the highest deck of the *Princess of Dogjaw*. She'd have the best view of what was happening from up there. No wonder he'd felt he should know her. Madam Butterly being here was definitely brilliant. His parents knew her through business interests. For instance, they'd invented and made turntables for the stage, then adapted them for farmers to use in feeding hundreds of animals. Even the army and navy used Robiasson turntables now for their swivel guns. Madam Butterly and his parents were often at the same parties, with pictures in newspapers and magazines. She'd take better care of Rufkin than the Mucclacks. And, well, he'd try harder this time not to do anything dumb.

He caught a glimpse of Nissy and Calleena ahead, then lost them again. If Nissy met Madam Butterly she'd be so impressed she'd be speechless.

Harry was rushing Rufkin and Vosco along the deck of another barge, close to the *Fighting Hawk*, the latest warship of the Fontanian Navy. He stopped for a moment, checked ahead, then dragged them on. "Keep your head below the parapets, if you know what I mean. Let me repeat: just stay out of trouble. That goes for your sister as well, and the little nudger."

Rufkin nearly put Harry right about Nissy and Vosco but he'd do it later. He had to watch where to put his feet while they climbed down to a smaller freighter, then up another gangplank, all the time trying to make sure Vosco didn't fall into a cargo hold or down between a yacht and a medium-sized freighter or into a tiny fishing rowboat stuck way down there between them. Now Harry rushed them to another gangway—wooden again—past a third end-of-days party where the songs were melancholy—and over a stout old metal gangway tied between a cargo ship and the *Princess of Dogjaw* herself, as large as a castle in the middle of the drifting flotilla.

—

ON THE MENU

One summer, Rufkin's parents had done the family tour on a cruise ship. The food? Better than excellent. Cakes with icing twice as thick as an ogre's thumb. Jellies bright as ruby and emerald. Ice cream sprinkled with chocolate drops, or toffee nuggets grandly called *o'keh-po'keh*. The energy Rufkin's family used up performing (and Rufkin helping backstage) had kept them slender and fit.

His mouth watered now at what might be served on the *Princess of Dogjaw*. Hmm, yes, only *might*. With machinery not working, the chiller cupboards could have run out of ice. The ship's ovens mightn't be hot. There might not even be fresh water to wash any vegetables.

Calleena was in view again, hurrying Nissy through a double door. Harry hustled Rufkin along, though he didn't need hustling, and Rufkin kept hold of Vosco. They were all led into a great empty dining room, then through into a kitchen.

Darn. He was right. There were no roaring ovens. No chefs screamed orders at their assistants. One oven purred a bit. One chef sat on a stool, scratching his head and leafing through a recipe book. The waiters must all have been at an end-of-days party.

"Feed them," Calleena cried, then beckoned Harry aside—it looked like she was giving him orders.

The chef took no notice at all. But a kitchen hand staggered in clutching a cabbage. His eyes were those of a man who'd woken from a nightmare and found it true.

On a bench was a tray covered in paper napkins. The kitchen hand set down the cabbage and dragged the napkins off as if they were heavier than concrete slabs. Four cold sausage rolls sat on a plate. In a bowl, five apples looked as if someone had used them for juggling.

It would be nice to cheer the guy up. "I was on the *Princess of Wolfhead* two years ago," Rufkin said. "We had vegetable confetti rolls and spicy fruit tarts. Kangaroo steaks too. That was remarkable. There aren't any kangaroos in all of Fontania."

The kitchen hand squinted at him. "The *Princess of Wolfhead*. Out of ten cruises and sixty thousand passengers, I remember one boy in particular."

Rufkin took a step back.

"The boy who skimmed a fruit tart to see how high he could do it. Seven of us had taken three days to build that tower of champagne glasses."

Nissy snorted. Rufkin decided this was a good moment to take one of the sausage rolls and mutter *thank you*. Nissy took one too—the biggest, of course.

The kitchen hand still made Vosco a peanut butter sandwich. He even cut off the crusts. But the bread was dry and curled up at the corners like wings. Vosco, the sleeves of the jacket too long, had a wary nibble. He kept glancing at Harry and the trumpet.

Calleena whispered a last order to Harry and swung out the door. The beads on her tunic clattered. Harry gave Rufkin a grim salute, then he and the trumpet were out the door too.

The kitchen hand spoke again in a Tone-sarcastic. "So sorry, I'm sure. This is all we've got."

"It's delicious and I mean it, compared to starving." Rufkin did a clown-sorry face, then passed his hand up over his mouth to reveal a clown-smile.

The kitchen hand softened. "We're down to this last cabbage. We were due to restock in Port Feather. There'll be pandemonium when the passengers find out that starvation is next on the menu."

"Pandemonium," said Nissy to Rufkin, "means—"

"Uproar and riot." Rufkin knew hundreds of difficult words, just not all of them.

The kitchen hand blew a breath of long-suffering. "The end-of-days. It's what happens at the end of progress."

"Progress isn't things getting worse," said Nissy. "It means they get better."

The kitchen hand turned his head from side to side. "The dragon-eagles could maybe stop the end-of-days if they were asked. But the King's on vacation. The Queen, in my unwanted opinion, was daft to try and tackle it on her own."

"Oo," said Vosco. It was the first time he'd said anything other than *help*. Rufkin stared at him. Did he mean *Oo, the poor chap has a sore neck?* Or was it *Oo, I just remembered?*

The guy continued with a joyless smile. "But it's not the problem of our lowly selves to solve. It is only up to us to suffer through it. I hope that means we'll come out the other end alive and kicking." He picked up the plate with the pastry crumbs and wandered off to a sink piled with unwashed dishes.

A sailor with a blue B on a yellow and black striped sweater elbowed through the dining-room door. "Children. Wanted by Madam Butterly. Now."

At last, progress of a pleasanter sort.

The sailor led them back into the dining room. Vosco tugged to go through the door they'd come in by, back to the barge. But the sailor turned to another door into a foyer. The biggest staircase Rufkin had ever seen, white marble and twisty polished wood, led upwards.

"I knew it. Madam Butterly is here on the *Princess*, not on her super-yacht," said Rufkin.

Nissy looked as impressed as he had imagined, though not at all speechless. "It might be the end-of-days but her dolleros still count for something. I'm going to meet her. Oh, my, Nissy Symore meets Madam Butterly."

"Hurry up," said the sailor. "She's waiting."

But Vosco eyed the stairs as if he might do some silent kicking that meant no-no-no.

"Let's be growlable cats," said Rufkin to Vosco (he felt silly but it was the kind of nonsense little kids liked). "They scramble up like anything. Or else I'll carry you."

"For heaven's sake," said Nissy. "Come on."

On hands and knees Rufkin started to climb. "*Arr-owrrhh.*"

Vosco blinked at him and again looked back the way they'd come.

"*Arr-owrh,*" went Rufkin. "This growlable's lonely."

Vosco chuckled and started to copy.

⌒

THE KNOT IMPOSSIBLE

BUSINESS TIPS

At the top of the staircase was a celebrity corridor. The violet carpet had tufts so thick that if Rufkin had bare feet it would bury his toes. The sailor strode to a door and knocked. A butler opened it and the sailor handed them over. Then the butler ushered them in to the biggest suite Rufkin had ever seen, and he'd seen plenty.

In the main room Calleena waited on the arm of one of three red velvet sofas. Still grim-faced, Harry was sitting on a silver chair, the trumpet on the floor. There was a dining room, huge. Side-tables, shelves, fancy ornaments shaped like fish or boats, that sort of thing. A small kitchen of its own too. Good. It would be stocked with food that Madam Butterly would be glad to share with the son of her friends and colleagues, Tobias and Maria Robiasson. She might not be so delighted by Nissy, who stood next to Rufkin, her mouth open, that spotted notebook ready in her hands.

But Rufkin bet Madam Butterly would be amazed to learn that the little boy was the youngest duke. She'd be proud to help return him to Lady Polly and Lord Trump.

Rufkin was happy for the first time since—well, since his parents had opened his Statement of Success. The day before he'd been packed off to the Mucclacks. Soon, very soon, all would be well.

He glimpsed Madam Butterly now, through glass sliding doors, still on the private deck, watching the sea.

Calleena tapped on the glass and Madam Butterly turned. Her hair was the smoothest shiny blonde. She had red fingernails and red lipstick. Her face was remarkably smooth too. He couldn't say why, but he didn't think she looked quite like her pictures. In her hands was a notebook of her own, luminous blue. A red ribbon marked her place. The fur coat, so long it touched her shoes, had a collar that looked like a whole fox. One lapel was the head, its tail the other. Rufkin hoped it was fake. He couldn't be sure.

She came in from the deck, smiled at Nissy, then at Rufkin with particular attention. She glanced at Vosco's dirty face and widened her eyes at the butler.

"Ma'am." The butler guided Vosco, still bundled up like a comic-book kid, past an alcove with a desk and into the bathroom.

"I'm sorry, Madam Butterly." Rufkin gave the Nod-respectful that he'd worked on for *The Good, the Ugly, the Terribly Cheeky*. "We are rather grubby."

Madam Butterly's eyes were such a deep brown. "So you're all on your own." Her voice was almost a purr, which suited the fur coat. Foxes were good parents. They sang purring songs to their cubs and the cubs would purr back.

Rufkin nodded again. "This is Nissy Symore. Her mother runs the engineering yard and marina on the estuary."

"Far away near the City of Spires." Madam Butterly's

smile was very welcoming. It seemed to Rufkin he even heard a deep purr while she spoke.

"And my name's Rufkin. I'm a Robiasson."

She looked startled. Well, it would be a shock to find the son of people she knew in this situation. He ought to say it wasn't his parents' fault.

She smiled again and raised her hands. "This is a strange place to meet."

"It's like a slow whirlpool that the ships are stirred into," said Rufkin, playing up the Blink-innocent. It often worked on grown-ups. Yep, she seemed to fall for it, though her face was not easy to read. He repeated the Blink-innocent and added a tiny head-tilt. "I saw your super-yacht stuck there. Even the *Fighting Hawk* is caught up in it. I hope it isn't really the end-of-days."

Nissy gave a *tut* as if he'd said something obvious. Of course he had. She ought to know you have to start a conversation somehow.

"It has caught us by surprise. But it is not the end yet." Madam Butterfly's smooth face managed an inspiring Smile-determined. She put her notebook on the desk and sat at last on a sofa that faced out to sea. "Nissy," she said. "A pretty name."

Nissy blushed.

"She wants to be as successful as you, if it doesn't turn out to be the end-of-days." Ah, Rufkin knew how to get Madam Butterfly definitely on their side... "If you have a moment, maybe you could give her some tips."

Nissy went even redder. Rufkin wanted to laugh. He kept his lips together, eyes wide.

Madam Butterly chuckled. "Another apprentice? Calleena's been my excellent assistant for years but Harry's new." She tossed a quick smile in his direction. "Watch out, Harry. Nissy could be competition for you." She turned back to Nissy. "Tips? Of course. Start as young as you can. By the time I was twenty, I was working for a woman of astonishing talent and I learned a lot. Grab any chances. No dolleros spent on research are ever lost, remember that. When you do your research, all sorts of surprises spring up, but you avoid costly mistakes. Hey ho, look at us now—no research predicted this exactly, did it? But never let anything stand in your way. And last—" her smile at Nissy almost turned sassy— "present yourself well. Your turn for the bathroom when the little boy's finished. Let's see how you clean up."

Nissy didn't look too pleased at that. Rufkin knew he was grimy too, and probably smelly. He had a little sniff of his own shoulder. *Phoo*, bad mistake.

"Who did you work for?" asked Nissy. "Who started you off?"

There was a flicker in Madam Butterly's eyes. "No one you would remember." She smiled again. "Don't worry, the pair of you. What we have here, the tangle of ships, isn't the end-of-days yet. We'll figure it out."

Rufkin felt warmth in his chest. She was too nice to upset him or Nissy by saying things that might not be true, such as *Our prospects are grim, hopeless and dire.*

"So," she continued, "none of you are with your parents. Rufkin, didn't I read that your family was about to set out on tour?"

It had been in the society pages. Rufkin could only nod. His throat choked up with missing them all.

"You can stay with me till we hear something. Perhaps all we need is a change in the weather." Madam Butterly stroked her fur collar. "Now, Nissy. Tell me more about yourself."

Rufkin went to the window and shoved his hands deep in his pants pockets.

From this high, the view was staggering. People below looked like dolls. They swarmed on the walkways between the yachts, freighters, and barges. They were staring at the swivel guns on the *Fighting Hawk*, up at the sky, out at Old Ocean. Beyond the hundreds of ships, Rufkin could almost see the movement of current that kept all the vessels penned.

He narrowed his eyes to see better. No, that wasn't a current—it was a shadow passing below the surface. The same shape that had scared him before. Too long for a whale. The wrong outline for a giant squid. For just a moment the shape looked like a dragon sniffing the great knot of shipping.

It must be illusion. It had to be. But again a feeling of loneliness knifed deep into him. His knees nearly buckled. Then the shape seemed to head away under the ocean. Rufkin let out a gasp which was covered by the click of a door. He turned back to the room.

Vosco was ushered out of the bathroom and Nissy marched in.

The butler carried Rufkin's jacket over his arm and offered it to him. "Yours, I believe, sir? I have sponged it."

"Thank you." Rufkin put it on and checked the pocket

for the Lord Hodie figurine. The butler also passed him the purple beanie as if it was something disgusting. It was. Rufkin tucked it behind a sofa cushion.

Vosco's face and hands had been spruced up and his waistcoat wiped too. He didn't look happy about it. He spotted the trumpet, marched straight over and picked it up. Harry frowned at the kid through his dark curls.

The butler looked at Madam Butterly with lifted eyebrows. "So here is little mister made as tidy as I can manage, Ma'am. He seems not to have shoes. And that sticky rust with the dust of blue is industrial dirt, Ma'am, never easy to remove."

Madam Butterly looked at Vosco more closely. Calleena leaned forward on the sofa. Harry had tensed like a catcher ready for serious slogball. Was there something special about the little kid's waistcoat? The industrial dirt?

"How did you get yourself in such a state?" asked Madam Butterly. "Over all that lovely pattern. Of feathers, is it? Come closer. Let me see."

Oh—they must have spotted a royal design. It would be dragon-eagle feathers.

But Vosco ignored her. He fished the beanie back out from behind the cushion and pulled it on. Then he leaned against the sofa and pushed the finger stops on the trumpet.

"She wants you closer." Calleena's voice was rather sharp.

"Little boy?" Madam Butterly used a softer tone. She opened a shiny box with words on the lid saying *Treats of Dogjaw.* "Goodness me. I found some peppermints."

Vosco cocked his head. From under a sofa crept a large fluffy cat, golden and purring. So there had been a real purr.

It slunk up to Madam Butterly, but she pushed it away with her soft yellow shoe.

"Not for you. Come on, little boy, these are the best peppermints in all the world." She beckoned Vosco again, eyes on his waistcoat.

Rufkin kept a grin to himself and waited for the big reveal—*this was the youngest duke!* The cat meowed. Vosco glanced at it. The cat nudged him with its head. Rufkin noticed Nissy come out of the bathroom. It was his turn for it now, but he couldn't miss the moment.

"This is my pet. See how it matches my coat." Madam Butterly smiled at Vosco. "Have you got a cat at home?"

"Ee-ow," said Vosco.

The cat meowed again.

The little boy took a step backwards, then another, still holding the trumpet. Then he turned, grabbed the door handle, and was out and away.

Harry took off after him.

"Vosco, wait!" Rufkin pounded out too, along the celebrity corridor, down the great flight of stairs. In the foyer Vosco headed for the deck.

No, cried Rufkin inside, *not back near the ocean—not near that shape.*

—

CRAZY WEATHER

Rufkin kept running. The dragon shape couldn't be real but nothing was safe anyway. Old Ocean wasn't safe. As soon as the weather changed, the knot would break up. The ships might be damaged from being crushed together. How many of them might start to sink? But he had to get Vosco.

His feet carried him over the old metal gangway, over the deck of a yacht. Harry should have caught Vosco by now but Rufkin himself passed Harry easily.

The end-of-days parties still rollicked. From somewhere he heard a violin, wild with energy and as lovely as when Oscar played, one moment making the listener want to shout with laughter, the next to sob. It was joined by a voice so pure it loosened his heart-strings. Ahria's voice! His family was here? The *Lordly Sword* was caught in the tangle?

Vosco was heading to a gangplank onto a freighter. He staggered—he would fall in! With a slogball dive, Rufkin seized Vosco at last. He knelt with him to catch his breath.

Above him was a shout. "Rufkin!"

He glanced up. His brother Oscar stared down from an upper deck, pointing with the bow of his violin. "How did you get here?"

THE KNOT IMPOSSIBLE

Rufkin only just heard him amid the roar of parties—and the growing howl of wind at last. He waved his arms and hands in the code they used mucking about backstage when their parents were performing. *Are you all right?*

Oscar pointed with the bow and violin. "Wait right there!" He disappeared.

Someone grabbed Rufkin's shoulder. It was Harry. "Keep going!" He yanked Vosco from Rufkin's arms, but then set the kid down on the deck and scooted him off on his own like a wind-up toy—in the direction they'd first come from the barge? The man must be crazy! Vosco was out of sight in a moment. Rufkin sped after him.

Ahead, Oscar slithered down a set of metal stairs and came running. Harry pushed him aside. The violin went spinning over the deck and through a doorway.

"Run!" Harry shouted to Rufkin. "Get Vosco. Run!"

There wasn't a choice. Rufkin took off again.

When he glanced back, he couldn't see Oscar, but Calleena and the butler were pounding behind Harry. Harry was weaving about as if he was trying to head them off, pointing them all the wrong ways. Definitely crazy!

Rufkin raced along the deck of a freighter beside the *Fighting Hawk*, over a plank to a yacht—another freighter—but it was hard to spot Vosco, such a small boy among all the grown-ups—

There was a flash of something purple, like a bouncing ball. The pom-pom.

Rufkin leapt and landed on the red barge where he'd played the trumpet. He glanced behind again. Calleena in her scarlet boots was still following Harry. By now, so was Nissy.

"Little thief! That's not your trumpet," Harry cried in the wail of wind. But he flapped his hand as if he was desperate for Vosco to keep running.

By now the little boy was staggering with every step, making for the rope ladder still hooked over the side to the rusty old launch. Rufkin reached the railing at the same time and held him steady.

Harry stopped Calleena a fair distance back, but he let Nissy sprint on. It seemed as if he was beginning to say something, but he glanced at the sky. Calleena stared up too and stiffened with shock.

The cloud bank was purple-gray now, heavy with rain, but on the bottom a sort of prong had started to form. In an instant it lengthened into a rope of dense cloud reaching down for the sea. The ocean below started to churn, then it too began to rise in a rope of spray. It was forming a waterspout.

Vosco's shoulders trembled under Rufkin's hands. Gasping, Nissy arrived. Rufkin pointed at the cloud.

The ropes of water and cloud met and made a high twisting funnel. At first it looked like a toy—now it grew like some sort of magician's trick—and now it sent out flashes like a scientist's crazy experiment. A second waterspout began to form. The first was speeding across the ocean for the knot of ships.

Something shoved Rufkin. It was Harry again. "Get down there!" He hustled him to the rope ladder.

But they wouldn't be safe in the launch. "Look at the waterspouts!" Rufkin cried.

"Get down!" Harry shoved Rufkin again. "All of you."

Nissy bashed Harry's arm. "Let him go!"

"Take Vosco," cried Harry. "Get him away!"

Bending and snaking, the first spout flew right at the ships. A blast of gunfire came from the *Fighting Hawk*. The sailors ran about like rats on a hotplate. The guns fired again.

"They can't shoot the wind!" shouted Rufkin.

"The guns are firing by themselves. The men can't stop it."

It was true. The swivel-gun turntable was breaking apart, guns discharging in all directions.

Harry wrestled Rufkin onto the ladder at last. He loaded Vosco into Rufkin's arms, and pushed.

A scream of wind like a monstrous engine nearly burst Rufkin's ears. Sliding—rope burn—Vosco's little legs kicking—Rufkin landed flat on his back in the launch beside the sled and the puppet. The trumpet was under his legs and the kid on top of him. As he lifted his head, Nissy's binoculars flew past and smashed. Then Nissy tumbled down the ladder and sprawled next to him.

Harry stared down from the top.

He'd called Vosco by name—he knew Vosco was the little duke and he'd tried to kill him!

The roar of wind slammed over the barge. Its red side rocked. The launch knocked against it with a screech of metal. Open-mouthed, Rufkin saw Harry loosen the rope ladder and fling it down into the launch. In the spray and wind, the terrible roaring, the hook of the grappling iron tore away and broke off part of the rail. The wall of the barge swayed above. Rufkin knew they would be crushed—

Vosco cried out, scrambled into the sled and huddled next to the puppet.

Harry had a foot on the railing, ready to jump—but his face was suddenly shocked, then furious. He gathered himself again to leap down. But the launch was already floating well away.

The distance from the barge grew greater and greater. In the sky, each waterspout circled like a monstrous lasso. The tangle of ships was breaking apart, gangplanks and walkways wrenching and splitting as the vessels separated. Even through the booming wind came the *crack!* of timber and groans of metal, the reverberating *twang!* of great ropes snapping.

The launch somehow moved on its own smooth current. White stones as big as hens' eggs began rattling on the water. Hailstones—hard and icy. But even as Rufkin ducked, he saw that after the first one or two, they fell only on the sea, not into the launch.

He picked himself up. The launch must be in some sort of invisible bubble. This had to be magic—it must be because Vosco was royal. Hail kept pelting from the black clouds, but Rufkin, Nissy, and Vosco were warm and dry.

—

CRAZY PANTS

For half a second Rufkin was terrified—magic. Then he went giddy—they were safe.

But then he thought—safe for the moment. What about next? Magic might not last very long. Madam Butterly would have protected them. She had food. She was on the sturdy *Princess of Dogjaw*, not a tub that would start to leak in the next five minutes. Harry had forced them over the side and hoped they would die.

And at last he let himself think—his family was there. He'd heard his sister's voice. He'd seen Oscar. He might even have made Oscar lose his violin.

He tried to make out the *Lordly Sword* through the hail, through fountains of spray whirled up by the waterspouts. He'd been furious and sick to be sent to the Mucclacks, but a lump as big as a duck egg stuck in his throat. *Be safe*, he thought to his parents, Oscar, and Ahria, *please, be safe*.

The splashing of hailstones eased to a scatter, then nothing. The waterspouts vanished. The rage of the wind died right away.

For a second Rufkin remembered the shock of seeing the two necks of tornado. His whole body trembled as it had when that shape moved past in the ocean. Maybe it had somehow been a reflection of the coming waterspouts?

Far off, dozens of ships dotted the sea. Even the biggest of them—it must be the *Princess of Dogjaw*—diminished in the distance. He hoped the boats were all the right way up, especially the *Sword*. He wanted Calleena and Madam Butterfly to be safe too, wherever they were now. He didn't give a ten-cent stuff what had happened to Harry.

Nissy was huddled on the deck, eyes closed. Sleeping, or fainting. At least she was breathing. Vosco, the beanie down to his eyebrows, was sitting beside the shabby puppet, playing with the keys of the trumpet. Serve Harry right that he'd lost it for good. The puppet's face was covered by the yellow sun hat. Whoever Rufkin had seen wearing it must have popped it there for a joke. He hoped they hadn't stolen the oat-bars while they were about it. He checked. The packet was there, opened, with one bar missing. He should save the rest till they were really starving, when the awful things might taste delicious.

But what next? He climbed onto the cabin roof. Way, way back, he could just make out the last of the tangle of ships breaking away. Lucky that the wind had helped move them to safety—well, luck, mixed with magic.

He felt exhausted, so he climbed down. Vosco was sleeping now, with his legs under the coverlet. Rufkin lay on the foot of the sled and tried to sleep too. But Nissy gave a grumble and either woke or stopped fainting.

She sat up and stared at the vast emptiness of Old Ocean. "What happened?"

"Did you faint?" Rufkin asked. "What did it feel like?"

She frowned. "Things went sort of gray, that's all." She jutted her chin at the smashed binoculars. Then she blinked at the puppet. "Why did you give it the hat?"

"I didn't," said Rufkin.

Nissy crawled over and picked the hat off. She looked closely at the puppet's blue face and rusty hair.

"What?" Rufkin peered at it too. The light wasn't good.

"Don't scoff before I've finished talking…" Nissy chewed her bottom lip. "It looks a bit like the Queen. What a mess it's in. You know—if Vosco's a duke, then that riverboat might be the one that went upriver with Queen Sibilla and the scientists. So the puppet could be a decoy. That rusty dust could be from mining. The cave-lizards come from an underground mine, don't they?"

"No, they just live in mud. And all mines are underground," said Rufkin.

"Don't you know anything? Some mining is on the surface. All right, I should have said from *near* an underground mine." Nissy dropped the hat back. "Anyway, I said don't scoff till I've finished. Maybe the Queen was too scared to go herself. Or maybe the Council of Wisdom said it was wise to send a decoy."

He had to clench his teeth so he wouldn't jeer. Why would anyone take a four-year-old royal nephew on a plague-solving mission? But why would a kid be so keen on a battered old puppet, decoy or not? And he'd wondered before if the puppet could be mechanical, or even magical.

"Have you touched it?"

Nissy shook her head, so he guessed she was too scared. So was he. They'd be in terrible trouble if they broke it.

Though Rufkin was frightened, and felt awkward, he drew the coverlet down to see more of the puppet. It wore a red cardigan with blue buttons and trim. That had been fashionable last year—Ahria had whined and moaned till she had one like it. The puppet also had a leather belt with a kind of pouch tucked under its side. It had baggy red trousers in thick material with leopard skin knee-patches. It had to be a toy. Not even a mechanical decoy would wear those on official business.

For a moment Rufkin touched a finger to the puppet's hand. It wasn't like wood. It was definitely not metal. It was very like a real hand, firm but soft, a clever construction.

Before he dared to touch it again, Vosco woke up. He patted the beanie, then the puppet's arm, and pointed at Rufkin. "Help."

"He's telling it that I'm sent to help!" Rufkin had to laugh.

"I'm here too." Nissy sounded put out.

"That's right," he said, still laughing. "Nissy's a huge help."

"Shut up." She scowled. Then she frowned. "How would a little kid get involved with a clockwork decoy?"

"I've asked myself that and I don't know." However, he remembered one of those things that are funny but awful as well, and really embarrassing. He rubbed his face.

"What?" asked Nissy.

"Nothing… Well, okay. Kids can get anywhere. Apparently I actually appeared on stage once. It was by accident. I was only two. My dad was playing Dread Pirate

Christopher-Richard and he threw back the lid of a treasure chest, expecting to find, I don't know, treasure. But it was me."

"So?" asked Nissy.

He wasn't going to say any more. Two-year-old Rufkin had stood up, wearing absolutely nothing but a beanie, and waved a stolen packet of chocolates. The audience had screamed with delight. He had no memory of it at all. But his family went on and on about it. He was sure that was the reason he was still crippled by stage-fright.

"Is this a puppet?" he asked Vosco now. "How does it work?"

The little boy shucked his shoulders and bent to the puppet's ear. "Ee-ow," he said.

Very slowly the figure stiffened, like someone stretching when they wake up. The sun hat settled more on its head. "How did—Vosco—get here." The voice stayed on one level. In jerky movements the puppet's head and shoulders rose off the cushion, then toppled back. "The Eastern. Isle. I must. Get."

Rufkin had a glimpse of its open eyes before they closed again.

"Broken," said Nissy. "I bet it's still worth a lot. But it's not really like the Queen at all. It might be their first try at her. You know, a prototype."

Its eyes had been blue as the sea on a sunny day, darker rings like storm clouds around the irises. If the real Queen's eyes were like that, Rufkin reckoned anyone would believe in her magical link with natural things like the wind and the wonders of the air, as Mistress Mucclack had put it.

The puppet's lips parted again. "Where. Are we."

"Maybe five or even more days drifting from the City of Spires. Maybe fairly close to Battle Island but who knows?" Rufkin felt nutty talking to a puppet. Nissy looked disgusted with him.

"North—East—Port Feather," said the puppet's flat voice. "The Mayor of Port..." One of its hands lifted and fumbled at the strings of the sun hat, the knot under its chin. Then it lay silent.

Vosco glanced at the sky and tugged up the coverlet.

Wind started to ruffle Rufkin's hair. Ripples surrounded the rusty hull. It took a few moments to be sure, but although there was no engine or sail, the boat seemed to have changed direction.

—

THE LAST
END-OF-DAYS

"Why are you grinning?" said Nissy.

"It's okay," Rufkin said. "We're heading north-east. For land."

"So what happens when we get there?"

How would he know?

After a moment she fetched the notebook from her pocket and scribbled in it. She was lucky she hadn't lost it.

"What are you doing?" he asked.

She frowned. "Trying to remember something. About Madam Butterly."

"Oh, the tips on how to get rich. Did you get enough out of her? I could tell she really meant it about research. Taking time on it."

"It's not that," said Nissy. "You didn't see her notebook."

"Nor did you," said Rufkin.

"I did. When I came out of the bathroom. When Vosco took off."

"You shouldn't read other people's notebooks," cried Rufkin. "You might want to be as rich as her, but you don't get there by spying."

"What would you know?" asked Nissy. "You're rich but only because of your parents being good actors and gorgeous. You can't understand how ordinary people have to live. Or what they have to do to get by, let alone get ahead." Face tight, she pointed at Vosco. "He's rich and he's royal as well. He's never going to know how ordinary people feel or what they need. Neither of you have any problems."

"I'm in a problem right here!" shouted Rufkin. "So is my family." He didn't want to say his family's ship had been in the tangle. It was none of Nissy's business.

Nissy burst into tears, put her hands over her eyes, and almost jabbed herself with the pencil. "Where's my mam? I want my mam."

When Ahria cried like this, Rufkin disappeared to the most faraway end of the house. Now all he could do was face the ocean and bunch his fingers into his ears. It wasn't as useful. Of course Nissy was scared for her mother, but she had no right to say that about him.

At last Nissy quietened. She wiped her face on her sleeve. "But truly—Madam Butterly—what is she doing? If I jot down what I remember I might make sense of it. I only had a moment to see, but I'm used to numbers." She started scribbling again. "Everyone knows she's making that new metal. You know, zirbonium. It's cheap to produce. But things that are made without it are taxed really high. That's why my mam's finding life tough." Her voice went jagged with fresh tears.

Rufkin really wished he could escape. "So just use zirbonium."

Nissy let out a scream. "You're as thick as two planks. My mam doesn't like zirbonium. She says it's not good enough. And I've just told you, ordinary metal costs too much because of the taxes. Stupid rules by the Council of Wisdom." She flung into the cabin and wrapped herself in Mistress Mucclack's blanket.

She was bewildering. He climbed back to the roof of the cabin.

Light faded till the ocean had the sheen of crumpled foil. His eye caught a movement that wasn't a wave. For a second his heart drummed in case it was that dragon shape. When the movement came a second time, it looked like a sailboat. He rested his eyes, then tried again.

After a moment of nothing, it reappeared. Yes, it was a sailboat. It was too far away to be sure, but maybe two people were in it. His breath went quivery with relief. If there were two survivors from the tangle, there were sure to be more.

~

Night came. It passed for Rufkin on the foot of the sled again, with fitful dreams, a smooth rocking of waves, the huffing of wind.

The sky turned dawn-yellow. He watched it turn dawn-pink and lavender. As the sun finally started to lift, it painted a road of light over the water. Rufkin wished they could ride along it and find his family. If this was a play, that's what he'd suggest to the director. You could do such things on stage—the magical passing of time in a way that made an audience sigh with wonder.

Nissy was still a lump of blanket on the cabin floor. Vosco was curled up with the puppet and the stolen trumpet. By the time the sun was high and the sky blue, Rufkin hadn't seen anything again that might be the sailboat.

Nissy's voice made him jump. "Fontania had an end-of-days before. Nearly thirty years ago, I think. The Great Accident." She was looking up at him, still wrapped in the blanket. "We recovered from that."

"I suppose," said Rufkin. "Are you being encouraging?"

"Lady Gall led Fontania through it," she said. "She was a scientist. And clever at business."

He let out a snort. "She was a cheat. A liar and evil. Incredibly vain. Her emblem was *forever beautiful.*"

"So don't be encouraged." Nissy rolled over again.

The wind stopped blowing. The launch wobbled without direction. He had a nasty thump of fright like a fist in his chest. The boat seemed lower in the waves.

But soon a fuzzy patch appeared on the northern horizon. Was the tide hauling the launch towards the coast? The waves continued to crumple around so that gradually the fuzzy patch became a white line of surf. Then the shapes of roofs appeared, and the long wharves that made Port Feather famous. Rufkin remembered racing Oscar along them on their trip two years ago. Oscar won, of course. His family had dined with the Mayor.

Nissy woke and so did Vosco. Neither spoke to Rufkin. With Vosco, that was no surprise. Actually it was no surprise either that Nissy was sulking.

The launch was lower and lower in the water. Rufkin

hoped Nissy could swim. He could, a bit. But he wouldn't be able to help Vosco, and definitely not her as well.

He clenched his hands on the rail and another piece splintered off.

Hurry up, Rufkin said to the tide. *Take us to the docks.*

Hold up, he said to the launch. *Just a bit further, please, then you can rest.*

Careful now, he said when the tide brought the launch in sight of the wharves with their booths painted red, purple, and blue like candy in a sweet shop.

Very careful now, he said when the tide took the launch under the wharves.

Clusters of limpets and barnacles wreathed around the piles. In the creak and groan of wood, the launch nosed up to a couple of posts. Rufkin tried to grab an old metal ladder but a wave came smashing through and the launch swung sideways. It wedged tight with a crunch. Scabs of rust flaked off.

"Idiot," cried Nissy.

"It wasn't my fault," he yelled back.

"Then whose was it? I'll be happy to see the last of you."

"Same!" shouted Rufkin.

"Help!" Vosco shrieked. "Help!"

The puppet sat bolt upright. Without its lips moving, the royal curse came out of it. "*Brisket!*"

—

NOBODY HERE

Metal graunched and crumpled again. The launch jolted and dropped lower. Water began to gurgle up through the deck. The puppet lurched right off the cushion and nearly toppled over the side. One of its arms had stuck in the rungs of the ladder. It was in Rufkin's way. All he could do was shove at its leather belt to bundle it upwards.

"Grab Vosco!" he shouted. "Hurry!"

Waves thwacked and splashed on the piles. Somehow Rufkin found himself on a small platform under the wharf, the puppet in a heap beside him. Nissy appeared, hauling Vosco, who had slung the trumpet round his neck.

The murky water below had signs in it that Rufkin didn't like. The swish of a tail—he hoped it was only a floating rope. The glimpse of a cave-lizard's claw—just a broken comb?

Pushing Vosco in front of him now, he scrambled for a set of steps that led to the top of the wharf. After the seventh step they weren't so slimy. He thought it was Nissy behind him, but when he reached the top he saw it was the puppet. It sagged sideways over a bale marked WOOL. Nissy's head appeared. She was crawling.

They were all safe. The cave-lizard plague wouldn't have reached this far, surely. Things were fine. Any moment a kind stranger would whisk them to the authorities. Things would be taken care of.

He looked around. There was nobody here. No one at all.

Why not? It must be, oh, about nine in the morning? Last time he'd been in Port Feather, the wharves were a riot of market stalls from dawn to dusk and after. There'd been performance booths, living statues and mimes, advertisers yelling that their steam-coach was the best to anywhere and the fare included a free pumpkin sandwich.

The sailboat was out there but a long way from the port...

Something bumped under the wharf.

Rufkin ran. Down to the blue gates, out to the quay—he slowed and stopped. There was still nobody there. The road was pock-marked as if things had burst up from below. He couldn't run on—he couldn't run back—

Something rattled behind him. It was Nissy coming through the blue gate, pushing a trundler. On it sprawled the puppet. Vosco sat with it, toe sticking out from the sock, and a smug look on his face under the beanie.

~

The trundler smelled like a fish cart. "It's ancient," said Nissy. "But it's wood, even the wheels."

She was already rattling it out to the quay. If Nissy could dare the possibility of cave-lizards, Rufkin had to as well. He ran to catch up. She'd draped a sack over the puppet.

"You don't need to keep it warm," said Rufkin.

She stuck out her chin. "I know. Tell Vosco. Do you want to cope with him in a tantrum?"

"You want a reward for the puppet," Rufkin muttered. "And for getting Vosco back to his parents."

Nissy's look could have fried him alive. "So I leave him with just you to look after him?"

"You've changed your tune," he muttered.

"If you're scared, stay behind. Otherwise, help push." She marched off.

So he had to hurry and put hands to the trundler as well. He kept one eye on the road because of the lizard-holes, the other eye out for familiar landmarks. If they reached First Avenue, he was pretty sure he would find City Hall.

The wind gusted now and then. The sky was cloudy but the day was warm and growing hotter. A black cat crouched in a doorway and hissed. Vosco blinked at it. A tabby meowed at something that wriggled under its paw. But not one person was on the streets. They passed steam-cars on expired meters but there was not even a parking warden. Cars, carts, buses, and steam-trucks lay abandoned along the roads. Parcels and backpacks, bags of shopping, various hats lay here and there.

So—the mechanical breakdown had reached here as well. Rufkin remembered what he'd heard on the tangle of ships—*Why couldn't we have had the end-of-days on dry land?*

They passed a toy duck with the stuffing pulled out. Rufkin was glad Vosco showed no interest in that. The little kid had found an old newspaper under the puppet and played with that, tearing strips, seeing them flutter, then letting them drop. Most ended up back in the cart. Some fell to the road, but what did it matter? The whole city looked deserted. Or maybe everyone was sulking indoors because they couldn't use their coffee makers and telephones or enjoy any ice cream. On a building site, three yellow cranes stood tangled as if they'd jammed in a mechanical ballet.

"I wonder if the breakdown is connected with the plague," Rufkin said.

Nissy shrugged. "Don't see how. The cave-lizards only ever used to live up Lazy River."

"Now they're spreading everywhere," he said. "Like the breakdown."

She nodded. "At least it's good you can sell their casts."

Rufkin let out a shout. "Who on earth wants lizard droppings?"

"Why do you think they're blue?" She gave a superior smile. "Because of traces of lazulite in them. I told you the lizards came from an underground mine."

She was so wrong. They came from river mud. Though Mistress Mucclack had said she blamed the mining for the cave-lizards. A lazulite mine near the river? Lazulite—Lazy River. That's where the name came from? He'd always thought Lazy seemed the wrong name for a wide strong waterway. "But flesh and blood creatures don't have metal bits."

"What about dragon-eagles? Their feathers are silver. Real silver that floats in the air." Her cheeks were plump and smug again.

He felt like an argument. "You'd have to know for sure that cave-lizards everywhere have blue metal droppings."

"True," said Nissy.

"And of course the dragon-eagles are magic," he said.

She smiled. "Your Lord Hodie once said that magic is only science that hasn't been explained yet. So he's clever as well as brave. That makes him more interesting."

Now Rufkin was really annoyed.

Nissy stopped for a rest, so he stopped too. They'd reached Hippo-goose Drive.

A crash from somewhere made him jump. A dog ran past and disappeared. They traipsed on.

"Which way?" Nissy asked. They were under a sign saying Quill Street.

"I'm sure First Avenue crosses this soon." At least he hoped so.

"I'm sweating," said Nissy.

It would waste energy to say that he'd been sweating since he saw the state of the road and even before.

Now and then the wheels bumped over potholes. Now and then a wheel wedged and they had to kick it or wrench it straight. Now and then, when the trundler grew heavy, they tried to make Vosco walk. Mostly he had a silent tantrum so they let him keep riding. He'd torn up all the newspaper. A pile of streamers was still in the trundler.

"You look like a mouse in a nest," Rufkin said.

Vosco grinned. "Ee-ow."

Nissy laughed.

At last, here was First Avenue. The trundler crunched over a broken message-bird. In the gutter three dogs growled over something gray and rubbery-looking. One of the strays shook its head, and pieces flew out of the struggle. They looked like the leg and tail of a lizard.

City Hall with its banner of blue and gold feathers came into view. Thank goodness Rufkin's memory didn't rely on machinery or that would have broken down too. Oh...the big double doors of City Hall used a sensor. Last time he was here, a guard had told him off for running in and out to make it work. Blast. If the doors weren't open, they'd have to shout till somebody heard.

It was hard work heaving the trundler and Vosco up the steps to reach the double doors. Lucky moment—a little shoe held the door ajar by the width of a nose. Rufkin put his through the crack. Darkness. He put his ear to it. Silence. Nissy pushed beside him.

"Hello. Excuse me," she called.

A creaky voice answered. "What do you want?"

Want—want—echoed an echo.

"Go in." Nissy shoved him.

Rufkin stumbled through. A thin rectangle of daylight showed the marble floor and gilded panels of the foyer. He still couldn't see anyone.

"Can someone take me to the Mayor?"

"There's nobody here."

Here—here—echoed the echo.

—

OUTSKIRTS AHEAD

"That's not logical." Nissy's breath steamed in Rufkin's ear. "There's him who's speaking."

"There's you," Rufkin called into the gloom of City Hall. "And here's us. Please, we need to talk to someone in charge."

Silence.

Nissy jabbed him with a finger. "Say it's a blot on the pride of the city if children must fend for themselves."

"You say it," Rufkin snapped. "Better still, shut up." He took another step into the darkness. "Can you tell me how to find Mayor Jolliman? My family had dinner with him once."

There was a pause, then a faint scraping. A light flared in the shadows. It steadied into a flame in a bedtime candle holder. Through an open door at the end of the foyer, Rufkin saw a small man at a large desk. It looked like Mayor Jolliman himself, tiny, with sleek dark hair and the pointed ears of someone of dwarf nobility. Even two years ago Rufkin had been taller than him, overawed that someone so tiny had such a powerful position.

Rufkin bowed with the Nod-respectful. "Mister Mayor, you may remember me. I'm Rufkin Robiasson."

"Robiasson!" The Mayor stood up.

Rufkin stepped back onto Nissy's foot.

"*Ow.*" She jabbed him again.

"I remember every one of your family, young Master Robiasson." The candle lit the Mayor's face in an ominous way until he smiled. "An ordinary younger boy—you. A clever older boy, a talented sister. Your charming mother's smile melted our ice cream. Most of all, I recall your father. How we laughed and joked together. What do you want?"

Yes, that was a warm, obliging smile. "Help," said Rufkin.

"Sadly, there's none to be had. I am Mayor of an empty city. I cannot desert it. A mayor must be the last to leave his city." Mayor Jolliman stuck a palm out towards the east. "The citizens have fled to the river on the outskirts."

"If everyone's gone, you are the last," said Nissy. "And what do you mean by *his* city? What about *her* city? There are lady mayors in the City of Much Glass and Port Marshall. There's a really intelligent one in Monkeyhop."

The Mayor sat down and chewed a thumbnail.

Rufkin felt like a balloon with the air hissing out. All he could do was give a second respectful nod and stride outside. He carried himself like the forsaken child, dignified in distress, in *All Is Never Lost: Search for a Way*.

The clouds had stretched into sketches under a pale sky. Two mongrel dogs scampered below the City Hall steps on their own business, which, thank goodness, didn't include dashing up for a nip at Rufkin. Or Vosco. Okay, or Nissy.

"He said people had fled to the outskirts," she said at his shoulder. "That might include the police."

Rufkin let his arms rise and drop in a gesture than meant

without hope. "He pointed east. We may as well try."

In the cart Vosco put the wrong end of the trumpet to his mouth and gave a huff.

At the foot of the steps they nearly lost their grip on the trundler. Vosco didn't seem bothered. In fact he looked hopeful that the jolt would happen again. But it would have been awful if the cart and Vosco and the puppet had rattled across the road, crashed through the window of the Butterly & Finnick Department Store, and bowled over the mannequins.

They set off along First Avenue.

"Stop!" The shout came from behind them.

Rufkin turned. The Mayor waved his arms from the top of the steps.

He caught up, puffing. "Forgive me, I seemed unfriendly." He thrust his hands into his jacket pockets and pulled out two brown paper bags. "Chocolate raisins. Peanut toffees. It's all I have, without my staff. I don't know where they hide the keys to the City Hall kitchen."

Nissy took the toffees but didn't say thanks.

"Much appreciated. Thank you." Rufkin accepted the raisins and shot a pointed look at Nissy. She ignored it.

The Mayor was red-faced from running. "I was just thinking. And what I thought came down to this. Does my city consist of its buildings or its people? Girl, you are right. If the people have moved to the fringes, I can go too. I'll show you the way."

~

"It'll be faster if we all push," Nissy said to Mayor Jolliman.

The Mayor took proper notice of the cart for the first

time and peered at Vosco in the newspaper nest.

"I didn't know you had a little brother." He blinked at Nissy—she too was much taller than he. "How's your beautiful singing voice?"

"I'm Nissy Symore." She sounded as stern as her mother and didn't try to explain Vosco.

Rufkin wasn't sure if Vosco could be explained. How did the kid come to be in the riverboat all by himself? Was it industrial dirt on his face and waistcoat like the butler said? Had Vosco been to the mine? And why wouldn't he talk? When Rufkin was four he'd been such a gabbler that Oscar and Ahria used to promise him ten dolleros if he'd only shut up for ten minutes. He never made it and never cared.

"Don't mention the puppet to the Mayor," hissed Nissy. "I reckon he'd take all the credit, and any dolleros."

She just wanted half of any reward for herself. She could have it all if she liked. But of course he wouldn't say anything. He felt stupid by now for bringing the darn puppet along in the first place.

Because the Mayor was so small, he fitted neatly beside Nissy and Rufkin at the trundler handle. It still took ages to go a few blocks. They had to keep dodging forsaken vehicles, spilled potatoes, dropped bags, and baggage.

While they stopped for another breath, Rufkin offered chocolate raisins. Vosco laid the trumpet on his lap and put his handful into the bell, which made a temporary and very useless dish. He picked the raisins out again one by one, with delicate pinches.

"I do wish you'd walk," Rufkin muttered.

Vosco did a good Look-reproachful and leaned on the sack over the puppet.

A front wheel stuck on another lump in the road. The Mayor put his shoulder to the handle and shoved till the cart ran straight again. "*Oof.* The cart must be full of schoolbooks and homework. Ha ha! Are you doing a project on fish?" He seemed proud of his joking amid hardship.

They had to shove over more blisters and bumps, then they reached a hill. It was much harder to push up. Rufkin's heart sank when he heard faint mutters under the sack. The juddering must have started the puppet's mechanism.

Nissy spoke loudly to cover the sound. "We'd like to send a message to the City of Spires. How soon can we do that?"

"City of Spires? Why not to the moon?" The Mayor heaved the cart over another crater.

"Can't you contact anyone?" Nissy asked. "Nobody anywhere?"

"Not unless we find new parts for the phone exchanges. And new phones. Not unless we find new parts for postman's bicycles and even new flaps for the letter boxes." He shoved the cart forward with all the energy of justified anger.

"And you won't have any old message-birds, that's a pity. So it's the same as back home." Nissy stopped and pulled out her notebook. "Do you remember the Great Accident that nearly killed the dragon-eagles? Because like I said to Rufkin, the country recovered from that. We have to be positive…"

Rufkin let out a choking sound. "She reckons Lady Gall's business sense saved the nation."

"Oh no," said the Mayor. "One could be in trouble if

one said that." The lobes of his pixie ears had turned red from exercise.

"So what do you think is causing this end-of-days?' Nissy asked. "Lack of research, poor metal, or wickedness like it was then? One or all of the above?"

"What are you doing?" The Mayor eyed the notebook as if it might bite.

"She takes notes," said Rufkin. "She wants to be a business woman too when she grows up."

"I'm one already." Nissy's face was lumpy with dislike.

"Hardly. You lost the lizard rings," said Rufkin. "You dropped the basket."

"There's still some in a box under my bed." She checked her notebook. "Sixty-three. That's nearly worth a dollero."

"Money." The Mayor sighed. "They do say the dirty dollero is the bottom of all evil."

"Money isn't evil in itself," said Nissy. "It's what people do with it that might be bad. When I'm really in business, I plan to be fair."

"Good girl. It's not all about money. For instance, take that." The Mayor waved at a disused area with a heap of broken metal. "I planned playgrounds with beautiful fountains all over Port Feather. Two years after this one was built, it crumbled and rusted. The first thing to go was a roundabout with a Robiasson turntable." The tips of his ears had turned red too. "Your father himself, of course, had nothing to do with it."

"I hope you got a refund," said Nissy. "You'd have kept the receipt."

The Mayor's ears turned red around the rims. "The city paperwork can be a muddle." He shunted the cart harder.

A growl sounded somewhere. The Mayor looked startled. Vosco, eyes wide as eggs, stared over Rufkin's shoulder back down the rise. Rufkin turned. At the foot of the hill about twenty strays were wrestling with something. A ragged man came into view, then another figure, equally ragtag, edging against the walls, facing the dogs.

"Looters?" whispered Mayor Jolliman.

More snarling dogs raced out of nowhere and joined the fight. But even from up here Rufkin saw paving bulge and burst under the pack. Out scrambled a cluster of cave-lizards. Dogs yelped and took off. Others snapped at the lizards, and the lizards snapped back.

"Quick," said Nissy.

Rufkin helped shove the trundler to the top of the rise but it jolted on the edge of the sidewalk. The puppet's mechanism made a noise like a burp.

"What is that?" Mayor Jolliman looked sharply into the trundler and pushed the streamers aside. Vosco hit him with the trumpet.

"*Ow*," said the Mayor. "Behave yourself." He glowered at Vosco, who glowered back, but Mayor Jolliman pulled the sack down anyway. His head went up like a chicken's when it spots something curious.

"Goodness." He gave Rufkin a swat that hurt a bit, though he probably only meant a Slap-playful. "What clever children. You made this puppet yourselves? It would be impressive if it had a paint job and a better costume."

DOWNHILL AHEAD

"It's a present for Rufkin's rich dad," Nissy said. "He can use it in a performance."

Rufkin couldn't help but admire her firm lie, and he hid a chuckle.

Vosco gave the Mayor a Look-disdainful and pulled the sack back into place. Then he stuck a hand right up the bell of the trumpet where he must have lost a chocolate raisin.

The two ragged people were halfway up the rise now but didn't seem to have noticed Rufkin and the others. One might be a woman. They staggered as if they'd had a night scared of what was hiding under their beds. Perhaps they were from the sailboat and had seen the dragon shape.

Mayor Jolliman got the cart moving and Rufkin lost sight of the people. "Nearly at the top, put some muscle into it." The Mayor himself stopped pushing. "Listen carefully. I've been thinking again. I have a plan. It will take the people's minds off any problems with the city coffers."

"What's wrong with the coffers?" asked Nissy.

The Mayor bunched a fist, then punched the air. "I want a performance that will encourage them to build Port Feather anew, build up the funds again, and fight the cave-lizards."

Fight the lizards. No way. Rufkin sped up.

"The thing is, the puppet's a little like the Queen," continued the Mayor, "though it needs an imposing costume. We're sure to pass a suitable garment lying about. Then when we reach the camp, we'll put on a show. Boy, you'll know rousing lines from various plays. Put some together. Girl—Nissy—write the lines in your notebook. We'll rehearse as we go." The Mayor kept talking though he was puffing. "We show the puppet, limp and lifeless. We recite lines about hope. Courage. Community. At the right moment we haul the puppet up in its new costume. People will cheer. It will act as a symbol of hope."

It was a good idea, though Rufkin didn't really see how it could work.

Mayor Jolliman bounced along. "It'll be a wonderful boost. Tell me I'm right."

Rufkin felt sorry for him. But he smiled, as brave and encouraging as the heroic boy in the play where Ocean Toads lumber up to smother the village bakery.

"Good acting," Nissy murmured.

"Help," whispered Vosco.

~

At the top of the rise, Nissy let go of the handle and took out her notebook. "Have you come up with any lines for the play yet?"

"No," said Rufkin.

She kept her pencil ready.

When the road started down, the trundler stuck again. The Mayor pulled out a handkerchief to wipe his forehead.

"Keep a tight hold," Nissy told Rufkin.

"I'm gripping so tight my shoulders hurt." He jiggled the cart, but one of the wheels was thoroughly jammed. "It would help if you kept both of your hands on the handle too."

Below, the road turned a corner and appeared again further on.

The Mayor put away his handkerchief and pointed. "That's the park where the camp is. Down by Jovial River. Boy, do come up with an opening line."

Rufkin kicked the wheel as hard as he could. *Bam!* The cart lurched, the Mayor let go entirely, and the handle slipped from Rufkin's fingers. He grabbed for it, missed—and fell over. *Oof!*

"Foolish boy!" The Mayor lunged for the handle and tripped over Rufkin. Nissy grabbed for it too and tripped over the Mayor. The trundler began to rattle down the slope.

"You idiot!" Nissy ran for it, but tripped again. The notebook flapped out of her hand.

Rufkin scrambled to his feet and snatched up the notebook to hurl it at her, but the cart gained speed—more speed—it was thundering away for the bend.

Beside Rufkin the ground split open. A cave-lizard emerged—even on the top of the hill? The Mayor shrieked and scampered off, away from the lizard or after the trundler, it didn't matter. It was obvious to Rufkin he'd never catch it.

The trundler swerved round the bend and out of sight. In the distance, amid the clatter of wooden wheels, Vosco was screaming like a normal four-year-old.

—

HUNTING FOR VOSCO

Rufkin jumped over Nissy and raced down around the bend. He stuffed the notebook into his shirt as he went and scanned the pavement for cave-lizard pock-marks. Not as many—very few now—none here at all...

Another corner came up, blocked with broken-down vehicles. He skidded to a stop—the cart hadn't bashed into them. Had it jolted off down that side road? He ran to check—no—hurtled back. There was a path between the vehicles after all. He sped through it and on. The Mayor was nowhere to be seen. All the buildings were shut, shops on the roadside boarded up. No craters or pock-marks at all now.

Nissy's footsteps pounded behind him. He made for a gap between more wreckage and a *Fancy Vests* shop. On the other side, the street flattened out. There was still no sign of the cart or the kid.

"Vosco!" he yelled. "Vosco!" He raced past a small deserted playground with another collapsed heap of equipment—more side streets, two broken-down steam-buses, another corner. When he snatched a look, Nissy was further behind but still running.

Ahead at last was Jovial River. For a horrible minute Rufkin was scared that he'd been responsible for sending the youngest duke to a watery end. Full-tilt with desperation, he took a final bend and entered the park—trees, flower beds, a statue or two, three fountains, though they weren't splashing.

There was no trundler. There were rows of tents of all shapes and sizes. People too, all sizes and shapes. Some in wrinkled pajamas. Some in wrinkled business suits. Some in paint-spattered exercise pants or what anyone might wear for doing the housework. It was quaint. But all Rufkin wanted was a small boy, unharmed, holding a trumpet.

~

There were two obvious places to look. First, a playground. It was old, swings and slides and a climbing frame. No Vosco. Only one plump little girl pushing herself on a sturdy old merry-go-round. Everyone else, grown-up and child, was in a line at the second obvious place Vosco might be: a row of trestle tables set out on the grass. The people were dolloping food from enormous bowls onto blue plastic plates.

Nissy's sweaty hand clutched Rufkin's arm. "Where's the trundler?"

"How should I know?" He jogged away to check the lunch line. There were several small boys in beanies, none of them purple.

He didn't know what was on the tables either. Dollops of green in the bowls. Slabs of pale brown that might be bread. A bean-looking slush.

When the people had filled their plates, they sat on the

rims of the fountains, on benches or the grass. They looked as mystified about the food as he was.

A grandmotherly woman jumped onto a platform. A young man with red spiky hair leapt up beside her and rubbed his hands.

"Welcome to the New Port Feather picnic!" the woman cried.

Rufkin ducked under a table to see if...*ow*. He'd bumped heads with Nissy.

She rubbed her forehead, scowling. "It's stupid if we both check the same places."

He set his teeth. "I'll take the side of the park nearest the river. You take the rest."

"Do it, then." She backed out.

Rufkin crawled out frontwards.

The grandmotherly woman was gesturing like a traffic cop. "We have warm thistle salad. We have bread from ground dandelion root."

"Port Feather has failed us," cried the spiky-haired man. "Who needs a mayor or council? We'll be self-sufficient."

"Eat and enjoy!" cried the woman.

Everyone dug forks into their food. The air hummed with people pondering their first tastes.

Rufkin heard Nissy's voice. "What happens when the thistles are used up? Or when it's not dandelion-root season?"

"Good point," cried a fat man. "We'll starve."

"We'll swell up if there's only beans," called a thin woman.

A bellow came from the other side of the crowd. "Look! Here's Jolliman."

The Mayor was limping into the park. Good—he'd sort everyone out and…

"Spendthrift!" cried the white-haired woman. "Architect of our ruin! Mayor and council have bungled our finances."

"True!" shouted the red-haired man. "City rates should have been spent on a lizard protection plan."

"Not on sets of swings and merry-go-rounds that cost three million dolleros," yelled an ogre.

"They didn't," cried the grandmotherly woman. "Somebody lined his own pocket with most of that money."

The Mayor spread his hands wide. "I agree we must sort out the accounts. But you can't stay here."

"Who says?" somebody shouted.

"You won't like it when it rains and your tents blow down," the Mayor shouted back.

That was a good point. They really should listen to him. Rufkin hated camping in bad weather.

Nissy gave a sudden wave at a bike rack. Between it and a hedge was the trundler. Vosco was sitting next to it on the grass, still wearing the beanie. And holding the trumpet.

Rufkin was stuck behind a table for a moment. "Vosco!" he cried.

The kid grinned. He raised the right end of the trumpet to his mouth and blew hard. The sound that rumped out was very like a troll who needed the bathroom.

—

26

SPRINKLING
THE BLAME

As the rumptipaze died away, Rufkin saw the puppet sit up in the cart, the sack round its shoulders. The downhill rush must have righted the clockwork. It coughed like an out-of-date message-bird. Its head in the yellow sun hat turned this way and that. From the grass Vosco beamed up at it.

"Where is the mine?" said the puppet's rusty voice.

"Where's its what?" asked a man.

"Where's Professor Perkitty?" This time the puppet sounded more realistic. It even stood up in the trundler. "What happened to the engineers? Where am I?"

"The park," shouted a child in the crowd.

Other children joined in. "Next to Jovial River."

"Port Feather."

"In silly trousers."

"In a fish cart."

A tiny hiccup shook the puppet. "Port Feather," said the mechanism.

Someone laughed. "It's escaped from Butterly & Finnick's window."

"It sounds like a delegate on the Council of Wisdom," a

THE KNOT IMPOSSIBLE

man cried. "But look at those clown pants."

The crowd had mostly turned to watch.

"It's a royal on vacation," somebody shouted.

Everyone burst into laughter. The puppet hiccupped once more as if it had stage-fright. It was sure to collapse again any second. Vosco had started to look as if the crowd worried him. Rufkin wondered if he should get him out of the way.

But there was no time. Mayor Jolliman stood in front of the bike rack and raised his arms. "Brave people of Port Feather. I have put together this performance myself for your enjoyment. It is an apology for any mismanagement by misguided members of the city council." He beckoned Rufkin. "Quick, boy. Give me a line to say."

Rufkin took a step or two, faltering. The crowd was a weight, prickling and freezing. A few paces from the trundler, he couldn't move.

The puppet pulled off the sun hat and stared at it. Rufkin could almost see how its clockwork brain moved. It must be like one of those mechanical pianos that played a different set of notes depending on what metal cylinder the gears clicked into place. Then it blinked at the crowd.

For the first time he thought, *It could be real now.* This could truly be a mechanical figure gradually transformed by royal magic into somebody real.

"Does it tell 'Once Upon a Time?'" called a little girl.

The puppet's mouth opened and twitched. "Once upon—a time…"

The crowd settled down, nudging one another.

The puppet blinked again. "…the King and Queen,

brother and sister, decided—it was high time for the people to govern themselves."

"Lazy twerps!" called a woman.

"Shut up!" cried someone else. "Let it go on."

For a moment the mechanism seemed to strike a hitch. Then the puppet continued. "They took advice from every quarter and brought together a group of talented people. But—a grave danger came..." As if the puppet couldn't remember the right words, it raised both hands and snapped its fingers like pretend alligators.

The crowd roared the answer. "Cave-lizards!"

The puppet's voice settled into husky and soft, though it carried well. "The—um—minuscule saurian mud-dwelling sharp-tooth, in great numbers. The Council of Wisdom spent many weeks deciding what should be done. Fire-lizards began to appear. The King was exhausted by years of struggle and the council packed him off on vacation..."

"Shut the thing up!" shouted a man. "It's just Jolliman hoping to jolly us."

"Chuck him in the river!" roared somebody else.

The Mayor spread his arms again. "I agree there is serious fault. But the fault is not mine. I blame..." He caught sight of Rufkin. "Ah! I blame the man who sold us those over-priced roundabouts!" He spread his arms wider. "I blame Tobias Robiasson!"

Rufkin's breath stopped up in his chest.

"You can't blame a star," somebody yelled.

"He's so proud of his handsome face he despises the rest of us!" cried the Mayor.

All Rufkin could do was stare at Nissy—she was staring at the Mayor as if he'd gone crazy.

"I blame the bigwigs in the City of Spires!" continued the Mayor. "I blame the royals with their high-flying ways, lording it over us!"

"So what's this puppet meant to be?" yelled a young man. "Brainless bigwig politician or a lazy royal?"

Half the crowd roared and rolled about as if it was truly funny. The other half squinted and wrinkled their noses as if nobody should make fun of a royal. The puppet put a jerky hand to its head again, then looked at its fingers. Some of the rust and blue dust had come off its hair.

Vosco stood up and tapped the puppet's arm with the trumpet. It glanced down and its eyes widened. "Vosco?" it said. "*Ew*. What a filthy beanie."

Nissy looked as if she'd just figured out something. Probably the amount she could have made on the puppet. Rufkin reckoned it was disgusting how everyone cared so much about dolleros. It was doubly disgusting how the Mayor threw blame everywhere and ducked it himself.

"Lazy royal!" bellowed a man. "We should rip it to bits."

"Interactive drama!" somebody cried. "Give me first go!"

This had turned dangerous. Rufkin moved closer to Vosco.

A deep voice rang out. "Hey!"

The crowd turned, startled. The ragged pair from First Avenue was staggering into the park. It was Calleena and Harry. He looked angry enough to throttle a hippo-goose.

He shouted again. "Wait! Calm down. Listen to me!"

Wait for Murdering Harry? No way!

Rufkin grabbed Vosco's hand and started running past the bikes and bushes.

"Vosco!" cried the puppet.

The whole crowd exclaimed and cried out.

"Rufkin!" barked Harry. "Wait! Let me through to him!"

The crowd laughed and screamed. "Blame the Mayor!"

"Blame the royals!"

"Blame the Robiassons!"

Rufkin hauled Vosco past a bed of red roses. Here was the edge of Jovial River. A notice said *Canoe Rental*. In the water were skiffs, red pedal-boats, canoes, and kayaks. Someone seemed right behind them—he had a look—blast—of course, Vosco had dragged the puppet along too. Rufkin grabbed the thing by its belt and heaved it into a rowboat. He shoved Vosco after it, tried to jump in himself, slipped and went under. He spluttered up and fell into the boat—*ow!* He'd bashed an elbow.

The boat-hire man was scrambling from his booth. "Hey! You have to pay first."

But the oars were in place. Rufkin pushed off from the bank. "Here's twenty dolleros!" He fished in his jacket pocket—no, he'd given the money away days ago. "I'll pay later. Promise." He splashed the oars into the water.

"Blast you," the man yelled. "Make sure you do. One adult, two kids. Stay this side of the sign! Watch out for the current—you won't be strong enough. Watch out for..."

Rufkin's ears were full of water. But Harry's voice was still bellowing. So was the crowd.

One stroke—two—a third—and Rufkin was well out into Jovial River. He glanced behind to make sure Vosco was all right.

The kid still held the trumpet. He was sitting in the puppet's lap and it had the sun hat on again. All Rufkin could see of its face was the pointed chin.

"Boy," said the puppet. "When you catch your breath, please explain what's going on."

Vosco grinned. "Help."

The puppet hugged Vosco and let out a sob.

At last, Rufkin got it. The puppet was real. There in red clown pants was Sibilla, Queen of Fontania.

—

RESTLESS
ADVENTURERS

JAWS IN
THE RIVER

Rufkin almost lost his grip on an oar. He tried to keep rowing. But it was wrong to turn his back on the Queen. For a stroke or two he kept facing her. *Ow*, it twisted his neck.

"Explain, please!" cried the puppet—Her Majesty.

But he was fighting with the current now. The hire man had warned him. The park was already out of sight. How far was it from here to the mouth of the river? He didn't want to be swept down to Old Ocean.

"Vosco," said the Queen, "where's your mother? Where's your dad? How on earth did you get here? How did I get…?" She stopped and coughed.

Rufkin fought for the bank. He couldn't manage. His shoulders ached.

The Queen tapped his shoulder. "Vosco seems to know you. Has he said anything?"

"Only *help* and *meow*," Rufkin answered. "What's wrong with him?"

"He can talk, he just doesn't bother." The rowboat wobbled. The Queen must be jiggling Vosco. "His mother manages charity lunches for a thousand schools—his father's a diplomat—no time to chat, so he isn't encouraged. I wish he'd talk now." It sounded as if the Queen wanted a little cry. "Please, boy—what are we doing here?"

"Just a moment." He had to keep battling the current.

The water looked sweaty with oil. Clumps of tar lay on the banks. A corner of Nissy's notebook pressed into his ribs. It was soaked, and too bad. The dinghy passed a sign. He didn't spot it soon enough to read what it said, but it had red lettering. That usually meant danger, or at least *You're stupid if you don't read this*. He started to worry—but no, whatever it said, he was with the Queen. She'd had plenty of royal adventures, some with Lord Hodie. Magic and the dragon-eagles would protect her. So he and Vosco would be all right too. Of course they would. Probably. He just had to row to the bank.

"Oh, I'm dizzy," said the Queen. "Limp as jelly. Was I really in a fish cart?"

"You've been unconscious for—I don't know, days." Rufkin could hardly lift the oars out of the water now. He let the boat drift for a minute. She'd be too weak to help.

Jovial River had widened. Pink parakeets whirred overhead. Blue willows and red spiky grasses lined the riverside. Even if he could manage the current, Rufkin didn't see a safe spot to land.

"Boy?" The Queen sounded stronger.

"Yes, Ma'am," he said. "My name's Rufkin. Please excuse my back to you, Ma'am."

"Don't fuss," said Queen Sibilla. "Just tell me, Rufkin, what's going on?"

"Ma'am, if you'll excuse me, I hoped you could tell me."

"This is not promising," muttered the Queen.

Rufkin rowed several strokes with the right oar to move nearer the west bank. It didn't work too well. But they'd reached a slower patch of water. He had a part-rest again and tried to explain what he could. How he'd found the riverboat stuck in the mangroves. How everything, phones, traffic, the Great Bridge of Size, had been undermined or broken down, slowly at first then all at once. How the rusty launch drifted or sometimes the wind seemed to push it. The knot of shipping. How everything at Port Feather had broken down too.

"Captain Thunderhead called it the end-of-days..." He shouldn't say this but it blurted out anyway. "You were meant to examine the cave-lizards and put things right."

The Queen gave a sad little laugh. "I know what the newspapers said. It was never going to work so easily. Yes, I can communicate with the dragon-eagles. But the world's changing so fast, I think they just want to be left alone. I don't blame them. We had to see where the cave-lizards first came from, to figure out what had caused the plague and how to end it. So I set off. Some people—" it sounded as if she said that through clenched teeth— "warned me against it. But it didn't seem so very dangerous. I had a professor of biology, other scientists, advisers from the Council of Wisdom, chief engineers from the mine. That's the Butterfly Ventures mine up Lazy River.'

She went on an expedition in her crazy pants? Rufkin couldn't help but glance round at them.

She laughed in a more truly amused way. "They're ridiculous and tough and I love them."

"Sorry," stammered Rufkin.

His jacket had dried a bit, which made things more comfortable. At last he was near the bank. But the water swirled over rocks, so he eased away. A broken branch floated down and nearly struck one of the oars out of his grip.

The Queen kept talking in those little bursts of trying to remember. "Outside the mine—very dirty holding ponds where they wash the lazulite—then we went inside, down in little trucks—around on turntables—further down in a safety cage—I pretended very hard that I wasn't scared. We had masks on, protective gear. And there were lanterns. We reached a cavern—one of the engineers said it was where the miners refused to continue, nearly three years ago. Madam Butterly herself had to go down and make them break through. It turned out to be the biggest lazulite deposit ever known. Then what happened? Not to her—what happened to me? Deep, very deep, we heard an explosion. All I remember—I sensed something huge. I saw a glow, was it…green?"

He glanced back. Her hand was gesturing near her forehead as if she touched an invisible crown.

"For a moment I felt so lonely," she murmured. "Deserted. Desolate. Then another explosion…"

"Boom," said Vosco.

"I remember a safety cage again—was I going back up?" she muttered. "Another turntable—they were Robiasson turntables. That dreadful little man in the park mentioned Robiasson, didn't he?"

Rufkin felt sick. He might even be sick over the side if he

166   THE KNOT IMPOSSIBLE

heard any more against his parents. He should have told the Queen his surname. He couldn't now.

He cleared his throat. "So, someone must have got you back onto the riverboat. Then—I don't know, maybe they were all overcome by fumes or something. After all, the explosion must have made you unconscious. You were like that for days."

"So lonely," breathed the Queen. "Hurting with grief."

She'd better not mention his parents again, that was all. Rufkin leaned as far forward as he could, dipped the oars and hauled back. The current was swift in the middle of the river but not as strong here near the bank. Thick curtains of the blue willows trailed in the water. He thought of the red-lettered sign, and something made him change course.

From nearby came a growl like an engine. If it was working, it must be an old one. That might mean they'd be rescued. He cheered up a little and rested the oars.

There, through some branches, beyond a curve in the river and coming upstream, was the hull of a large yacht. She might have been using an engine but she was also under sail, a jib, and a mainsail full-bellied and brave. On the funnel a blue sign glinted. As she rounded the curve, Rufkin could see three decks.

"Vosco, it's help! Real help at last. That's the *Sea Honey*," he told the Queen. "She was there in the tangle. With luck, Madam Butterly might have got herself back on board. Even if she didn't, whoever is there will take care of Vosco and you, Ma'am…" He couldn't be perfect-polite any longer. "They'll take care of me too. Madam Butterly knows my parents. I am the son of Tobias and Maria Robiasson. They're very well known of course. And they make the turntables." It was taking a risk. But Rufkin felt smug.

~

The engine-like growl came again surprisingly close.

"Help!" shrieked Vosco.

Rufkin swung himself around. A swirl of water at the side of the boat almost looked like a long head, its nose sniffing him.

The Queen let out a scream. "Keep your hands inside the boat! Give me an oar!"

The swirl burst up. In the spray Rufkin saw leathery lips, a jaw crammed with teeth. Alligator! It was half-grown but still enormous.

He thrust out an oar. The teeth crunched together, sinking into the shaft. The Queen ripped the other oar from its rowlock, held it in both hands and bashed the snout. Rufkin's oar started to splinter between the jaws.

"Let go!" He couldn't believe he was screaming at a monster in a tug-of-war. "Get off!"

The rowboat rocked. The Queen yelled and bashed the snout a second time.

Rufkin's oar shattered in half, but he still held one end. The alligator dropped underwater, then surged at the dinghy again. Its teeth were spikes, its tongue dotted with warts, its gullet a tube of horror.

Rufkin stabbed the creature with the jagged end of oar. Its eyes bulged and rolled up in the sockets. It let out a hiss—for a moment he almost felt sorry for it—then it sank into the stream. The last thing he saw were the nostrils like two dark pipes.

"Which they are." He struggled for breath. "Nostrils lead into pipes that go to your lungs."

"Are you all right?" the Queen asked.

He was shaking. "I don't know."

She didn't look good herself. In fact, she looked more like a puppet than ever.

"I didn't know there were alligators so close to Port Feather," gasped Rufkin.

"There never used to be." The Queen shaded her eyes with a shaky hand and peered at the riverbanks. "There are heaps of iron mines in the hills behind Port Feather. That might have something to do with it, I don't know." She shuddered. "It made a noise like an engine. A horrible purr."

Vosco leaned against her and patted her. She patted him too. "Help's nearly here," she said. "We'll get you home to your parents and brothers and sisters as soon as we can."

Past the drapes of willows, the super-yacht glided into full sight.

—

AN UPHELD OATH

Rufkin raised an arm to signal the *Sea Honey*.

"Brave boy," breathed Queen Sibilla.

He wasn't. He still couldn't believe he'd fought an alligator.

The Queen folded down, knees on the floorboards, her head on the seat. She looked very weak, like a pile of old rags. No wonder, if she'd been in an explosion, unconscious for so many days, then bashed an alligator as hard as that. She ought to have something to eat and drink. Rufkin wished he and Nissy had known she was real. They could have stuck bits of oat-bar into her mouth while she seemed asleep.

Four men stood on the super-yacht's bow deck. A boat that size must have a big crew. He didn't dare hope they'd saved at least some of his family. The Queen's talk of Vosco's parents and brothers and sisters had reminded him how much he missed his own.

He beckoned again. "Over here. Help!"

The yacht went into a tack—and Rufkin huffed with laughs that were almost sobs. See? All he'd had to do was trust that someone would come.

"There mightn't be ice cream," he said to Vosco. "But

they'll have ham and pickles. Sailors on yachts always have ham and pickles."

Vosco made a rude sound and shook his head.

"Pickles and cheese?" asked Rufkin.

Vosco grinned. He settled the sun hat on the Queen, wrapped the sack over her. She didn't stir. Vosco put a finger to his lips.

"Keep her a secret?" asked Rufkin. "Or let her sleep? Good idea."

Vosco sat and watched the yacht, trumpet slung on his shoulder.

The *Sea Honey* slowed. Rufkin would like to ask how they did that with sails. Several crew in yellow and black jerseys were working hard at ropes, and the sails went flat.

That face pickled by sea-salt peered down from the bridge deck and looked delighted. "A piece of luck. Tiddlers again!" said Captain Thunderhead.

A much bigger blue and green face topped by a deerstalker hat popped over the main rail. "The very same, though lacking the girl," cried Doctor Goodabod.

The captain yelled for someone to take the wheel. Next thing was a lot of rocking and creaking, orders to the crew and *aye aye sirs*. Rufkin eased the dinghy around to the stern of the super-yacht where there was a small platform. A couple of sailors there tossed him a rope. He tied it to the rowboat and they hauled it close. The doctor and captain arrived to watch.

It was lucky the doctor was as strong as an ogre. With one arm he reached down to lift Vosco and the trumpet.

With one arm again, he heaved Rufkin. It nearly yanked Rufkin's own arm out of its socket.

Doctor Goodabod set him down not very gently next to Vosco. Another dinghy was stowed there on the platform. Two pairs of oars hung in brass clamps, with a coil of rope, a fire extinguisher, that sort of thing.

"Thank you," gasped Rufkin. He rubbed his shoulder. "Now we're even."

"You played 'Song of the Ogre,' I saved you from Jovial River? Very good even-ing—*ah-ha!* I make a joke." Goodabod laughed and kept laughing, using the buckets of air he must have in his chest.

Rufkin had better explain carefully about the Queen. They might think he was joking too and slash the rowboat loose to tease him.

Captain Thunderhead was still looking pleased. "That gypsy fool Harry said he'd fetch you. He set off in a sailboat. Refused to wait. Keen to please Madam Butterfly. Calleena said she'd keep tabs on him. So where's Harry now with those dark, watching eyes of his? Where's Calleena? At sea! *Ha-ah!* So it's Thunderhead and Goodabod who'll get the credit. And it's not just credit, it's heaps of dolleros."

"Dollero dollero!" Doctor Goodabod sounded like an even bigger engine than the alligator. "I have done no harm, not to myself, not to man, woman, child, ogre, troll, dwarf, or what-not. I have upheld my medical oath."

Captain Thunderhead rocked with laughter. "All you'll do is hand the children to Madam Butterfly, for her to choose."

Choose? Choose what—how?

Goodabod wagged a giant forefinger at Thunderhead. "It is no harm to hand children to someone who will feed and water them. It is Madam Butterfly who makes the next steps. A parent—a youngling. That is the deal. It is not I who does any harm."

Harm? Rufkin looked at the crew. Their faces had no expression to help him understand what the doctor was saying, not a wink for a boy, no flash of teeth for a toddler.

The rumble like a motor sounded again.

"Joke's over, Goodabod," said Captain Thunderhead.

"I am no longer laughing," said the doctor.

The roar came louder like an engine revving.

The ogre's skin turned eggshell blue between the green bits. "Alligator," he whispered. "Iron-fed alligator. That is its war-cry." He scanned the stream, scanned up the bank.

"There are no alligators of any kind in this part of—" But the roar sounded again. The captain tensed.

A large swirl of water from the left bank was bearing down on the *Sea Honey*.

"Alligator to port," roared the captain. "All hands on deck! But keep your hands in! Ready your pistols. Don't fire till you see its bloodshot eyes."

Doctor Goodabod drew a huge pistol from his belt and held it aloft. "I'll fire the second I set eyes on its ugly snout."

Vosco started a long high scream.

"The Queen—" Rufkin's voice was only a flutter. "The dinghy—save the Queen…"

But Captain Thunderhead was thundering orders to all the crew, Goodabod shouting, the crew shouting at one another. The yacht began to sweep in a half-circle, rowboat dragging behind her.

Rufkin pulled Vosco to the back of the platform. Thunderhead kept yelling orders. Madam Butterly's butler appeared down some outside steps and at once disappeared up again. Thunderhead ripped an oar from the brass clamps and brandished it like a club, ready to strike.

The water churned close to the rowboat. A snout emerged.

"Observe me do harm!"

Goodabod fired.

The alligator's head heaved up. The ogre fired a second time—and missed again.

The deep *quonk* of a hippo-goose resounded from the bank—there the giant bird stood two-square in the mud. The alligator swung its muzzle round and sank under the river. A swirl showed it speeding for battle. The hippo-goose clacked its beak, wide as a suitcase and far more dangerous. It stamped one thick gray foot and then the other. The alligator rushed at it in a fountain of spray.

The hippo-goose crashed its beak, the alligator splashed backwards into the river, another surge, thrashing of scaly tail, another crash and crunch of beak, a turmoil of water. The alligator arrowed away, the hippo-goose arrowed after it (though it really looked more like a fast-moving shovel). More splash and more crash—a *quonk*, a roar—at last the great bird flapped into the air, trailing muddy droplets of escape and victory.

Rufkin looked over the stern. Vosco shivered beside him. The rowboat was quiet. Unharmed.

FOREVER
VICTORIOUS

Captain Thunderhead mopped sweat off his forehead. "Sammo, rush the tiddlers to the cabin lounge. If Madam Butterly's not ready, feed 'em some hard-tack." He gave a short chuckle.

By now Rufkin didn't really trust the captain and the doctor. Vosco had a very tight grip on his hand again—the kid wasn't happy about them either. Maybe Rufkin wouldn't tell these two that the Queen was still slumped in the rowboat under the sack. Madam Butterly was on board—he could tell her first.

The same crewman—Sammo, was it?—who'd led them to Madam Butterly on the *Princess of Dogjaw* carted Vosco up the outside steps. Rufkin sped after. The lounge had padded benches more like sofas. The windows and glass sliders to the bow deck looked as silky as lozenges.

"Keep out of trouble," said Sammo. "When Madam Butterly does appear, she'll have a headache. Watch your manners for all you're worth." He hurried out through another door and didn't come back, not with hard-tack or anything else that might be more comfortable chewing.

They sat on a padded bench. There was nothing to do: a pile of society magazines on a side-table, a wall of mirrors. Rufkin didn't want to look at fancy people nor at himself. There was a large book with a shiny blue cover. It might be a business notebook. No—it was one of those folders for picturegraphs or mementos. It could still be private. He left it alone.

A clock had one face with the time of day and another that said the date including the year. He supposed business folk needed full details.

What was keeping Madam Butterly? The *Sea Honey* had finished the turn and was heading downriver. Through the lounge window the channel looked deeper, coppery red between sandy banks edged with red rocks.

Rufkin wanted to get home as fast as possible. But when the yacht reached Old Ocean, she should take Queen Sibilla on to the Eastern Isle. The dragon-eagles were there, and they would—if he and everyone else was lucky—help the Queen return Fontania to peace and stability. Only then might he go back home.

Vosco had fallen asleep, purple beanie askew. For a few minutes, instead of watching the riverbanks through the windows, Rufkin watched the reflections in the wall of mirrors. There was a big circular frame too, draped in silk so he couldn't see the picture. Maybe it was Madam Butterly's parents, or some famous person she admired.

Somewhere the cat started to purr. It wriggled out on its back from under an easy chair, hopped on the bench, and sniffed Vosco's skinny wrist.

"Don't be a pest," said Rufkin. "Let him sleep."

The cat settled down on the cushion, paws tucked to its chest, and just watched.

Rufkin watched again too—the riverbanks, for signs of life. High in the sky floated white clouds. He watched them in case of waterspouts. From here he couldn't see the *Sea Honey*'s stern or down into the rowboat. But he kept listening to hear if the Queen had wakened or anyone had discovered her. Vosco made snuffling sounds. The cat purred.

An inside door opened. It was only the butler. He nodded to Rufkin, hurried on deck, brought Doctor Goodabod back with him and closed the door again. More minutes ticked by.

Finally, Madam Butterfly came in, leaning on the doctor's arm. Rufkin stood up.

She wore a handsome blue dressing gown instead of the coat. Around her face was a pink scarf, like the silk over the circular picture. Had she been hurt in the waterspout? That would be awful.

The ogre helped her sit in the easy chair. "Madam, dear Vida. I am confident I have achieved exactly what you wished. It has taken many months, but wait five more minutes, if you please, before you look."

Rufkin sat down again next to Vosco. The butler came in and handed the doctor a tumbler with a fizzy liquid. The ogre examined it, then passed it to Madam Butterfly. She waved for both men to leave.

"Call if you need me," the doctor said as he closed the door.

"Are you all right?" Rufkin hoped so. He must tell her about the Queen.

She spoke carefully. "It is no more than a final treatment. The good doctor is clever and thorough."

He could tell she didn't want to say any more. His parent's friends were sometimes embarrassed if anyone knew they'd had their wrinkles frozen with beauteen. Lady Gall—"forever beautiful"—had done that. So it was something you kept quiet about. His mother didn't use beauteen even in secret. She said an actor needed a face that expressed emotion. In fact, she said, so did anyone.

Madam Butterly dropped the scarf enough to take a careful sip of the fizzy medicine. Rufkin snuck a look. Her cheekbones seemed more pointy perhaps, her chin rounder. She reminded him of someone else but he couldn't think who.

"Rufkin, I was afraid you'd all drowned," she said in her kind aunt voice. Vosco snuffled in his sleep again and she glanced at him. "Why didn't you tell me that this is the little duke? I heard he'd gone missing just before I left the City of Spires, six nights ago now. And where is Nissy?"

He'd had more important things to think about. "Oh, she was fine earlier. I hope she still is. She'll probably make sure of it."

"If she has a good business head, she certainly will." Madam Butterly took a second cautious sip of her medicine.

The cat gave Vosco a lick on the hand. He startled awake and drew back from its tickling whiskers. Rufkin didn't blame him. The last animal the kid had seen was an alligator wanting a snack.

Madam Butterly reached out with her foot—in a blue silk

slipper—and pushed the cat to the floor. "You'd have been more comfy if you'd stayed with me, Rufkin. But top points. You stayed alert and took advantage of the waterspouts to get yourself moving."

She gave that lovely smile, so whatever the treatment was, her face must be starting to feel better. Actually, it seemed a bit odd that she'd bothered with beauteen or anything like that in the middle of a crisis.

Now she was smiling at Vosco, who wouldn't look at her. "Can you play the trumpet yet, little Duke Vosco?"

The kid tucked it behind him.

"It's the one he nicked from Harry," Rufkin said. "He hardly lets go of it."

"We'll give it back when things are normal again," said Madam Butterly. "When we find Harry. If Harry deserves it." Her eyebrow went up in a little quirk.

Good, she knew Harry was dodgy. Rufkin would tell her the man really was dangerous. But first, tell her about the Queen.

The cat jumped up again, rubbed its head on Vosco's chest and meowed.

"Ee-ow," said Vosco.

Madam Butterly touched a hand to the pink scarf round her face, as if her jaw still ached. Then she reached for the blue folder Rufkin had thought was a book. She took a deep breath, opened the folder and smiled at something in it.

"Um," he began, "as soon as you're all right, I've something to tell you."

A knock sounded. Sammo entered and bowed. It made

his black and yellow stripes fold up, so for a moment his jersey looked completely black. "The small cabin's ready for the boys, Ma'am." He stood waiting.

Madam Butterly nodded, not at all bossy and smug like many people were to a servant.

She stood the folder open next to the magazines. Each side held a picture. The first was the face of a very beautiful woman—not Madam Butterly, though it had smooth blonde hair. The second one was the same woman's face in a circular frame with wording around it. At the top it said LADY GALL. At the bottom it said FOREVER BEAUTIFUL.

Lady Gall—long gone, but forever remembered. The most wicked ruler ever in Fontania. She'd even tried to poison the baby Sibilla. And Madam Butterly treasured that woman's pictures?

His heart started jolting. He couldn't tell her about the Queen—could he?

Madam Butterly glanced at Rufkin. "Oh. You have something to say?"

He hesitated. "I—I should return the rowboat to Port Feather. I—didn't pay for it. If it's lost, I'll owe the boat-hire man for a new one. Actually, I suppose he has lost it. But I've got no…" He patted his pockets. No money of course. Only Nissy's notebook down his shirt, and the hero figurine. By now one of its legs was loose.

Madam Butterly gave her golden smile. "Certainly, everyone should pay their debts. I'll have money sent to the boat-hire man. Seven dolleros should be more than enough."

Rufkin blinked. Nissy had said wealthy people had no idea. Only seven? For a whole new rowboat? It should be more like fifty or even a hundred. But what could he say? He got to his feet again.

"Wait. Let me think," Madam Butterly said. For a second she looked scary. But she smiled at once. "Just a minute."

She turned away, let the scarf drop around her shoulders, and took paper and pen from the side-table. She started to write. Rufkin had told Nissy it was not polite to look, but he was more and more worried. He couldn't help glancing over Madam Butterly's shoulder.

The letter was to Mayor Jolliman, asking him to give the boat-hire man seven dolleros from her account. She added something about *Rose Island*, in quotation marks. She must be having some sort of joke. She also told the Mayor she'd found what she needed, so he could relax. Then the note praised Rufkin.

His whole face went hot. Madam Butterly liked him. Nobody had ever called him *necessary* before. She thought he was important. Why had he worried for even a second? Of course he could trust her.

Madam Butterly folded the letter and passed it to Sammo. "Pigeon post to our friend in Port Feather."

She gave Rufkin another smile. For the first time since she'd come in, he saw her face clearly. He thought his eyes had gone weird. Then he blinked back at the open blue folder.

Doctor Goodabod's treatment had made Madam Butterly's face look like Lady Gall's.

"I was abrupt just now. Rufkin, I apologise," she was saying. "Sammo, amuse the boys. They can see the pigeons. Then tell the chef to make oven fries and hamburger. I want them tucked in very safe indeed before we reach open sea. Off you go."

Madam Butterly took herself to the circular picture, hooked back the veil and gave an excited and satisfied smile. It wasn't a picture at all. It was a mirror with words carved around the frame. At the top was her name: VIDA BUTTERLY. Below were the words: FOREVER VICTORIOUS.

—

BACK-UPS
TO BACK-UPS

Sammo hustled Rufkin and Vosco out of the lounge. The cat padded with them. The yacht was even bigger than it looked from outside. Many cabins led off the internal passageway.

They stopped at a small door and Rufkin smelled the sharp feathery odour of bird. Sammo unlatched the door and led them in. Pigeons rustled and cooed in a large cage. The cat sat in the corridor, ears and whiskers back, tail twitching at the tip as if it was hungry.

Rufkin wasn't hungry at all. Not even for hamburger.

"Actually," he said, "Vosco and I have to check personally on the rowboat."

Sammo scowled. "Madam Butterly will be watching to see the birds released. If she doesn't, I'm for the chop." The scowl turned to the grimmest of grins. "That's not a lamb chop to go with the fries."

It was surprising how many thoughts could travel round Rufkin's head at the same time. Thunderhead's words—*a deal or reward*. The line of the front half of the pantomime horse in *Dark Heart of Greed*. "The face behind the mask of friendship is not offering free oats." The horse's back half blew a raspberry.

In his mind Rufkin saw the words again—FOREVER VICTORIOUS. A twist on Lady Gall's *forever beautiful*. He could guess whose assistant Vida Butterfly had been when she was young. Lady Gall, selfish and cruel. And that blue folder. Madam Butterfly didn't just use beauteen to freeze her wrinkles. Doctor Goodabod, with elastic surgery, had also given her a round chin and pointed cheekbones exactly like the chin and cheekbones of Lady Gall.

Rufkin had to get the Queen and Vosco out of here.

Sammo rolled the letter into a tiny brass cartridge. From a bench he picked up a little knife with a safety sleeve, cut a piece of tape, then put the knife back. He chose a sleek pigeon. It uttered a *coo* when he began binding the cartridge to one of its legs.

"It's amaa-aazing that she's still got pigeons." Rufkin knew that being cute would annoy the man. "Everyone else gave up pigeons years ago. But the old ways are best again now phones don't work and nor do message-birds."

"She always has back-ups," Sammo muttered. "And back-ups to back-ups, then back-ups to them."

"How will the pigeon know where to go?" Rufkin asked. "I thought they only flew back to where they'd come from in the first place."

"Madam B has means and methods." The man was expressionless. But there were times when lack of expression screamed the truth. Rufkin had tried it at school and still got detention.

He kept his eyes wide in the Expression-cute. "It would be very clever if she guessed that phones would stop working all over the place. And to make sure she'd have the right pigeons to send to the right places."

Poker-faced, Sammo adjusted the cartridge.

Rufkin managed the Blink artless-and-innocent. "It could even mean that Madam Butterfly knows a lot about what's really at the bottom of the end-of-days."

The man looked right at Rufkin, a welter of thoughts in his eye now, none of them comforting. "Shut up. Stand back. You'll soon be in your cabin."

Pigeon in one hand, he fiddled with the latch of a porthole.

Rufkin snuck the little knife into his pocket and whispered to the birds in the cage, "Get ready. It's us or you." Then he yanked open the cage, grabbed the cat and threw it in among the pigeons. He seized Vosco by the wrist and started running.

A yowl and a screech from the cat, a yell from Sammo, a mad chirping and flapping of wings…

By now Rufkin and Vosco were back in the lounge. In front of the round mirror, Madam Butterfly turned. She dropped a new glass, tall and brimming with bubbles, and cried out in surprise.

Then they were through the other door onto the deck.

"Sammo! Thunderhead! Get the boys!" Madam Butterfly's cry had turned to rage.

Rufkin hurried Vosco down the outside stairs to the stern platform. He half-dropped and half-threw Vosco into the rowboat, still bobbing on the end of its rope. Then he wrenched one of the yacht's spare oars from the brass clamps and jammed it into the davits that held the dinghy.

He grabbed the other oar, and slithered from the platform into the rowboat. It wobbled like crazy. He whisked out the knife and sawed at the rope. A shout came from up on the bridge deck. He heard sailors running. But the knife was slicing through the rope like—well, like a knife through butter.

⁓

SCABBARD
AND DAGGER

Rufkin snatched up the oars—the one he'd just stolen and the one the alligator hadn't crunched—fitted them into the rowlocks and bent to work. Pigeons flew in spirals above the *Sea Honey*.

"About ship!" he heard Thunderhead roar. "Lower a rowboat!"

"Your Majesty," said Rufkin. "Wake up. Vosco, make her wake up."

He glanced over his shoulder. Vosco had dragged the sack off Queen Sibilla and was patting her face.

"Use the trumpet," Rufkin cried, "that'll do it." He dipped and raised the oars as hard as he could—which bank was nearer? The eastern one.

The trumpet blew, horribly rumptipaze. Rufkin glanced around again. The Queen continued to lie with her eyes closed, but he heard her murmur through the splash of the oars.

"Breakfast," she muttered. "Toast and peanut butter. Plum preserve cut into squares on my porridge."

She must be feeling better if she was hungry. Now he heard *ouches* and *ows* as she struggled up.

"It's evening?" she asked.

Yes, the sky was lavender. The pigeons had started to flap off in a dozen directions. The crew on the *Sea Honey* were struggling to lower the dinghy.

Rufkin scooped an oar, then rowed more steadily for the eastern bank. He tried to explain—that time had passed, he and Vosco had been on the yacht, what he'd seen and heard.

"'Forever victorious,'" said the Queen. "Kind and good Madam Butterly? The one who gives thousands of dolleros to charity every three months? The one with the smile that warms at two hundred paces?"

Rufkin kept rowing. She would think him an idiot. He had done the wrong thing.

"Good on you," said the Queen. "I knew she was too sweet to be true."

There was no time to waste on being self-satisfied. The *Sea Honey* was ending its turn and would soon bear down on them. And its dinghy was lowered at last, with five men. The rowers in their striped jerseys looked far too brawny for a fight to be fair.

Vosco made the trumpet blurt again. "Help," he said.

The Queen eyed the *Sea Honey*. "If Lady Gall is Vida Butterly's idol, that madam will have no time for dragon-eagles or common decency. We'll row for our lives. Give me an oar."

Together, she and Rufkin made far more quickly for the eastern bank. It was so rocky there, the *Sea Honey* wouldn't be able to get close—though its dinghy would be deadly if it carried a deadly weapon. Rufkin glanced at the sky, darker purple now. Unless Madam Butterfly's dinghy had a searchlight, their own little boat might stay hidden in the night.

What was beyond the red rocks of the riverbank? Sand, as far as Rufkin knew. That was all he'd seen from the super-yacht. He couldn't remember a scrap of geography.

The Queen must have been weak after her ordeal. But she still kept giving him tips and was darn good at rowing. With just a couple of oar-dips she had them between some sheltering boulders and out of sight from the main stream.

"Wait a moment," she said in a low voice.

She nipped over the side of the rowboat. On her stomach she wriggled up the rocky bank for a few queen-lengths. The pouch he'd seen on her leather belt actually looked like a scabbard. With a dagger in. Impressive.

He heard shouting in the distance. The Queen wriggled down again.

"The yacht's anchoring," she said. "The dinghy's taking in water, so they're giving up. They'll expect they can find us tomorrow. They won't dare come ashore in the dark."

"But we came ashore," said Rufkin. "I—I didn't see any more alligators once we left the willows behind, but…"

"Any noise we make should scare off—um—small things," she whispered. For a moment she held her head as if she was dizzy again. "Now. What have we got with us? It's always best to take stock. One Vosco and a trumpet." Vosco chuckled. "One Rufkin. Two whole oars, *phew*— good thinking, Rufkin. And half a chewed oar. There's me, still with a headache. And a sun hat. A sack. There's a coil of rope under the seat, but not a large one."

"And you've got a dagger," Rufkin said. "That's some sort of protection."

There was a pause. "Maybe." Then she smiled. "I'm sorry I can't be more reassuring. Now, we must speak quietly or our voices might carry. So quick, just do what I say."

~

The rowboat was very light indeed. Rufkin was glad he hadn't known how flimsy it was when the alligator's jaws were open beside it. Now, at least, it wasn't much effort to haul it out of the stream, then up through the boulders. It was hard to see good footing. But he managed. The Queen staggered only when they were up on flat stony ground at last. So did he.

"Sit quiet," she said to Vosco. "No trumpet. Or I'll take it away. I mean it." She gave him a grin and he grinned back.

She took off the sun hat, lay flat, and scanned the stream again. "Can you see them at all from here?"

Rufkin shook his head.

"Good," said the Queen. "As soon as it's really dark, I want to set an oar upright against the seat of the rowboat, with that sack tied to it."

"Here? On the stones?" Rufkin asked. "That'll be no use."

"Don't look at me like that," said Queen Sibilla. "The job's not impossible."

~

Of course it wasn't. Any stage-hand could fix an oar vertical in a few minutes. If someone gave Rufkin a bag of metal brackets and screws and a strong screwdriver, he'd do it too.

Well, maybe in an hour with the right swearwords and a few blood blisters. It would be easy if there was a bright light too, and snacks like cheese pastries and apple. But here? In the dark? Only him and the Queen?

"Can't you just use magic?" he asked.

"You know it doesn't work as easily as that." She sounded annoyed. In a moment she might ask if his Statements of Success were any good.

So he kept his mouth shut and did his best. There was the coil of rope. His little knife would cope with that. But *blast*, it was pretty small for making a notch in the edge of the seat so the oar could be set.

"I need the dagger," he said.

"No," she replied.

Double blast—

Then it was like a light switched on in his head—the dagger. The royal dagger. Of course, she would wear it on a dangerous mission. It was the sign of the monarch. No ordinary person should even touch it.

"Let's get on with it," she said softly.

He blinked, felt really dumb and—got on with it.

The little knife he'd stolen from Sammo did an okay job. There were small rocks to help wedge things in place. Rufkin wanted to use the beanie for extra packing, but Vosco refused to give it. The Queen let him use the sun hat though. She kept wanting to help. That made it tricky. He didn't want to jab her fingers by accident. He didn't want to give her a knock with the oar as they raised it.

There was no moon, but fitful starlight came through the

clouds. Out in the stream, lights glowed on the *Sea Honey*. The air moved gently as it had done since Rufkin began work. He had always known a boy having an adventure should be strong with muscles as well as his mind. It would have helped if he'd also been allowed a scrap of magic. But not the dagger. Never the dagger. He didn't want to touch that at all, no way.

Finally the oar was fixed like a mast. The sack was its sail.

"Rudder," she said. "The oar you stole will do for that."

He managed to fix that in place too.

She stood back and looked. "Good job."

He blushed hot. For this moment of being praised by the Queen, he was grateful. But what next? An average boy like him in such an adventure? It couldn't end well.

Queen Sibilla tucked Vosco and trumpet in the bow. "Rufkin, sit here with me." She arranged herself at one side at the stern, he sat at the other. She took a last look back at Jovial River and the glow from the yacht. Then she stared up at the sky in the west.

For a long moment nothing happened except that the air stopped moving entirely.

Then the Queen faced ahead to the east. She picked up an end of the rope attached to the sail and handed the other end to Rufkin.

A breath seemed to begin.

Rufkin felt it on his hair, his neck and shoulders. It became a soft huff that gathered strength but had no sound. The sacking sail filled then—impossibly—and the rowboat lifted a little above the sand as if it drifted on invisible water. Slowly, very slowly, the rowboat began floating eastwards over the stony land.

So—there was magic around him after all. It wasn't huge magic. But it wasn't the stage magic of illusion and clever machinery. This was real. This was the Queen in communion with the power of nature. She was heading at last to the dragon-eagles.

—

WHAT NEXT?

The moonless night made the journey into a waking dream. They had to ease around large rocks and skirt past crevices, tugging the rope attached to each side of the sail to angle it this way or that. The wind kept the rowboat moving at no more than the speed of a donkey-saunter. Speed—not the best word. But Rufkin had to admit the sacking sail would collapse in any strong gust.

Steam rose from a crevice as they floated towards it. Far down another, Rufkin caught flashes that might be the luminous tails of lizards, small and large. In the next, coils of steam were gathering before some underground boiling might shoot them up in a geyser. In the strange simmering and purring from underground he also heard the *oo-oo* of a night bird, a far-off clopping that could be horses on stony ground, the distant churning of waves on the shore of Old Ocean.

A faint snore from Vosco turned into a sob. The little boy sat up. Tears and nose-drip glistened in the night.

"Manage the sail," the Queen murmured to Rufkin. She climbed over to talk softly to Vosco.

Rufkin thought he heard horses again. Nomads, maybe.

To their right Old Ocean boomed on in the distance. On their left a dark line of hills lay like dozing dragons. Ahead would be dawn and the end of the stony flat. What was Nissy doing by now? Where might she be heading?

Vosco slept again. The Queen clambered back to the stern. "He misses his parents."

Rufkin wanted to say *That's natural* but his voice didn't feel reliable. It took a few minutes to be sure it wouldn't wobble.

"Ma'am, I know you have to go east. But we can't get to the Eastern Isle in one night."

She shook her head.

"So what happens next?"

"I don't know," said the Queen.

Even while he was asking, he'd known the answer. It would be great if whatever amount of magic she'd been granted or earned could solve everything. But he supposed that would be too easy.

Anyway, what was going on? He tried to think it through. He'd always wondered about stories and plays where villains wanted to rule the whole world. What would they do if they succeeded? There'd be nothing left for them to want. The stories were any good only if the villains lost. It was highly satisfying to see a thwarted villain. But those were just stories. He couldn't see any particular villain at work in this adventure. Madam Butterly was a crook, he was sure of it, and Nissy's notebook, still down his shirt, might hold some useful clues when the Queen could look at it. But Madam Butterly wouldn't have created the end-of-days deliberately.

Not even the worst villain would do that.

The Queen swayed where she sat.

"Do you need to sleep again?" Rufkin asked.

"I've been sleeping for days." Her voice was so tired. "We have to go on as far as possible. I can't stop yet."

Rufkin wasn't clever like Oscar and Ahria, but he didn't think being unconscious was the same as sleeping. "You haven't had anything to eat since the explosion. You were probably poisoned by all that blue stuff over your face."

"Blue stuff?" She rubbed her cheeks. "It must be lazulite dust. I must get a message to my brother. And to Vosco's parents and the Council of Wisdom."

She could have done that at Port Feather, if he hadn't run off with Vosco. He had a stab of guilt. "You need a doctor. A good one, not like Goodabod—he might be a good elastic surgeon but he's not..." He tailed off.

As they glided by a crevice, a rumble began and out gushed a fountain of steam. Hot drops sprinkled down. Vosco awoke with a squeal. The sacking sail flapped like crazy. The Queen lost her grip on the rope. Rufkin managed to hang on to his bit and grab hers as well. The rowboat banged on the ground twice but wobbled back into the air.

The shade of the sky began changing at last. He could make out the Queen's face again. She looked as haggard as a sketch drawn with old scrappy pencils. The wind faltered for a moment, then blew just as steadily.

Rufkin kept his eyes on the stony sand flat and tugged the rope to by-pass a deep cleft, then edge past a cluster of rocks. He tried to scan the path they had journeyed. It was still too dark to see anything much except darkness—if he wrote that in a school essay, the teacher would say, *Keep your jokes out of school work, I've warned you before.*

He scanned ahead again. Now a rim of gold showed the horizon. A few pointy bits and shapes like cauliflower might be distant trees. As the sun lifted, a shaft of light beamed into his eyes. This was like the road he'd hoped for back on the launch. All it showed to the south was a rumple of grass-covered dunes. To the north, trees and hills. Ahead was a scatter of rocks like a natural barrier. Then tussock. The end of the stone flat.

"What's the next town?" Rufkin asked.

The Queen looked too exhausted even to think.

He closed his eyes to help him remember the map on his classroom wall. "This is the Coast of Beaks. The next big city…um, it's called Rocky something. Before that…a few smallish rivers. Not many towns…a few small settlements." He dredged his brain for more. "There is some farming and…cheese-making? There's a factory that makes preserves and pickles. There are vineyards. So that's wine to go with the cheese."

"Rest," murmured the Queen.

"I've remembered more than I expected," said Rufkin. "But that's it."

"Rest," said the Queen again.

"Oh, sorry. There won't be much choice once the rowboat has to stop," said Rufkin.

The Queen sat up straighter. "No. Adventurers rest."

"Everyone has to rest," said Rufkin. "Not just adventurers."

The rising sun made her face glow. In her red pants, ragged cardigans, and frizzy rust-and-blue hair, her smile would have warmed a crowd at a thousand paces. "Funny boy. No—we're heading for Simmering River. Not far upstream is Adventurers' Rest. It's a lodge. It's a vineyard. All we have to do is reach the river."

Another spurt of steam blasted behind them with a shower of scalding mud.

"*Ouch*," said Rufkin.

"*Ow*," said Vosco.

In a stuttering yawn the wind faded. The rowboat stopped floating and dropped—*thwack*—to the ground.

The Queen had fainted again.

—

WHAT'S THIS?

How far they had come? Where were they? The sea boomed behind red rocks on their right, foothills rose to their left. Rufkin buried his head in his hands.

The day was warming already, making him sweat. They couldn't stay here on rough ground beside the boulder bank. The sun would fry them alive. He was exhausted. And the Queen was shattered right through, in body and spirit.

Why didn't the dragon-eagles come to rescue her (and Vosco and him)? Why didn't a friendly bird fly up to her now to say she'd be saved if she waited a bit? Getting home had to be the least likely event in the world. It was far more probable that he'd be blistered to death by hot mud. Or starve till he was a husk of skin. Or, before then, fly into a rage and yell things he'd be ashamed of his parents hearing. If he swore in front of the Queen he'd be disgraced. He took in a breath anyway—

Some distance away amid the tussock was a leafless tree. Three birds perched in its branches. Their wings were raised in such high curves they looked like umbrellas. He thought he heard faint whistles like singing kettles.

He shook the Queen gently. "Come on. Please. The

rowboat's stuck. We have to reach the river before the sun's too high. The Simmering River, you said. Look, there are some birds. They'll be near fresh water, I'm sure of it." That was a lie. He wasn't sure. He only hoped. "Come on, Your Majesty. Please."

She stirred, then like a puppet she climbed from the rowboat. She stumbled off for the tree, keeping to easier ground near the bank of red boulders. Rukfin and Vosco followed. Rufkin felt stiff from sitting so long but he soon caught up with her. Vosco, carting the trumpet, explored as he went, random and scatty. He said *ow* again a few times when he tripped over a tussock.

"He's improving," gasped the Queen.

Rufkin didn't suggest she saved her breath. He was saving his own.

At last, they all neared the tree. He'd never seen such birds before, not even in pictures. They were as large as geese but their bodies more delicate. Their purple wing feathers gleamed like amethyst, and their throats were creamy with light blue spots. One had blue spots down its chest too. Their tails were long and curved like balances, their beaks long and thin.

A faint whistle sounded again. One of the birds flapped like an umbrella battling the wind but its wings settled upwards. Probably its feathers had needed adjustment like pants that slip sideways.

"Are they dangerous?" he whispered. "Should we try getting under the tree for some shade?"

The Queen lay on the rough ground with her eyes closed and didn't reply.

It wasn't fair that he was the only one who could do anything. Wait out here while the day grew hotter—bad idea. Chase the birds away? They might chase him back. Head inland—that didn't seem wise. Go nearer the ocean— really bad idea. The *Sea Honey* might have followed along the coast. He should do some research.

Rufkin ran a few steps, then wriggled up the boulder bank. Far out on the lazy waves lay a large yacht. He couldn't see a blue B but he guessed it was the *Sea Honey*. Lucky his hair was dirty and straight. Even if Thunderhead was peering through a telescope, he'd think Rufkin's head was just a small brown boulder out of place.

But if Thunderhead did spot him and send Sammo and the crew to bring them in, there'd be food and water.

Rufkin nearly stood and beckoned the *Sea Honey*.

He gritted his teeth, slid away and ran back to the Queen.

"Your Majesty," he said gently and clearly. "Are you absolutely sure we need to get to Adventurers' Rest?"

"No," she snapped, still with her eyes closed.

Even royal grown-ups could be difficult. "So what should we do?"

She looked as cross as two sticks. "All we need is to find someone to help us. It might happen before we get to Adventurers' Rest."

Rufkin made a face at Vosco and spread his hands. Vosco put the trumpet to his lips and made it fart.

"Very funny, no." But Rufkin snorted.

The birds shuffled in the tree and turned to consider them. From somewhere else, a high whistle filled the air again. The birds whistled too. Was there a fourth bird somewhere out of sight?

Vosco blew the trumpet again in a dying groan. A *hee-haw* answered some distance off. The three birds shook their wings into normal flying position and soared away.

"Hey!" A white-haired guy in hunting gear came into sight. He was leading a donkey. He stopped and peered at them through binoculars. "You've scared off the first blue-spotted bower birds round here for five hundred years!" he shouted.

~

In the next five minutes the man loaded the Queen, who could only groan, on the donkey's back. Her rusty, ragged hair was over her face. "There there," the man muttered through his wispy beard. Whether he said it to the donkey or the Queen, Rufkin hadn't a clue. At least it was a kindly word, repeated. Then the man bundled Vosco in front of the Queen.

"That's enough load for the beast." His old brown eyes peered at Rufkin. "You don't look as if you'll last the distance, but you'll have to try. I'm Swan. Swan the bird man, and this is Tiger." He slapped the donkey. "The name is ironic but you see the faint stripe in his coat."

He had a pistol holster on his belt—and a pistol in it. Big and old like the man. Should Rufkin trust him? Swan might be the help the Queen had hoped for.

The donkey set off through the tussock. Swan had no questions, not even about who they were—rare for a grown-up. He just kept griping to himself. "How to upset a scientist. Make his research flap off to the blue yonder. Jog along, Tiger."

The donkey continued to be the opposite of ferocious. If it dawdled any slower it would be no more than twitching in its sleep. Rufkin began to feel as if he were asleep too.

"It's hard enough to study transformation," Swan bellyached. "Not to mention studying changing back again to what came first. D'you hear me, boy?"

"Er," said Rufkin.

"Tiger, jog along. What? What was that, boy?"

"Er," said Rufkin.

"Help," whispered Vosco.

Rufkin nearly tripped over Tiger's droppings. He fell back a few paces and made himself wake up. It still felt like one of his part-nightmares. The man seemed okay, but at first so had Thunderhead and Goodabod. The tiny knife was still in his pocket but not much of a weapon—and anyway he wasn't much of a fighter. Rufkin tried to get a better glimpse of the Queen's dagger but her cardigan covered the belt.

"Those blue-spotted bower birds—" Swan tugged on the donkey's bridle— "One of them was a man once. Spotty chest feathers, that's the sign."

"Fascinating," Rufkin managed.

"Two were holding their wings like umbrellas." Swan waved a hand in description. "But the third, wings up like a parasol." The wave looked identical. "Important differences. Small but significant. What do you say?" he barked. "Comment, boy. Out with it."

Rufkin struggled to keep his feet moving. "Umbrellas

and parasols look very alike. And you can use an umbrella to keep off the sun as well as the rain. But a parasol might let the rain through."

Swan's smile showed a set of teeth as straight as tombstones. "You have the makings of a scientist."

"I doubt it. They need to be clever," Rufkin muttered.

"Time reveals." Swan hitched up his hunting pants and patted the pistol. Rufkin took in a sharp breath, but the old man just kept walking on.

They reached the line of trees that Rufkin had seen in the dawn, the bunchy ones, a skinny cypress or two, and normal green willows thick with leaf. A narrow road wound along the top of a steep bank. A strong river flowed below.

"Er," said Rufkin again. "Thanks. We're fine on our own now."

"Rubbish. Jog along, Tiger." Swan led them upriver. "See, he has the scent of home in those big nostrils."

It was true that Tiger had sped up to a sluggish walk.

A mist stinking of rotten egg rose from crannies by the roadside. The Simmering River. Rufkin had done a report on it for Brilliant Academy. He'd glued yellow wool onto the cover page to indicate the sulphur that made the rotten egg smell. He'd used sparkly pens to write END in the middle of the end page. He'd made fancy chapter headings and left space for when he finally wrote the report. There was still plenty of space. It was too late to get a better grade. Now he was at Simmering River for some personal experience. His report would never have included an old man with an ancient pistol and a striped donkey.

On the opposite riverbank was a wharf, with a launch and an antique sailing ship. It showed how deep the channel must be. Ahead was a bridge, long and high. Rufkin's skin prickled. The bridge looked new. Shiny blue.

Tiger sped up to a dawdle.

"No!" shouted Rufkin.

Tiger startled, *hee-haw*, and sat down. The Queen slid off.

Vosco clung to Tiger's harness like a jockey. "Help," he cried, "help."

Swan flapped round, growling. "Tiger, you're not in a circus now. Up on your hooves. Boy, have you never seen a bridge before?"

Rufkin had to explain. The problem with any new metal. Cave-lizards.

Swan showed his teeth again. "A nationwide problem? Not here, boy. Don't worry, this bridge is old. It's just new paint. The adventurers did it last week—swinging on work cradles over the torrent, shinning up ladders. It was a whiff of the good old days."

He hauled the donkey's reins to make it stand again, and loaded the Queen—still unconscious—onto its back. "Poor lass, you're no use to anyone. We'll have to fix that."

Next Swan picked up Vosco with gentle hands and set him on his own hip. Then he coaxed Tiger, trip-trapping, over the bridge.

When Rufkin was sure the Queen, Vosco, Swan, and the donkey were safe on the other side, he raced over as fast as he could. So far, so good. Maybe he could trust the old man further.

"I'm sorry about the birds," he muttered.

Whiskers twitched on Swan's chin as he lifted Vosco back on the donkey. "It wasn't your sin, it was the little chap's. But if you expunge it by giving me a decent tune on that trumpet, you might get breakfast."

A word Rufkin didn't know—*expunge*. Did it mean sponge the sin away, like when you dropped something sloppy? Rufkin hoped Swan was joking, but he could never be sure with old people.

On this side of the river the road wound on past more willows, but Swan turned aside to a gate. Beside it two slender trees with leaves in a lilac shade had twined together as they grew. A sign in old bronze letters read *Adventurers' Rest*.

Tiger's bottom, donkey-shade, swayed in front of Rufkin. A white stone path crunched under his feet. Around a corner was a wooden house three levels high. The path took him past a garden with pink and red roses, pink and red geraniums, and a lawn where old people were unfolding deck chairs. They were saying things like "They're not expected" and "They're late for breakfast. We ate all the eggs."

Rufkin's legs hurt. So did his feet. His eyes and brain hurt. He no longer gave a ratty dollero for who could be trusted and who couldn't. All he cared about was keeping a tight jaw so he wouldn't burst into a sob in front of all those retired buccaneers and mountain climbers, explorers and gray-haired bandits.

—

FIRE AHEAD

Tiger shuffled to a halt. Rufkin saw a tree with spiky branches, steps to a veranda, then a door. He fell up and over, and his legs gave out. He sprawled on a hall carpet.

"They're young adventurers," he heard Swan say. "They scared off the bower birds."

Rufkin managed to crawl over and prop himself up near a hall stand full of walking sticks. Strong old men carried the Queen and Vosco through into what looked like a day room. Rufkin could see them—rusty hair, purple beanie—being laid on cane sofas with red and purple cushions. Then his eyes closed.

"They're very young indeed, all three of these mysteries," came an ogre's voice. He sounded as old as Swan and just as vigorous.

"Is the phone fixed yet?" asked Swan. "There'll be parents to contact, loved ones to reassure."

A moist cloth wiped Rufkin's forehead. Something wet trickled into his mouth. It was only water but tasted like sunshine.

His eyes opened. Peering at him were men, women, ogres, trolls, and dwarfs, all gray- or white-haired or bald.

Their eyes shone with concern and at the same time glowed with the excitements and triumphs of past exploits.

"The boy's promised to pay for their breakfast with a tune on the trumpet," Swan said through a chuckle.

Promised? Rufkin set his shoulders against the wall, shoved up to standing and tried to look dignified. His parents had shunted him off to the Mucclacks. He'd been pushed around by the wind, ocean currents, and Nissy. He'd been shoved around by Captain Thunderhead, Goodabod, and the terrible Harry, who'd tried to drop him and the others feet first in the ocean. He'd had enough.

"Sir, I am not a performer. I'll pay for help in the usual way." He fished for some dolleros in his...his pockets were empty. Except for the hero figurine, with its leg loose.

A tiny lady with a white ponytail squinted at Rufkin. "No money. I remember that look from the inside. Had it myself at a difficult moment."

"Me too, Delilah," mumbled a dwarf man. "Many times at difficult moments."

Swan's tombstone teeth grinned through the wispy beard. "Theft or forgetfulness? Bad luck or just being dim-witted? Never mind. I'll forgive you for chasing off my research, though I'll never forget it. So it's a free breakfast. Put the boy in a chair, Littlewink."

An ogre so ancient that even the bumps on his face were crisscrossed with wrinkles cradled Rufkin into the day room and dumped him in an armchair. Again Swan and the old folk crowded around.

"The boy has tales of a knot of ships," said Swan. "The

Bridge of Size on foundations as useful as custard."

"I take anything said by a boy with a grain of salt," said the ogre Littlewink. "The mind of a boy is riddled with pitfalls, crammed with surprises."

"I trust any boy as far as I can fling him," said the dwarf. "How far could I throw this one?"

"The boy's scowling," said tiny Delilah.

"Perhaps we intimidate?" asked Littlewink.

Swan grinned again. "If he thinks we're gruff, wait till he meets the manager."

Delilah snorted. "Love's turned the manager soft. These days, he's never gruff."

"Only if we tease him about young Hodie," said Littlewink.

They knew Lord Hodie?

On the sofa, the Queen let out a groan and thumped a fist.

The sound of rustling leaves came through a window. Whistles and chirps made a chattering chorus.

"The bower birds!" Swan tiptoed out with his binoculars.

Rufkin saw the birds from where he sat. They lifted their wings over their heads, two in umbrella position, one possibly parasol if Swan was right.

He wasn't sure how keen he was on the old adventurers. But they seemed kind enough. Now the Queen could send a message to King Jasper. As soon as she came to, she'd explain who she was. And someone could look after him for a change too. This time he'd do nothing rash. Like crash a sled over a gangplank and send a launch out into the ocean. Or jump into a rowboat.

~

"The young woman and little boy need attention," said Delilah.

Rufkin would actually like some attention himself. *Ow*, he ached. Were they going to ignore him?

"Where's Doctor Maisie?" continued Delilah. "Helping in the winery? Where is the Empress?"

Empress?

High voices rang outside, laughing and calling like in the playground of Brilliant Academy. Children?

He looked around properly. Large windows. A toy box against the opposite wall. A big dining table. A painting of both dragon-eagles, the older and the younger. On a bookshelf below it sat a small box with a medal displayed. He eased himself up to have a look: *For services to Queen Sibilla and King Jasper.*

This place had to be safe. He could tell the old people himself it was the Queen lying there in her clown pants...

An explosion rattled the windows. A smash of glass followed. The old adventurers stiffened. The bower birds flew up out of view.

Vosco sat upright. "Help!"

The Queen put both arms over her head and rolled over to face the wall.

"The winery!" Some adventurers dashed outside. Some rushed to the windows.

Rufkin lurched to a window too. Across the lawn, a low building with a fancy roof was covered in heat haze and curls of white smoke. Out of its main door staggered a sturdy figure in a white boilersuit and white cap.

"Blistering junk!" he roared. "Bring shovels and brooms!"

Behind him staggered a tall woman, her boilersuit and cap splattered with red. She shooed a clutch of small children together and scooted them on. "Look after babies. Keep orphans out of mess!"

The five children, all younger than Rufkin, ran through the day room into the back of the house.

Vosco watched them till they'd disappeared, then hopped off his sofa. He straightened the purple beanie, tiptoed a few steps, stopped dead—then took a deep breath and pattered after them.

The sturdy man in the boilersuit pounded up the steps and into the day room. "The batch of bloodberry wine exploded," he cried. "The temperature desk overheated."

"How? It was new last week," Delilah said. "I installed it myself."

Oh no. And Swan had asked earlier if the phone had been fixed. Blood started to drum in Rufkin's ears.

The tall woman strode in and pulled off her own cap. Her hair was a pile of dark loops. She saw Rufkin and Vosco. "*Argk!* Must make room for other orphans?" She spotted the Queen. "And what is this?"

Another roar like sudden flame burst in the air. Black smoke laced with flickering red spouted from the winery skylights. A swirl of flame licked out under the eaves—five swirls of fire—now a dozen. Large flakes of ash drifted—no, it was birds—no, the shapes of lizards, lizards with wings. Fire-lizards.

"Buckets, hoses! Keep the orphans well under cover and out of the way," bellowed the man.

The old people started to stream across to the winery. Like parts of well-oiled machinery, there was no dither or stutter among them. But explosions burst again inside the building. A skylight shattered and flames began gushing. *Bang!* Another skylight exploded. Fire licked the length of the roof as if it too were a great lizard with a spine of flame. Sparks whizzed through the air, dancing close to the house.

"Get the old folk out of the hospital wing and down to the river," Littlewink boomed.

"Play hoses on the house," cried Swan's voice. "Save the house!"

By now everyone else was busy with buckets and hoses. Rufkin flung himself down beside the Queen.

"Fire. It's a fire, Your Majesty. The house will burn. Please! Summon the wind."

It was too much to ask of her. He hated himself for doing it.

"The end-of-days is here too," he cried. "And fire-lizards."

She turned her head. "Fire," she whispered. "The wind…"

He helped her to the open window. The smell of smoke made them both cough.

The Queen put her hands to her lips almost like a prayer. She closed her eyes. A small breeze began to blow. Rufkin saw fire flakes headed this way begin to veer off. Could she contain the embers and sparks? Could she keep it up till the fire was out?

Flames continued to lap from the roof of the winery.

Fire-lizards soared above like living bombs. The Queen leaned on Rufkin, and he struggled to stand firm. But at last the roaring and explosions started to dwindle. The blooming and licking of flame died away. No fire-lizards flitted, just a thick scatter of ash.

The Queen was as pale and drained as when they'd arrived. Her hair was limp. Rufkin helped her stumble back to the sofa. He ran to find the kitchen and fetched a glass of water. He was trying to dribble some into her mouth when the sturdy man and tall woman returned.

The man flopped in a chair and dragged off his white cap. His head was bald, speckled with freckles. "Like magic. The breeze came at just the right time, for just long enough."

The woman folded her arms and frowned at Rufkin. "The extra orphans. And the ill person. Must find Doctor Maisie." She turned to leave again.

"Excuse me!" Rufkin forced himself to stand in the Attitude-respectful. "I'm sorry. I know you're in a crisis. But there's a bigger crisis. If you're the managers, I have something to say."

The man didn't move but his eyes narrowed as if he liked life better through a frown of distrust.

Rufkin wanted to roll up and hide. "My name's Rufkin Robiasson and the little kid with me is really Duke Vosco..."

The man sat up and looked the very pinnacle of suspicious.

"And the lady—" Rufkin pointed to the Queen, still lying flat.

"Speak up!" said the man.

"Do not scare boy to his death," the woman said. "Rufkin Robiasson, please to continue."

She was so imposing, even in her red-spattered boilersuit, that Rufkin bowed. "I know she doesn't look it," he said. "But that lady is Queen Sibilla.'

In the next instant the man was out of the chair to kneel by the Queen. "So it is." He rested a hand on her rust-covered hair. "Oh, little Queen. And you're bearing the royal dagger. What kind of guts and glory have you got yourself into now?"

Rufkin teetered where he stood with sheer relief. He should have known— the man was Special Major Murgott, retired. He was once a pirate too. He'd get the better of any murdering Harry. And the woman was Murgott's wife, former Empress Lu'nedda of Um'Binnia, who had abdicated her throne for love and democracy. The former Empress was sure to get the better of Thunderhead, Goodabod, and Madam Butterly.

—

VILLAIN AHEAD

Major Murgott and the ex-Empress began fussing over the Queen. Rufkin heard whistles and cries from the blue-spotted bower birds as they settled again in the tree.

Before the thought was fully formed, he raced out and called to them. "One of you was a man, is that right? Please get a message to King Jasper. Can you do that?"

Cinders and ash still drifted. But the bower birds looked down at him, eyes bright as beads.

"We have to try to stop the end-of-days," he said. "Please tell King Jasper. And, if you can, fly to the dragon-eagles."

The purple wings of a bower bird floated down and brushed his forehead. Then the bird disappeared up and over the roof of Adventurers' Rest. In the direction of Old Ocean? Then over the Watchers and Lake Riversea to King Jasper in the City of Canals? Oh, he hoped so.

The other two birds had left the tree and were circling in the last tendrils of smoke. They dipped their wings like a salute and flew off over rows and rows of fresh young vines, away to the east.

He'd done all he could. Actually he felt he'd done well. He stumbled inside again.

Murgott had the Queen sitting now, and was rubbing her hands. "More water," he called.

"She hasn't eaten for days, either," Rufkin said.

"Bread," said Lu'nedda. "A sip of milk. A cashew nut. And little Vosco? He has not eaten either?" She hurried out.

Very soon she returned with another old person, Doctor Maisie (so Rufkin supposed), who bent over the Queen. The oldest orphan pattered in too with a blue glass mug. Murgott helped the Queen sit and held the mug to her lips as if she were made of glass herself. She sipped, and a pink flush appeared in her cheeks.

Small feet drummed in from the kitchen. Vosco and the orphans. An old dwarf lady followed, carrying a red tray with a pitcher of milk and a platter of sandwiches. Rufkin guessed at least some would be pickle and cheese. She set the tray on the table.

Vosco settled himself on a chair. He hunched his skinny shoulders, sat on his large hands, and blinked at the platter. The smallest orphan climbed on the chair next to his, grabbed the first sandwich, and slapped it in front of Vosco.

"Good," said the old lady dwarf. "Pipsqueak helps others first, then helps himself."

Rufkin hoped he'd be offered a sandwich too. They looked packed with delicious mouthfuls. But it took a few moments for the old lady to remember him and beckon. He slid into a chair.

The sandwich was better with each bite. Lettuce for crispness, avocado for velvet on the tongue, tomato for the sweetness of sun. Salami and pickle for richness and tang.

The bread was fresh and homemade. His teeth sank into the cheese exactly the way teeth should.

Thank goodness. Grown-ups were in charge. The Queen had Murgott and Lu'nedda to help sort out the end-of-days. Vosco would be hurried back to his parents, there'd be kissing and hugging. Lady Polly and Lord Trump would blame themselves for what had happened to Vosco. They'd encourage their kid to talk. They'd make sure to be good parents to all seven of their children equally from now on.

Rufkin dropped the last piece of sandwich on his plate and stiffened his chest so he wouldn't cry. It wasn't always wise to think of happy families. Would he get ever home again himself? His parents had packed him off to the salvage yard. He was only as good as his Statement of Success, and that was rotten.

'What'th the matter?' Face rosy and clean, one of the middle-sized orphans stared across the table.

Rufkin tried a Laugh-resolute but sounded feeble. "Oh, nothing. Every good play needs a character whose story doesn't end well." Oh no, that came out as self-pitying.

The orphan showed young gaps in its teeth. "Pip-thqueak had a bad ending."

"He's started again though," said another orphan. "Now he's on a journey to a good one."

"You took the best sandwich!" screamed a smaller orphan to goodness-knew-who, and burst into tears.

"All the sandwiches were the same," said the old lady dwarf.

"Outside to the swings," called Lu'nedda.

The orphans and Vosco ran out through the hall. From the winery across the garden came the song of old adventurers as they hosed down the last of the embers.

Rufkin slouched into an armchair. The hero figurine dug into him. The real Hodie would be heroic even with a wonky leg. He'd never be self-pitying. But the real Hodie would never be ignored and not thanked for all he had done. Rufkin's leg twitched. He wanted to kick something so hard that it hurt.

He glanced at Queen Sibilla. She was still murmuring with Murgott and Doctor Maisie.

"Vosco must have stowed away on the expedition to the mines, Ma'am." That was Murgott. "It's very possible. After all, you're one of the few people who play with him, poor little beggar—begging the royal pardon, so to speak."

The Queen chuckled.

Murgott patted her hand. "The first thing is to send a message to Polly and Trump. And to Jasper. And the dragon-eagles."

Rufkin should tell them he already had. But he didn't think they'd take any notice of him right now, or any time.

By the main door came a clatter of an adventurer trying to fit her walking stick into the rack. "Wretched thing, life's so annoying."

Rufkin agreed.

Tiny Delilah staggered into the day room, still with her stick; it had a brass handle. She fell into a chair beside Rufkin's. "Three gypsies are tying their horses down at the gate. It's a shame we've just tidied the mess after the fire.

They might have helped for a few dolleros." She closed her eyes. A snore whuffled out of her.

Rufkin sank deeper into his chair.

Footsteps crunched on the path outside. They stopped.

For some reason Rufkin felt wary.

"Hello," a man's voice called. It was obvious to Rufkin it was trying to sound deeper than usual. "Anyone home?"

Old Delilah stayed asleep. But Murgott stood up with a puzzled frown. The Queen rose as well. She looked caught out but her eyes were alert.

"Hello," the man called again. "Murgott? Mistress Lu'nedda? Anyone? I'm coming in anyway."

By now Rufkin knew it—a Voice-familiar. He linked it with danger. He linked it with being dropped over the side of a barge. What would Lord Hodie do if he were here? Not sit and mope.

Rufkin edged from the chair. His fingers found the old lady's stick, its handle of brass, and slipped down to grasp the other end. He snuck against the doorway into the hall. Murgott made furious gestures. Rufkin ignored them.

The man's boots sounded on the veranda steps, then in the hall. Harry's curly hair came around the door. Murgott seemed to brace himself. The Queen looked baffled. Lu'nedda let out a scream.

Rufkin gripped the stick as he'd been taught for the part he'd never played as a brigand in *Love or Dolleros*.

Harry took another step. Rufkin lifted the stick high— but he couldn't hit someone for real, not even a man who'd nearly drowned him.

He thrust the stick out at ankle level. Harry tripped over it. Then Rufkin was on Harry's back, pressing the stick across his shoulders as hard as he could. "You tried to kill me! You tried to kill Vosco!"

—

HEADY DAYS

Strong hands tugged Rufkin away, then seized the stick. Murgott. Old hero. Rufkin's chest swelled. He leapt to his feet. No one could overlook him now.

"Stand up. Slowly. Whoever you are," Murgott ordered.

Harry clambered up and towered over him, his wild curls thick with sea salt.

Murgott squinted, looked closer and lowered the stick. "Stars above, what's on your head? Are you wearing a poodle?"

Lu'nedda clapped her hands together once. "Lord Hodie!"

"It is not! He's murdering Harry!" Rufkin snatched back the walking stick and swung with both hands.

Harry batted the stick off as if it were a toothpick and held Rufkin with an arm around the shoulders. Rufkin struggled and kicked, but Harry's grip was iron-strong. Murgott watched, hands on hips, scowl on his forehead but mouth in a grin, as Harry shoved Rufkin aside so he tripped over his own feet and fell to the floor. The air squashed out of him.

Then Harry seemed to notice the Queen for the first

time. He went still for a moment. "Your Majesty." He gave a cool bow and a furious look.

With a calm smile Queen Sibilla raised her chin. "Lord Hodie," she said in her husky voice.

What? If the Queen knew Harry as Hodie—he probably was. Rufkin wanted to drop away through a crack in the floor. But Harry-poodle-head had nearly drowned him! The Queen must be wrong—

"Come in," Hodie called over his shoulder. "It's safe."

"Why would it not be?" Lu'nedda asked.

More footsteps sounded on the veranda. Another "gypsy" staggered in through the day-room door—Calleena, travel-stained, with her red beaded bag.

Nissy stumbled in too. She seemed crosser than usual, as if everything ached. But she was safe! She jumped when she saw Rufkin, though she also looked pleased.

"Who are your friends, Lord Hodie?" asked the Queen.

Calleena gave a jolt of surprise. "Harry!" she said with a sharp frown.

Nissy's jaw dropped. She blinked down at Rufkin again. "He's Lord Hodie?" she mouthed.

"Ma'am." Lord Hodie bowed to the Queen again. "This is Madam Butterly's assistant, Calleena Beagle. This girl is Nissy Symore. Until now they've known me as Harry."

"Thunderhead was right. You were a spy." With a little laugh Calleena blinked the frown away. "And I said you weren't."

Hodie drew himself up and looked scary. He jerked his head at Calleena. "Keep an eye on that one," he said to Murgott.

Murgott nodded. Rufkin didn't agree. Hodie had tricked Calleena, like he'd tricked Rufkin. She had every right to be mad. She wouldn't have known her boss, Madam Butterly, was a villain.

Nissy caught Rufkin's eye again and pointed at the Queen.

"Queen Sibilla," he whispered back.

Nissy mimed *Duh-uh, the pair of us.*

Rufkin, still on the floor, put a hand to his stomach. Nissy's notebook, still inside his shirt, another surprise waiting for her.

By now Calleena had curtseyed to the Queen and stepped to the side. Her fingers fiddled with the red bag, just as Rufkin fidgeted in his pocket when he was nervous. She stayed close to the door, eyeing the room and everything in it. Hodie held a hand out to Murgott and they gripped in a soldierly arm-shake.

Lu'nedda gave Hodie a hug and a great smacking kiss on both cheeks. "Everyone, sit down," she said. "We are having exciting morning. Now, refreshments for new guests."

Tiny Delilah opened her eyes. "Lunch at last for the grown-ups." With a thumbs-up she marched for the kitchen, white ponytail bouncing.

Rufkin slid up off the floor at last and hoped Lord Hodie wouldn't notice him.

The orphans and Vosco scurried in like a flock of chickens. Hodie bowed and greeted them all from smallest to tallest. "Pipsqueak. Buffin and Jonty. Mungo. Petulia." He grinned at Vosco, white teeth startling in his smudged face. "And Vosco. Yes, it was me."

The little boy was holding back, gray eyes wary under the very disgusting beanie. Lord Hodie hunkered down and offered his hand. "I'm happy to see you again and to see you well. Good on you, mate, for getting through. You're a little champion. Do you still have the trumpet? You're welcome to keep it."

With the ghost of a smile, Vosco backed off till he was leaning against the Queen again.

"Little duke needs shoes," said Lu'nedda. "He had adventure in holey sock. Pipsqueak, bring pair of your sneakers."

The little boy raced off.

Rufkin eased further to the edge of the room. He'd hand Nissy her notebook later when he had a chance. It would save more embarrassment if he stayed incredibly quiet for the rest of the day. He should sneak outside. But he'd like to hear what happened next.

Lord Hodie, grim-faced again, stood at ease like an army officer. Which of course he was. It was scary to see a hero in the middle of a job.

"As you know, Your Majesty, I thought it important to investigate Madam Butterfly before doing anything else." Lord Hodie glanced at Calleena.

She held her hands up like pretty paws and settled in an armchair at last. She did look weary.

The Queen gave her a calm stare, then turned back to Hodie. "And as you know, Lord Hodie, I thought it essential to check out the lazulite mine."

"The mine exploded," said Hodie. "If I'd known you

were…thank the stars nobody was killed. But look at the state of you."

"And look at you." The Queen glanced at his hair. "I didn't know you at all."

Hodie's hands clenched, and he spoke as if his heart hurt. "I recognized you the second I saw you lying for dead. In that boat with the kids."

"That is love," Lu'nedda said.

"It is not," snapped the Queen.

"Utter rubbish!" said Hodie at once.

Lu'nedda patted the top of her splattered boilersuit. "Ah, always remember these heady days of early romance."

The day room went into an interesting stillness. Hodie and the Queen looked at each other under lowered brows.

"She didn't recognize you at Jovial River either…" Blast. Rufkin had meant to keep quiet. They were both scowling at him now.

Despite himself he prattled on. "But she might not have seen you. She was dizzy. And Vosco grabbed her hand and dragged her with him…" Lord Hodie's fists clenched and loosened. "And you'd tried to drown him."

It was probably the most dangerous thing Rufkin had ever said. Hodie had looked grim before. Now he looked terrifying.

"I deliberately dropped the three of you very carefully to keep you away from Madam Butterly."

"Why?" asked Murgott.

"All right. Listen," Lord Hodie said.

"First, children can play. Outside," said Lu'nedda. "Little ones, choose balls."

The little kids scrambled around the toy box. Pipsqueak ran in with spare sneakers for Vosco and helped put them on. Then they were all out on the grass near the deck chairs, beyond the tree.

Rufkin glanced at Nissy. They stayed where they were.

Hodie began. "Madam Butterly knows the mine is causing pollution but she hasn't admitted it. She's also bribing Mayor Jolliman to speed up deliveries of iron ore from the mines in the hills behind Port Feather. Her zirbonium refinery is working non-stop."

"For goodness' sake. If this were true, I would have known." In her armchair Calleena dabbed a finger to her eyes.

"You might not be aware of it." Hodie still seemed suspicious of her. "I couldn't find proof. But I'm sure it's true. I understand why she would be doing it—pure greed for more money. What I don't understand is to do with these three." He pointed outside at Vosco, then turned around till he found Nissy and Rufkin. He gave Rufkin a dark look, then continued.

"Vida Butterly is interested in finding a child. It seems to be just any child. But it's as important to her as the Lazy River mine and making zirbonium, as important as making her millions. Maybe a child is even more important. Calleena has dodged any of my questions. But you—" he pointed at Calleena— "Goodabod and Thunderhead were desperate to gather these kids. So was I when I realised Vosco was one of them."

He glared at Rufkin again. "I was about to drop down to the launch myself and do my best to keep you safe. Then I recognized Sibilla…" He threw such a frown at the Queen that Rufkin reckoned an old-fashioned monarch would shout, *Chain him at once and swallow the key!*

Calleena let out a brave little gasp. "And the waterspouts arrived and you couldn't reach her. You never told me that the Queen was involved. I suppose a spy would keep that to himself. As for Madam Butterly, it's not at all strange. It's truly sad. She has no child of her own and longs to adopt one. These three seemed spare." Calleena waved her hand again.

But now Rufkin didn't trust that pretty gesture. It was the wave of Missie Cute-Fox sending chickens to safety, ha ha, really into her lair.

Vosco and Pipsqueak ran in again to the toy box.

Rufkin's mouth opened. "Well, Madam Butterly can't have me. I've gone totally off her. She can't have Vosco. And Nissy's mam probably wouldn't let her have Nissy till she's old enough to be a real apprentice."

"Ee-ow," Vosco said, a green ball in his hand.

"Right," said Rufkin. "Madam Butterly's got a cat. She could just get another."

All the grown-ups stared as if he was nuts. So did Nissy.

"But Your Majesty, I think we forgot to tell them yet," he continued. "How she's had herself made to look like a second Lady Gall."

—

EW, SPOTTY
NOTEBOOK

Rufkin expected some attention now. But there was silence, except that Vosco and Pipsqueak zoomed outside again.

"So that's what Doctor Goodabod's been up to," said Lord Hodie at last.

"The elastic surgeon?" Murgott fell back in his chair. "Little Queen, if Vida Butterly wants to look like Lady Gall, she's as warped as a nest of vipers."

"This is crazy!" Calleena pulled a handkerchief out of her bag and dabbed her face.

Lord Hodie shook his tangle of hair and turned to the Queen. "Sibilla, I told you—"

"Have you learned nothing from me?" Murgott demanded. "You don't tell a monarch anything. You politely suggest."

"Pardon me for shouting," said Lord Hodie calmly. Then he shouted, "If you don't tell a monarch anything, why have we set up a Council of Wisdom?"

"For the sake of democracy." Lu'nedda spoke like an utter Empress. "But look at the youngest royal child playing with Pipsqueak, his little cousin—so sharing with toys.

By the time we agree, Vosco and Pipsqueak both be very old men. That is problem with Council of Wisdom. It takes too long to make suggestions. It argues but does not act."

Lord Hodie dragged a hand though his hair. "We're in the middle of a national disaster. There's no time to wait."

"You won't defeat anyone with that horrible hairstyle," said the Queen. "Sorry. That was petty but I couldn't resist. It really is an awful perm."

"I'll grow it out at once, Ma'am," Lord Hodie said in an excellent Tone-ironic.

Actually Rufkin didn't think the curls were so terrible, they just didn't suit Hodie. But he managed to bite his lips together.

A group of adventurers appeared from the winery to wash soot off themselves. A few others, already clean, wheeled trolleys heaped with food in from the kitchen. Swan came in and ladled soup for himself from a vast tureen.

Calleena must be starving but she was still sitting there, watching and listening. So was Nissy, head going back and forth as if she was watching a play. The smell of the soup was tempting but Rufkin didn't want to miss a word either. Things didn't feel right.

Murgott drew the Queen, Hodie, and the ex-Empress into a huddle. If he meant to be confidential, he should have whispered. "The situation is urgent. In this room are a dozen of the best brains in Fontania. Most of them are old but that's an advantage. They're crammed with experience. I count my own brain, in regard to tactics. No pirate won by blasting into a fight without a rock-solid plan."

"You told me you did," said Lu'nedda.

"That was luck," said Murgott. "But an army has never won by marching off willy-nilly. Well, hardly ever."

"But how to fix this end-of-days?" Lu'nedda asked. "Hodie, what is use of spying if you find no proof of a badness or plot? Wanting to look like Lady Gall is maybe big mental problem only."

"Actually, I might have proof," Nissy said.

The grown-ups stared, Calleena especially.

The Queen beckoned Nissy.

Before she went closer Nissy combed her hair with her fingers and rubbed at her face. "Madam Butterly said to stay alert and take risks. So I did. I wrote some actual information in my notebook. But I lost it."

"Here." Rufkin fished out the book at last.

"*Ew*," said Nissy. "It's been down your front?"

"You'd already dribbled on it," he said. "It got soggy in Jovial River. When the corners stopped digging in, I mostly forgot it." He held it out, smiling.

But she stuck her hands behind her back. "*Ew*," she said. "Double *ew!*"

The grown-ups peered at the notebook but didn't touch either.

"You open it," Lu'nedda said to him.

Rufkin wanted to chuck it on the floor and march out. But he didn't dare refuse an order from an ex-Empress. He wouldn't have refused an order from Lu'nedda whatever she'd been. She was pretty fearsome. He eased back the cover.

THE KNOT IMPOSSIBLE

"*Nissy Symore*," read Lu'nedda over his shoulder.

"Me," said Nissy.

Rufkin turned another page.

"It is in code," said Lu'nedda.

Nissy frowned. "I hope I can remember it."

"You can't remember your own code?" asked Rufkin.

Nissy straightened her shoulders. "The first pages are how much money I could make if I sold cave-lizard nuggets. If I was lucky, it would have been fifty-nine dolleros and twenty cents for about thirty bucketsful."

He turned more pages.

"*Ew*," she muttered again.

He came to the last pages she'd scribbled on.

"Yes," she said. "Madam Butterly was bringing in metal from Um'Binnia, made in the old ways, not with lazulite."

"You're all crazy," Calleena said. "You believe the notes of a child? What she thinks she remembered?"

Queen Sibilla lifted a hand. "Let Nissy speak."

"Madam Butterly was smuggling, probably." Nissy gave Lord Hodie a blink. "You suspected it, didn't you? Well, I wrote down exactly what I remembered from her notebook." She frowned at a tidy set of columns much neater than Rufkin's printing, and set a finger on the first one.

"This is iron, and that sign is what gets added to it to make regular steel. In other words, it's old metal. But this column is iron with lazulite added, so it's zirbonium. Now look at these dates. I think that three years ago she began buying up old metal at cheap prices, and at the same time she started selling the new stuff at a higher price."

Queen Sibilla's hands pressed together. "Nearly three years ago Vida Butterly suggested she would sit on the Council of Wisdom when it was created. She suggested taxes on imported metal—that's on metal without lazulite. But if she was smuggling, she avoided paying taxes on it herself."

"And almost exactly three years ago she had that trouble at the mine," said Hodie. "When the miners refused to go in."

Calleena started to protest again, but Murgott and Lu'nedda both glared at her.

Nissy set a finger on the last date. "And that was underlined three times and marked *deadline.*"

Hodie's brows pulled together. "That's the day after tomorrow."

Murgott flung up his arms. "But what does it mean?"

"It didn't say." Nissy chewed her lip for a moment. "But Madam Butterly had drawn lots of gleeful faces and spiky things in the margin."

"Show." Lu'nedda passed her a pencil. Nissy scribbled an example in her own margin.

Lu'nedda pulled a face. "Doodling shows personality. Very nasty."

"Where is Madam Butterly now?" asked Murgott.

"I have no idea," said Calleena in a sharp voice. "I really haven't."

Rufkin had better say something. "I saw the *Sea Honey* first thing this morning. Just before Swan found us."

"Swan?" called Murgott. "Where did you find them?"

"Near the mouth of Simmering River," Swan called back from the table.

"Would she be heading upriver?" Murgott asked. Rufkin almost saw his thoughts marching along. "The channel is deep enough—ah, no need to worry. Vida Butterly can't harm us."

Calleena, expressionless now, held on to her bag.

"Just a minute, Murgott," Lord Hodie said. "The *Sea Honey*'s crew would be a match for you and me. There are eight of them. Including one ogre. The captain would give anyone a tough run for their dollero. And the yacht's got a swivel gun on a solid old turntable. It's disguised as a telescope." He flashed a glance at Calleena. "Yes, I spotted it. There's also a loudspeaker system, very elaborate. Thunderhead was testing it out. It seems to me Madam Butterly has some unusual plans. Murgott, what weapons do you have on the property?"

Murgott's eyebrows came together in the frown Rufkin's dad had used in *The Aim is Victory*. His nostrils flared as if he smelled danger.

The Queen rested her forehead on her hand and old Doctor Maisie came and took her arm. "Too much talk and not enough rest. We must clean you up and give proper nourishment. Come along to the hospital wing." She and tiny Delilah helped the Queen leave.

Lord Hodie, with his own terrible frown, watched them go, then gave Calleena another glance.

Outside, one of the orphans was in shrieks of tears again. In the next second it turned to laughter. An orange ball bounced into a deck chair. A red one bounced into the tree and down the path. Vosco went running after it. He tried to pick it up but the trumpet got in his way. It would be much easier if he put the darn thing down now and then.

A *hee-haw* came from behind the house. Tiger, the donkey. The horses that Hodie and Calleena had left down by the gate gave a few snickers. They might need water. The day was overcast but it was hot.

Rufkin heard a familiar sound again—very heavy footsteps, a crunch on the path.

His breath sort of whispered back down his throat. He prickled all over.

~

Through the window, Rufkin saw the orphans wheel around on the grass and look at the path. They backed off and squeaked a bit. All the balls bounced to a stop. Vosco pushed the beanie up so he could see better and went very still.

Doctor Goodabod stepped into sight. "What is here? Outstanding surprise! Excellent specimen!" His huge hands whisked up Vosco as if he weighed nothing.

The orphans ran screaming from view. Murgott and Hodie made for the door, Lu'nedda with them. Rufkin dashed out as well, but skidded to a stop just before he bumped into her on the veranda.

Captain Thunderhead stood on the path beside Goodabod. Behind them were four sailors in yellow and black jerseys, rifles over their shoulders in a casual attitude.

Murgott stayed halfway down the veranda steps. 'Did you have a booking?'

Thunderhead's grin nearly split that sea-pickled face. "What a welcome. Harry the apprentice is already here. I see

Calleena too, there at the window. We think alike in Butterly Ventures. All roads led to Adventurers' Rest."

For a moment Rufkin thought it had all been a mix-up. Madam Butterly and her crew wanted a night at the lodge. He started to smile.

"And tiddlers again." Thunderhead rubbed his hands. "So many tiddlers when we only need one."

"Goodabod, you're scaring the boy," Hodie said. "Put him down."

The ogre tucked Vosco under one arm like a rolled-up blanket. "I do no harm."

"Help," whispered Vosco.

Rufkin pushed past Lu'nedda to the top of the steps. "Put him down!"

"Take you instead?" A wheeze of laughter from Thunderhead. "You'd be too much trouble."

"Please to put child down," Lu'nedda said. "What do you want?"

Captain Thunderhead's head reared back a bit. "What Harry and Calleena came for. Any spare orphan. But a spare royal child will suit better. Madam Butterly will be a happy woman, richer than ever."

Lord Hodie's shoulders had widened with anger but he spoke softly. "Put the boy down, Goodabod. You can't…"

Thunderhead had whisked a hand to his belt and brought out a pistol. Rufkin heard the click of the safety catch. The sailors unshouldered their rifles.

"Time's short," said Thunderhead. "You're in it for money or you're out. I'll just take your resignation back to Madam

Butterly. No place for kind hearts in Butterly Ventures."

With his ogre-size hand clamped over Vosco's mouth, Goodabod backed past an open window. The white-haired troll leapt from it and tried to bowl Goodabod—Hodie dived at Thunderhead—the pistol went flying—

"Stop!" came Calleena's voice. Something hard pressed into Rufkin's head, and sharp fingers had clutched his shoulder. "Mistress Murgott, stand well back, thank you. Mister Murgott too, stand well away."

The pressure left Rufkin's head and he stumbled. Beside him, Calleena, red bag over her shoulder, held a sleek silver pistol. In the doorway, Nissy looked stunned.

"Thunderhead, his name isn't Harry. He is a spy. It's Lord Hodie." Calleena aimed at Hodie now. "I'd shoot him, but the sound might bring out some tough old folk. The Queen's here too, but she can't do anything. Thank the stars you thought to come here. Now, quick. We have three days."

Calleena turned to Nissy and tugged her hair. "Madam Butterly liked you. This is your chance. Come along."

Nissy kicked Calleena and burst into sobs.

"Stupid girl," muttered Calleena.

"Cover us," Thunderhead barked to the *Sea Honey* crew.

The sailors formed a shield of rifles.

Calleena and Thunderhead strode away down the crunching path. The ogre lumbered after them for the gate, Vosco still under his arm. The trumpet dangled from the little kid's neck.

—

DO NO HARM

The moment they'd gone, Murgott dived up the steps into the house. "Weapons!" he roared.

"Nissy, go comfort orphans," said Lu'nedda. "Rufkin, fetch help from winery."

Even before he reached it adventurers were pouring out with their brooms, mops, and shovels. They ran faster and more steadily than most people younger would have managed. By the time he'd gathered them all together, Murgott and Hodie were ahead already, each with a pistol. Rufkin caught up at the gate by the twisted trees.

Goodabod was far down the road. Thunderhead and Calleena were just behind him. The sailors still formed a shield. There past the bridge was the wharf and the old wooden ship Rufkin had seen only this morning. There was a small launch and a couple of dinghies.

And there was the *Sea Honey* too. A crewman—it was Sammo—stood on the wharf, guarding the gangway.

"Keep under cover," muttered Murgott.

Rufkin, through blood beating in his ears, heard Vosco— *Help help*.

Swan stumbled up and aimed his pistol.

Murgott pushed his hand down. "Can't risk hurting the child."

Rufkin tried to run on, but Murgott grabbed him. Lu'nedda had caught up as well. One by one, all the old adventurers stopped beside them. The only thing to do was watch Goodabod cart Vosco onto the yacht. Not like a roll of blanket now—the kid was kicking. Good on him. Rufkin choked down a sob.

From the yacht, Calleena trained her pistol too on the adventurers. As the gangway was hauled up, Rufkin managed to squirm from Murgott's grip. He raced for the wharf. Thunderhead aimed above his head and fired. Someone tackled Rufkin from behind, and his face squashed into the dirt. It was Lord Hodie.

Rufkin struggled up again, spitting grass.

"You said we were even," he shouted to Goodabod. "We're not any more!"

Doctor Goodabod gave a finger-salute to his deerstalker hat. "You are right," he shouted back. "Therefore I tell you three somethings to be even again. One, Council of Wisdom is half council of honesty, half council of dark greediness. Two, King Jasper is absent and cannot be reached. Three, Queen Sibilla is stuck at Adventurers' Rest and can go nowhere. Thus—" He laughed and picked Vosco up by the scruff of his neck— "As Thunderhead said, royal sprat is perfect for the job."

"What job?" screamed Rufkin. "Madam Butterly can't adopt him!"

"Adopt? Ha! No, no. With him, Vida Butterly's greatest

business deal yet will be as sweet as a deal can be." That ogre's laugh was getting on Rufkin's nerves. "Run off, cower with the old folk and pray that you survive the end-of-days."

"You'd never hurt a little kid!" Rufkin cried.

The ogre nudged Thunderhead. The captain shrugged.

Goodabod beckoned Sammo and put a hand on his shoulder. "This is not a little kid, and a wetting such as I give him does no harm at all. But here's an example."

He shoved Sammo overboard into the river. Thunderhead aimed and fired. Sammo didn't surface. The *Sea Honey* with her quiet engine began moving downriver.

Murgott shoved Rufkin back into the grass. Shots blasted over their heads from adventurers behind, the yacht in front. The white-haired troll raised a rifle with a shiny barrel and pulled the trigger—then let out a roar as the rifle exploded, falling to pieces in his hands.

"Backfire," said the tiny old lady. "Of course —zirbonium barrel. Useless." She examined the troll's face. "That's the good thing about thick warty skin. Still pretty, my lad."

When Rufkin lifted his head again the *Sea Honey* was well away. Sammo still hadn't surfaced. Tears dripped down Rufkin's face. Some went back up his nose because of his gasping.

"War is no time for sentiment," Murgott growled.

"War?" said Rufkin.

Murgott scowled. "What else do you call it? There's us and there's them. They've stolen a child at gunpoint. They've shot one of their own to scare us off. Call it an ugly game if you like. I call it war."

Rufkin stumbled down past the wharf. There was no point in it—he just couldn't stop himself. The *Sea Honey* was rounding the bend now. If only he'd thought faster. If only he'd found a way to help Vosco.

Amid his gasps of hopelessness he heard a splash and a groan. He took a step nearer the edge—there lay Sammo, caught in a snag. Rufkin scrambled down and tried to lift his head out of the water.

Sammo smiled, a sad sort of smile, but Rufkin wouldn't have believed a jolly one. "I…I'll tell you," Sammo stammered. "Boys like to know. I would've liked knowing when I was a boy. There's a…a worse than a dragon. Bigger than—" his voice hitched as if something terrible pinched him inside— "than a dragon-eagle. I've never seen it…she calls it the deep-dragon."

Deep—the deep-dragon—could it be the shape in the ocean? The wonder of underground and undersea in Mistress Mucclack's ancient story?

"Lonely," Rufkin found himself whispering. "Terribly lonely…"

Sammo's eyes had closed. Was he dead? But he spoke again on a ragged breath. "More wealth and power than even your parents could dream of with…their big actors' heads. Famous big heads…" He lay still, chest barely moving.

⌒

PLAN AHEAD

There was nothing in all of the world that would help Vosco. Or Rufkin. Or even the world. But Rufkin found himself shouting.

"Lord Hodie! Help! Over here!"

It felt weird, wanting to help an enemy. But Sammo was wheeled back to Adventurers' Rest in a wooden trundler. Rufkin walked for about five steps, then a couple of old people half-carried him. Their kindness made him feel worse. What did kindness even matter any more?

They set him in the day room again, and sent Nissy and an orphan to fetch him some calming tea.

The Queen was out of bed, cleaned up at last but still a bit staggery. Her hair shone, mostly soft blonde curls down over her ears, though some were frizzy. She'd been given a white shirt so long it might as well be a dress, dark purple leggings, and blue boots. The belt with the scabbard and dagger was around her waist. She looked like a Queen now, but she'd always behaved like one even when he'd thought she was a puppet. Her cheeks were rose pink. It was awful to see them turn pale while Murgott told her Vosco had been kidnapped at gunpoint.

"For a business deal? But what can it be?"

"Your Majesty." Murgott rubbed her hand. "Youth and skill has won to this point. Old age and know-how can still win the day."

It was even more awful to see the Queen's face not brighten at all.

It was just about the worst thing of all to see Lord Hodie watching the Queen. As if it was written in the air above the poodle curls, Rufkin knew how Hodie's heart broke to accept he couldn't help the person he loved the most.

The ex-Empress Lu'nedda clapped her hands sharp as a gunshot. "Yes, dear Murgott. We must win day, week, month, and years to come. First, boy Rufkin needs a bath. So does girl." She squinted at Nissy who—of course—looked insulted. "Quick. Boy in ordinary bathroom. Girl who has been helpful with orphans can use luxury bathroom. Next we all have the nourishing soup. Then we make plans. All must be done at very much speed."

With an arm as strong as any aunt's, she shoved Rufkin to the back of the house and into the ordinary bathroom. He didn't care what bathroom he had. Oddly, it was a comfort of sorts to find the plumbing was strong old metal. It worked with groans to show it was on the job.

An orphan cracked the door and with a skinny arm passed Rufkin fresh clothes. The length of sleeve and leg was spot on. But they must have been borrowed from an aged dwarf. They were far too wide. He didn't care about that either.

Then he was allowed back to the day room and told to sit again at its long wooden table.

The old adventurers were saying how much better life always seems after an exploit when you have your first bite of something tasty and the rest of the plateful still waits under your nose.

Nobody seemed in much of a rush. And Rufkin didn't feel at all hungry. But Lu'nedda put a soup spoon into his hand as she walked past in a fresh white boilersuit. He had a sip. The scent of coriander, rich celery soup with not a whisker of stringy bits and thickened with the creamy weight of potato, did somehow lend strength back to his soul.

Before long Nissy came and stood next to him. Her hair was pig-tailed again and she wore a clean but also too-wide tunic in pretty leaf-green. "Just so you know. I never told Harry or Calleena that the puppet was the Queen."

"That's because you didn't know," said Rufkin.

"I did at Jovial River just before she ran with Vosco." She plumped down on the chair next to him. "Calleena was rubbish at riding a horse. So was I, but I'd never been on one. That was my first and last time, that's all I'm saying."

Lu'nedda swept up again. "Quick, finish soup. Then children must rest, play, and relax."

"No." At once Rufkin's face burned from daring to interrupt such a grand woman. "Sorry. But what about Sammo? About what he said?"

Lu'nedda frowned. "He is unconscious. Doctor Maisie has to operate." Her strong-aunt hand dragged him from his chair. "Rufkin, if you have more to tell us, do not say another word until you have the audience."

~

He had to face a circle of Murgott, ex-Empress Lu'nedda, Queen Sibilla, and Lord Hodie. Not to mention Swan, Delilah, Littlewink, and most of the others. Nissy hovered on the edge. Stage-fright stuck needles in his chest but Rufkin spoke up.

"Sammo didn't say much, so this won't take long." He continued—how Sammo had said there was a dragon far worse than a dragon. How he'd whispered about wealth and power. How Rufkin himself had twice seen a great shape in the ocean that struck the fear of being alone deep into him. When he said that part, his voice quivered. How Mistress Mucclack had told of old tales about the network of caverns underground and undersea.

Murgott's frown grew more and more suspicious. But the Queen—Rufkin had a feeling she understood. She sat and thought for a while. Her hair actually went bouffy with it—her changeable hair, one of the signs of her magical qualities.

At last she shook her head. "What Mistress Mucclack talked about must be the deep-dragon. But I think what you describe is too small."

"It was enormous! Bigger than this house, bigger than—" Oh, what would he know? He turned to go.

Lord Hodie laid a hand on his back. "Rufkin, wait. Sibilla, what do you know about the deep-dragon?"

"The story is so old. It's just a few fragments." She pressed her hands to her eyes and thought for another moment. "It was so huge that it liked to emerge from underground only at one place. The Eastern Isle. In the Eastern Lake,

I suppose. What bothers me is Rufkin saying he felt such a sense of loneliness in the midst of his fear. I felt it too."

She had? His back straightened a little.

"I dreamed about it when I was in the launch," Sibilla continued in her soft way. "That's what woke me while the children were up on the barge. I thought I was still dreaming. I ate an oat-bar to check. It tasted awful."

And she'd put on the sun hat. Rufkin glanced at Nissy— she seemed on the edge of a grin for a moment, just as he was.

"Did you feel it?" the Queen asked Nissy.

Nissy shrugged. So that was a no.

"What worries me," said Lu'nedda, "is tetchy and criminal assistant to Vida Butterly saying, 'We have three days.' And three days from now marked in Butterly's notebook. Three days to what? And what does greedy Butterly want with Vosco?"

"We must move as fast as we can," said Murgott. "We have to plan."

A plan would be great. As long as Rufkin didn't have to get back on Old Ocean. Not for anyone. Not at any time, nor anyhow. Especially not if there was some sort of dragon.

~

"A plan to survive in the end-of-days," rumbled Swan.

"A plan to subdue the enemy without fighting." Littlewink's eyes were damp with tears. "So we may continue to climb mountains for a peaceful dekko at the stars."

"He just means a look," Delilah muttered. "A squizz. Or a bit of a gander."

"Please to concentrate," said Lu'nedda.

"A plan for the return of King Jasper," Lord Hodie said. "Her Majesty is still too weak…"

"But she stopped the fire in the winery spreading to the house," said Rufkin. "Didn't you, Ma'am? You summoned the wind."

"Rufkin helped me to the window," said the Queen. "He understood what was needed and made me do it."

The look Hodie gave Rufkin turned his insides to water. He'd never known what that really meant. It wasn't pleasant.

Delilah clenched her tiny fist. "But Your Majesty must not do any more for a while. We need a plan to send a message to the dragon-eagles."

"Oh—I've done that," said Rufkin. "I hope. I told the bower birds. Two flew east. One went south as well to tell the King."

Hodie's fist was a knot of muscle and bone. "Do you have proof?"

"You've a nerve to talk about proof," muttered Murgott.

"No arguments," said Lu'nedda. "Say thanks to boy."

Various grumbles happened, a few pats on Rufkin's shoulder, that sort of thing. He could almost see his own face turn red from the inside.

The Queen raised a hand. Very good gesture. Very well timed. "This is worse than the Council of Wisdom. We have three days. It's mid-afternoon on day one. For goodness' sake. I want a plan."

The silence quivered with shame. Interesting to see grown-ups quenched a bit.

"I was already headed to the Eastern Isle and the dragon-eagles," continued the Queen. "I see two choices. Either keep going. Or follow Vosco."

All the grown-ups started to gabble.

The Queen lifted her hand again and they shut up. "Murgott first. I'd like your opinion."

He looked horribly put on the spot. "Ma'am. I'd rather go last."

"For goodness' sake," the Queen said again. "Lu'nedda?"

Lu'nedda drew herself up to her full height. "As Empress I would have chosen Eastern Isle. As mother of orphans, I choose follow the child."

"A military leader is forever alone in decisions of command," Littlewink said. "The choice is terrible. But it should be the Eastern Isle. If there is a deep-dragon, you might save the entire country."

"Delilah O'Lilah?" the Queen asked. "You were head of the Workroom of Knowledge. Your opinion is important."

"Logic says, the Eastern Isle," Delilah said.

"Science says, the Eastern Isle," said Swan.

The troll with bandages on his face from the rifle that backfired. And all of the rest. All of them said, "The Eastern Isle."

"Hodie?" the Queen asked.

For a moment Lord Hodie said nothing. Then, "For me there is no question. I would choose Vosco. But I must be logical. The Queen will be safer if we go east for the dragon-eagles. I have to choose east."

The Queen turned to Nissy.

"Me?" asked Nissy. "Oh, of course I say Vosco. Also,

of course, I'm going too. I want to see Madam Butterly done for."

"Neither of you two will be going," said the Queen. "It's far too dangerous. Rufkin?"

Whatever he said would be right and wrong. Whatever the Queen decided would be right and wrong too. But for him there was only one answer.

"Vosco," he said.

Murgott saluted. "And I say, Vosco."

Rufkin had kept count. Even if the Queen chose Vosco, it made only five. It was ten for the Eastern Isle.

—

TO BE SO
BOLD

"If I may be so bold," said Nissy, "and why wouldn't I be, you're going about this the wrong way."

The Queen looked entirely emptied of strength but her hair was still bouffy. Her smile had a glimmer.

"Madam Butterly might be going to the Eastern Isle anyway," continued Nissy. "You won't know till you reach the sea."

The Queen's smile widened. Rufkin reckoned she'd thought that all along.

"So if I were you," said Nissy, "I'd get a move on. Or you'll be too slow to catch a glimpse of the *Sea Honey* no matter where she's heading."

"Get a move on?" said Murgott. "Any clue about how?"

"There are boats down at the wharf," Nissy said. "I supposed they were yours."

Lu'nedda looked her empressy best but it wasn't encouraging. "The launch is too small and also had new engine two years ago, so we cannot trust it. It would be heroic to vanquish Madam Butterly using our rowboats, but most unlikely. We have horses that Hodie and Calleena arrived on. We have donkey Tiger. We have three large-size tricycles and several bikes—oh, they might break down too."

"One's broken already," said Littlewink.

"What about the wooden sailing ship?" asked Rufkin.

Queen Sibilla sat up. "Sailing ship?"

Murgott shook his head hard. "Ma'am, you know we have the *Golden Chalice* here. But she's far too old."

"Sibilla, you knew her when she was called *Travelling Restaurant*," said Lu'nedda. "I never like how Fontanians spell 'travelling'. In Um'Binnia we use only one l."

"Dear wife, however you spell it, the ship is a wreck." Murgott covered his freckled bald head with his hands.

"*Golden Chalice* is also very sentimental name," Lu'nedda added. "We argue many times but he is determined."

Murgott's fists came down and thumped the table. "She is the ship that helped save the baby Sibilla. She's a ship of history and adventure. But the hull has as many leaks as there are stars in the sky."

"Will she last for three days?" asked the Queen.

~

"Weapons of all sorts," cried Murgott. "Combat gear."

"Ropes and maps," said tiny Delilah.

"Changes of underwear in large sizes?" asked ancient Littlewink.

"Dried rations," said the white-haired troll. "Bananas in those individual curved boxes that stop them bruising."

How many people should go with the Queen? Only five: Murgott, Lord Hodie, Littlewink, Swan, and Delilah. Lord Hodie looked very dark on it.

The old people hurried off to storerooms and bottoms of wardrobes to gather the gear. Rufkin and Nissy were told to find the banana boxes. Rufkin was happy to help. This would be the last thing he did for the whole adventure.

Back in the day room, two voices grew louder and louder.

"If we're not going east, you're staying behind," Hodie shouted.

The Queen shouted back. "Till we catch sight of Madam Butterly we don't know if she's going east, west, or straight upwards. What are you going to do then? Chuck me overboard?"

"And the boy and girl are staying here with you!" he roared.

"I already said, they are staying behind!" cried the Queen.

Rufkin felt sick with relief that he wasn't allowed to go. But he noticed the jut of Nissy's chin.

—

ACT THE FOURTH

THE NECESSARY CHILD

ORDINARY
BOY TRICK

Rufkin stood at the handle of a trundler again, this time at the steps of Adventurers' Rest. Yes, this was the last thing he'd do. Then he'd really relax.

"Goodbye," the orphans cried from the veranda.

"Goodbye!" Lu'nedda held out her arms to Murgott and tidied the flaps on his combat jacket. "Good luck and good strength, unless you return in half an hour because ship sinks. That did not sound exactly right but you know what I mean."

Murgott kissed her farewell in a terrible rush. "Look after our babies." He kissed all the orphans and gave them bear-hugs. "Look after your Mamma Lu'nedda." Then he shouted, "Come on. We must reach the sea while it's still daylight." He pounded for the dock and the small sailing ship.

Lord Hodie's combat jacket, an old one of Murgott's, only just buttoned across his broad chest. It still looked ferocious, so many pockets and flaps all meaning military business. He eyed Rufkin. "Bring that cart, then hurry back here and stay out of trouble."

Old adventurers were already pushing carts off to the

wharf. Littlewink and Delilah O'Lilah went running past. The gate and tangled tree showed through a final tendril of smoke from the winery fire.

Rufkin shoved the packed cart. Beside him, Nissy hauled an enormous bag that held only pillows. At the wharf Lord Hodie and Swan were busy at once with ropes and the gangplank. The gray-haired troll was helping the Queen on board.

For the first time Rufkin had a good look at the vessel. What on earth were they thinking? She was more round than ship-shaped. Two masts were crooked. The third, with a crow's nest, stood straight only if he squinted. A shabby lifeboat hung on lop-sided davits. She might indeed be a ship of legend but she was so old. Well, "of legend" meant old but… His chest hurt from the last ashes, and from disappointment. Vosco had no chance of help. None at all.

Swan, in a seaman's sou'wester, came running off the ship. "Get that up the gangplank. What, are you scared?" He grabbed the handle from Rufkin and shoved it himself.

Rufkin stayed where he was, feet safe on the wharf.

Nissy and Delilah were wrestling over the bag of pillows. "I just want to stow them," Nissy cried. "Please, let me help."

Old Delilah threw up her hands and marched onto the ship. Nissy nudged Rufkin and grinned. Then she climbed on and disappeared into the cabin.

A shout came from the elderly troll. Rufkin looked up. A fire-lizard was circling the wooden ship. It dropped closer and peered with a bright red eye.

Tiny Delilah rushed into view with a pistol. She braced

herself on the deck, aimed, and fired. The lizard merely side-slipped in the air.

"It's a scout," cried Hodie from somewhere. "If we don't get rid of it, it'll summon the rest. This old wreck's a fire risk."

"Just get the wreck moving!" Murgott clambered the outside stairs to the wheelhouse. He spotted Rufkin there on the wharf. "Boy, get back to the house like you were told. Hodie, to the engine room. It's old metal, never repaired, but it needs attention."

"What about fuel?" shouted Hodie. "What kind of boilers…"

"Get down and find out," Murgott roared.

The fire-lizard scouted lower. Delilah shot a second time. The lizard soared up and spat out a spark.

"Blast you," she cried.

Rufkin tried to remember. What had killed cave-lizards in Port Feather? Dogs. They had no dogs. What had killed the one in the mud near the salvage yard? He had no idea. But if cave-lizards could be killed, so could fire-lizards.

He leapt to the troll and snatched a scarf from his neck. "Sorry. Pay you later," he gasped.

Then he slid down the bank to the edge of the river. As fast as he could, he scooped three gloops of mud into the centre of the scarf and twisted the long ends together. This had worked for the teacher escaping his pupils in *No Easy Lessons*.

He ran back to the wharf, swung the makeshift sling around his head and let it fly. The sling rocketed up. The fire-lizard dodged again but the mud package clipped the side of its head. The ends of the scarf flew out and tangled around the fire-lizard's wings. The package of wet mud, scarf, and lizard tumbled into Simmering River. The water fizzed.

Already Littlewink had hauled up the gangplank.

Murgott roared again from the wheelhouse. "Cast off!"

At a cabin window, Nissy's head popped up and down.

Murgott grabbed a speaking tube. "Steady ahead and you'd better be ready!" he bellowed to the engine room.

A thick mechanical cough sounded inside the hull. The ship juddered.

Rufkin saw twisting water between the wharf and the ship. The pit of his stomach filled with dread. But he dashed to the road, swung round, then sprinted back. He leapt over the gap and crashed onto the deck. *Ow.* Very *ow.* He hadn't meant to do that last bit. Actually he hadn't meant to do any of it.

~

Rufkin rolled in through the cabin door. This was stupid. Utterly stupid! He'd better hide from Murgott till the *Chalice* was so far downriver it couldn't return.

But in less than an hour, Murgott was roaring louder than Rufkin's father in the lead role of *The Beast who Had Lungs of Brass Bellows.* The curses were more horrible than in *Revenge of the Vengeful New Wife.*

Then Murgott saw Nissy was on board as well. The roar creaked to a stop and he rubbed his throat. He pointed to the galley and the boxes of cooking gear. It meant, *Store it away or you'll both be keel-hauled.* He slammed the wheelhouse door for some time on his own.

Nissy rubbed her ears, found some old menus in a kitchen drawer, and sat down to read them. "Yum," she muttered, "Chocolate Menace. *Ew*, Hot Lettuce Salad."

Rufkin sorted some cutlery into neat compartments. Why had he jumped? Why? He'd managed to beat one fire-lizard but there'd be much worse to come—like a deep-dragon. He'd been such an idiot! He crashed a fry-pan into its iron wall clamp.

"Good job." It was Queen Sibilla, a bunch of tea towels in her hand. "Where do these go?"

Rufkin had no idea but he pointed to a drawer.

"And thank you for dealing with the fire-lizard." She had an odd look in her eye, as if she was especially pleased that he'd done it with an ordinary boy trick.

His face felt as fiery as it could without actually scorching. She laughed and looked as beautiful as sunshine. Then she swung away up the internal ladder to the wheelhouse.

"You're blushing," said Nissy.

"Shut up," said Rufkin.

"She could have said thank you to me too. After all, I had proof of Madam Butterly's dealings. Not that it matters." Nissy did a terrible job of pretending she wasn't offended.

"If you want the Smile-careless, this is the way." Rufkin made a side of his mouth curl up just the right amount. She gave a little laugh, then copied perfectly.

"Ocean ahead!" Murgott's roar was hoarse from overuse, which made Rufkin feel guilty. "Littlewink! Find the life-jackets!"

The ogre shouldered in to rummage through the gear.

"Sort out the life-jackets," he grumbled. "Then bamboozle the enemy. Hoodwink and startle the foe, small or large, human or otherwise."

Rufkin tried a Smile-careless himself. It didn't stick to his mouth for half a second.

—

RAT-LINES

It was only moderately scary sailing through the estuary of Simmering River. The banks were too far away to see alligators.

Then it was hilarious listening to Swan and Littlewink. They spread the old green sails of the ship over the deck to check for rips and holes in case they'd be needed. The ancient swearwords and insults they'd gathered during research and adventures would have sent his mother into a fit. Rufkin bet they would need the sails. The fuel Lord Hodie had found in the engine room would run out before three days were up.

Now they'd reached Old Ocean. Rufkin stood on deck and watched the land shrink till it was a long dark line. The sea turned silvery, the sky like an upturned bowl of pewter with feathery clouds. How lovely it was—but Vosco, wherever he might be, must be confused and scared.

Murgott's head poked from the wheelhouse. "We'll spot the *Sea Honey*'s lights if they turn 'em on. But we won't if they don't. Boy, up to the crow's nest."

What? Him? "I've never climbed a mast," he called.

"The rule of a first time is that it's the first." Murgott

held up a finger to help make the point. "I didn't ask you to come. Now you're here, earn your keep."

Rufkin crossed his own fingers for luck. "Lord Hodie would do it better than me."

Bad luck. Lord Hodie just that moment came on deck, wiping greasy hands on a greasier cloth. "I'm wrestling with the engine."

Murgott glowered down. "And he's heavier than you, boy, with some years of muscle. We haven't checked the strength of those old masts. Go."

Delilah O'Lilah was lighter than Rufkin. But it was safest to say nothing even if his insides were water again.

He wiped his hands on the back of his pants and set his hands on the rope ladder—rat-lines, he thought they were called. The tiny platform of the crow's nest seemed...

"Don't look up!" Murgott shouted. "It'll make you dizzy."

True. Rufkin climbed a few rope-rungs.

"Don't look down!" Murgott roared. "It'll make you dizzier."

Also true. At the first cross-piece, he rested. Swan's and Littlewink's swear words swam through his head.

"Get off that yard!" bellowed Murgott. "The sun's setting fast."

At the second yard, he rested again.

"The sun's setting faster," came a cry from Swan.

Rufkin climbed for the third and final yard. There was the gap in the bowl of the crow's nest. He wriggled through. As if they'd waited for the moment, prickles of sweaty fear rushed over him.

He hauled himself upright, clung to old metal handles on the mast and closed his eyes. He begged that he wouldn't see the vast shadow. But he was up here to search the horizon. For that, his eyes had to be open.

It helped when he used both hands as a sort of porthole to help him focus. And it kept out some glare.

Nothing to the north—that was the direction they'd come from, so of course not. After all they hadn't overtaken the *Sea Honey*.

To the east, nothing but silvery waves.

Nor anything south, though this high up he saw the smallest blur on the horizon. If he'd had a map, he'd know if it was Battle Island.

West? By now his eyes couldn't be sure what they was seeing. The pink of the sky had begun painting the water.

Voices below broke into argument. Argument turned into shouts. He peered over the rim of the nest. At the first yard Nissy clung to the mast.

"Swan's binoculars," she called. "I've brought them this far and I'm not coming higher."

~

Rufkin muttered an ancient curse. He climbed down then up again very carefully. At last he was back in the nest, legs shaking with effort. Gulls bickered overhead. The crows' nest swayed. Wind whistled in his ears and made his face sting. Inside he was crying to be on deck again before darkness fell.

But he yanked on an ear to help him concentrate, then began a last scan of the waves. Nothing more to the north.

Nothing east. South—yes, it was Battle Island, which looked very peaceful. He firmed his back against the mast to focus on west.

There, far off, was the shape of a super-yacht. With the sun setting behind it, he couldn't see for sure if she was the *Sea Honey*. She wasn't using sails. The bow was pointing west. Rufkin trained the binoculars on the pennant flying on her highest mast.

Steady, he whispered to the old ship beneath him, *let me have one moment where it all comes clear*. The air stilled around him. The sound of voices below and birds above quietened too. And far off on Old Ocean a breeze lifted the pennant.

For a second he thought he saw a gleam of blue. The pennant folded in the breeze and the flash disappeared. As the sun dipped below the horizon, the pennant unfolded again. Rufkin saw a luminous B.

—

MAGNET AHEAD

The waves should rock a tired boy to sleep. The sleep should be filled with dreams of exploits and fun. The fun? Good times with family and friends, catching fish and telling lies about their size. Rufkin was chased to sleep by the sound of Hodie and Murgott arguing with Queen Sibilla. His sleep jumbled with dreams of trying to catch Madam Butterfly, but she slipped away like butter on a hot plate. The dreams changed to ones about loneliness.

The worst thing about the night was that it ended. He had to wake up.

The worst thing about breakfast? It was oat-bars.

The good thing was having breakfast at all. But none of the grown-ups dropped a clue about whether Madam Butterfly and Vosco still headed west.

Murgott said something with his mouth full of oat-bar.

"Swallow," said Swan. "It is scientifically proven, the voice is more easily understood if it comes from a mouth free of food."

"Excuse me," Rufkin began. "What direction…"

Murgott ignored him. "We've come a considerable distance overnight and I don't like it. Nor does Hodie."

Hodie frowned. "How did you know?"

"These days you don't like anything," said Queen Sibilla.

Hodie pointed an oat-bar at the Queen. "Fact: the engine is too old to be anywhere but a museum. Fact: we have two days' worth of toad-oil. Fact again: what happens at the end of three days? Where will we be? How far from land? Just for instance. If I may ask."

"Love," muttered Littlewink.

"And not me and you," Delilah wheezed.

Queen Sibilla's eyes went even darker than Hodie's. "Lord Hodie, if you don't like it, you may leave."

"If you didn't need my pair of shoulders along for the trip, Ma'am, I'd leave with pleasure." Hodie crunched into the oat-bar, then made a face at it.

Rufkin slid off his chair and hurried on deck.

Nissy followed. "What's up?"

He didn't want to talk to anyone. He definitely wouldn't say how afraid he was. But she looked at him so hard that words he didn't expect came rushing out. "Even if the Queen and Hodie are in love, even if it isn't the end-of-days and if there isn't a deep-dragon...all that would happen is they'd get married, have a family, and one of their kids would be useless and never fit in."

Nissy stared as if he was crazy. "What you ought to worry about is how long before they send you back to the crow's nest."

"Where's that boy?" came Murgott's voice. "There's work to do."

~

One good thing—the light was better now it was morning. Two—Rufkin had climbed the mast before, so it was easier. Three—he remembered the binoculars. Actually he didn't, Nissy reminded him. He steadied himself again in the crow's nest. The fourth good thing—this was all for Vosco with his skinny legs and puppy feet, his skinny neck.

To the north the binoculars showed bumps and blurs that must be the coast. A few small boats.

He swung east. In the never-ending crumple of the sea, sun struck the shapes of other ships, more than thirty all heading in the same direction as the *Chalice*. That seemed odd. He swung to look south, back to the east, then north again. From all over the ocean, at the same speed as the *Chalice*, ships were heading west. Dozens—even hundreds? One looked like a long riverboat. That one was a tug.

He didn't have much sense of direction. His Statement of Success in Geography made that obvious. But it seemed to him that the ships were all heading for the same place. If they were trying to reach the City of Spires, fair enough. Everyone would want to complain about all the disasters to the Council of Wisdom. But it looked as if none of the vessels were heading north-west to the City of Spires. They were—what was the word?—converging—on another point.

And there was no wind. If most of those ships had new engines or new repairs, how come they hadn't broken down? Deep currents wouldn't send them all along at such a pace.

Rufkin studied the ships a few minutes longer. There was the *Sea Honey* too, moving west at the same pace as the others.

At last he was sure. It was like an experiment he'd had

to watch because his science teacher had a grip on his ear. It had turned out to be really interesting: slivers of metal aligning themselves at the pull of a magnet. They just couldn't help it.

~

He slung the binoculars round his neck. The moment he set foot on the rat-lines a roar came up.

"Stay where you are!" Murgott, of course, and—

"Stay," rumbled Littlewink. "Stay!"

Rufkin wasn't a dog. Which one of them was in charge anyway? He kept climbing down with his ears closed.

"Let me in the wheelhouse." He swung himself the last distance onto the deck. "Let me see the map."

"The nautical term is *chart*, boy!" said Murgott.

"Murgott," the Queen said from the cabin doorway. Then she waved an arm in a beautiful curve, pointing Rufkin to the outside ladder. Before she changed her mind, he scrambled up.

In the wheelhouse, with its dull yellow walls and unpolished brass fittings, he stuck his chin out like Nissy's. He might be wrong, he might be stupid. But this might be important.

"Sir," he said. "I mean Captain. I mean sirs…" Littlewink and Swan had crammed in as well. The Queen had followed. "And Ma'am…"

"Get on with it." Murgott pointed to a handy sloping desk with narrow drawers. Clipped to the desktop was a chart of this area of Old Ocean.

Rufkin put his hands on it. "Where are we?"

The Queen bent over the chart and rested her finger between Port Feather and Battle Island. "Round about here."

With his own fingers Rufkin traced the direction of the *Sea Honey*, trying to match it up with lines he traced from north, west, and south. It didn't make sense.

"What is it?" asked the Queen in her husky way.

Rufkin explained about the hundreds of ships. "I thought they might be going to some special place. But if they meet up…" He checked again. "They might all keep going and pass each other. Or knot up in another big tangle. It's only that…I'm sure they'll cross at this place, where there's nothing."

It was just the central point of the direction circle showing North and South, East, and West.

"It's not nothing," muttered Murgott. "What do they teach you? That's the compass rose."

Littlewink's green lips turned up in a smile. "A gem of design in any chart, as if a star rested there. Or a rose, of course."

"So what's under the design?" asked Rufkin. "What's actually there?"

"Empty ocean in this case," said Murgott. "That's why the chartmaker drew it there. This boy left his brain in the crow's nest."

No. Rufkin could almost feel thoughts unfolding. "I told you I saw Madam Butterly's note. The one she sent with the pigeon to Mayor Jolliman. It said something about Rose Island."

"Never heard of any Rose Island." Murgott squinted at the waves. "Get back up the mast."

"Wait a moment." Lord Hodie had crowded in too. "Rufkin, what are you trying to say?"

"I don't know. I have to think." He stared at the compass rose, then at the spot the *Chalice* was now, and for a third time traced the paths of the other ships. "Sir, how many hours would it take to reach the middle of the rose at the pace we're going?"

"We call it knots, boy," said Murgott.

"That's nautical miles," Nissy called from the cabin. "The calculation is to do with the number of actual knots tied on a line thrown from the stern—"

"What's the girl doing in here?" growled Murgott.

"I'm actually down," Nissy said. "On the inside ladder."

"Full marks for being partly correct," said Murgott. "But thank you, shut up."

"Please!" shouted Rufkin. "Sir—Ma'am—I have to know. At this speed, how long would it take to reach where the lines cross?"

Murgott's eye, deep in the wrinkles of age and experience, twinkled a little. "It's rare to find a boy who'll stand up to me."

"None since Hodie," muttered the Queen. Then she blushed. So did Hodie. Rufkin felt himself blushing too.

Murgott bent over the chart with Hodie, the Queen, and Littlewink.

"Thirty hours," said Murgott at last.

"Thirty-two," said Littlewink.

"Give or take," added Hodie.

"Precisely," said Swan.

The Queen nodded. "Why?"

Again Rufkin described the way the ships seemed pulled by a magnet, converging somewhere at the same steady rate.

"Your point is?" asked Murgott.

"Let the boy explain," said the Queen and Lord Hodie as one.

Rufkin felt wobbly from first the praise and now the kindness. The wheelhouse walls seemed a brighter yellow. "It could be the start of another great tangle. But the *Sea Honey* didn't expect to be caught in the first one. It annoyed Madam Butterfly. I think it frightened her."

"He's right," called Nissy.

"She was frantic," said Hodie, "though her stiffened face and business experience didn't let her give that away easily."

"But whatever is pulling the ships now," said Rufkin, "I'm sure the *Sea Honey*'s not caught in it. She's heading deliberately. Or, if she is caught up, this time she expects it. Sorry—I'm not making sense. The thing is, we're not caught in it either because of the old engine. So we can sneak up. Sorry," he said again. "*Sneak* has to do. I don't know the nautical term."

Murgott's mouth twitched. "I'm fine with sneaking."

The wheelhouse walls almost glowed yellow as marigolds. Below, the railing of the deck almost glowed cherry-red. The masts had a glint of green.

The thing was—maybe the grown-ups had counted too, maybe they hadn't—thirty hours would take them into the third day.

RECIPE FOR
DISASTER

Someone touched Rufkin's shoulder. Lord Hodie. "Good job. Good thinking. I don't want the Queen to be doing this. At the same time, we have to help Vosco." He gave his startling grin. "Poor little beggar. He needs friends like you."

A complicated knot stuck in Rufkin's throat. He slid down the inside stairs and huddled in the dining cabin, not glancing at Nissy. The words in Madam Butterfly's note. As well as mentioning Rose Island, she'd written *the necessary child*. He'd thought she meant him, praised him and liked him. He'd flushed with pride and astonishment. Now he felt sick. The knot tied tighter in his throat.

From up in the wheelhouse came the bash of a fist on the chart table. "Time for some real planning," said Queen Sibilla.

Nissy sat behind the counter to listen. Rufkin couldn't let her get away with that on her own. He hid there too. Cross mutters. Argument. Planning, they called it? He supposed it covered as much as it could, when they knew so little.

The *Chalice* would travel under sail for a while to save on toad-oil. Lack of wind might become a problem. If the

THE KNOT IMPOSSIBLE

Queen rested now, she could help later if it was needed.

Her voice came down the internal stairs. "I am flaming strong enough now."

It didn't sound as if she especially believed it. Rufkin did. She'd managed the winds even while she'd been unconscious.

"I'd prefer to stay close to the Summerland coast while we can," Murgott shouted. "In case the Queen can't control the wind and the engine fails. Not so far to swim if we have to."

"You can't swim," Lord Hodie said.

"Boys," warned the Queen.

"Pessimism has sunk great nations as well as ships," declared Littlewink.

"This is no time for philosophy," said Delilah O'Lilah. "Who's tending the engine? Swan? Stars above, I must get below. Someone should have fixed the davits for that lifeboat."

An even bigger thump hit the chart table. Wood creaked in an ominous manner. Littlewink went on in a booming roar. "Too many leaders is a recipe for entanglement, failure, disaster. Who gives the orders? Who has the heart for being in charge?"

The air hummed with tension, as well as the hum of the engine.

"The Queen?" said Delilah after a moment.

"No," said Queen Sibilla. "We need someone skilled in military matters."

"Warfare is based on deception," Littlewink rumbled. "I'll take part but I cannot plan it."

"There's no question. It has to be Murgott," said Lord Hodie.

"Good," came Murgott's voice. "If you hadn't said that, I'd have thumped you."

~

The *Chalice* sailed with the Summerland coast just in sight. Rufkin had to climb the mast a third time, a fourth and fifth. The sails billowed and flapped. Ropes rang on the masts. It would have been nice to have helpful birds bring signs of comfort, such as a muffin. Better: to use the nest themselves and fly down with news.

But keeping a lookout was something to do while he felt sorry for himself.

He also felt cold. Cold was meant to be good for the brain. Could he think any better? He doubted it. But. Whatever was attracting the ships must be incredibly strong. It pulled barges and container ships; Rufkin saw three cruise ships and hundreds of small craft. Was the *Lordly Sword* somewhere among them? He shivered and forced his brain on. The shipping drawn into a tangle near Battle Island had been captured by the current, because each vessel had broken down. This time it looked like a sort of magnetic power at work as well. Was it the deep-dragon?

He shivered again. After all, Nissy had said the dragon-eagles, creatures of the air, had feathers of real silver as light as thistledown. The deep-dragon could have magnetic power of a sort never known. Lord Hodie had said—well, Nissy had reminded Rufkin on the launch—magic could just be science we don't understand yet.

Oh, his head was only good for scratching because he hadn't washed his hair when he had the chance at

Adventurers' Rest. He let the binoculars drop on their cord and stuffed his hands into his pockets for warmth. There was the hero figurine. In fact, the real Lord Hodie seemed an ordinary guy, though stronger than most. The Queen seemed completely normal too and really stubborn.

A seabird fluttered past with an *onk-onk*.

Onk, said Rufkin. Well, he had let himself in for tagging along while they tried to save Vosco. He'd be useless in any action. But at least for a while he hadn't had that dreadful hollow feeling of being alone.

—

DISGUISE
AND SNEAK

Rufkin awoke in a little cabin and lay for a moment. Though it was morning he couldn't hear anyone. He hurried to the main cabin and found it empty. The tablecloth was dabbed with gloop, so somebody must have had breakfast.

But somehow the dining room and galley looked brighter and fresher than yesterday. The bottoms of the fry-pans in the clamps sparkled and shone. Fretwork birds on a wooden beam seemed to be singing. A chirping of small seabirds, the call of gulls through the open door, the shimmer and pulse of the sea…he stretched his arms up, wishing he was the young King Jasper on his first adventure. Then he remembered. The third day.

Rufkin darted up to the wheelhouse. It was silent but crammed. Even Nissy was here. There was no coast in sight. The sails had been taken down and lay in tidy folds at the foot of the masts. Ready for sneaking.

"We've turned south-west. Look." The Queen let him use the telescope.

No wonder they were all silent. The ocean ahead had filled with ships, all heading for the meeting point.

Gradually the *Chalice*, her engine muffled, closed on the rest. Now she was just a few ship-lengths behind the last of the flotilla.

"All the other ships look more battered than the ones at the Mucclacks," said Nissy.

"If it's a magnet at work," whispered Rufkin, "there'll be a last-minute rush."

"Shut up," said Nissy.

"No shouting. No wild gesturing," said Murgott. "We'll stay astern of everyone else till we have some bearing on the *Sea Honey*. Then we'll sneak up on her. Boy, to the crows' nest."

Rufkin turned to go. "But Captain," he said. "Look."

The railing below glowed bright cherry-red. The masts gleamed green. The bird shapes in the brasswork outside the cabin seemed to move their wings to help the ship fly over the waves. The lifeboats, one each side, were as orange as fresh-picked oranges on bright orange davits.

The Queen's hair frizzed up like a halo. "Magic—magic is with us. But now people might know this is the *Chalice*."

"We stand out worse than a purple parrot in a bunch of bald ducks," said Swan.

Littlewink threw up his hands. "To put it bluntly, we're puckerooed."

"Another word from your travels to obscure and faraway lands," Delilah muttered. "Thwarted? Confounded?"

The ogre nodded. "Up the creek without a paddle."

Delilah tugged her white ponytail. "Other ships could well notice us. They'll also notice we're using an engine."

Murgott let out a growl. "The problem will be if Madam

Butterly and her thugs notice. I know thugs from a long way back. Notice, they will."

"Every problem has a solution," said Swan. "Right now…"

Silence fell again in the wheelhouse.

"The solution is tablecloths," Nissy said.

Murgott's usual expression grew darker.

She bounced on her feet. "The one we've used is messed with wet oat-bars because I tried making porridge. It's a good start."

"Could you explain a little more?" asked the Queen.

"There are dozens in the dining room," cried Nissy. "Striped, checked, edged in blue…"

"The aim is not interior decoration," Murgott began.

"No, it's disguise," said Nissy, "with dirty rags."

And it didn't take long. The Queen, Littlewink, Rufkin, and Nissy gathered the tablecloths and scuffed them over the engine-room floor. It made the floor cleaner and the tablecloths filthy.

"Don't rejoice too early," growled Murgott. "Hodie, engine as low as possible. Swan, break out the hammers."

Rufkin and Nissy helped nail the tablecloth rags on the cherry-red railings, the stern and the bow. They wrapped each mast to Swan-height. Now the ship looked like a gypsy down on her luck.

"Good job," Rufkin told Nissy. She smiled *thanks*.

It was good to see everyone look braver. Even he felt a bit better. They all wore the same glow of eagerness and determination…Oh.

Rufkin hurried up and turned the wheelhouse telescope on

the ships still a few lengths ahead. He checked on their crews.

"What's the matter?" the Queen asked at his shoulder. Hodie was right behind her.

"Captain," Rufkin said. "Ma'am. We've still got a problem."

Murgott's knuckles whitened on the wheel. "What more do you want?"

"We—maybe even me—look too heroic," Rufkin explained.

Murgott's face would curdle oat-bars. "What? Pretend we're helpless? You expect me to sniffle and cry?"

"Rufkin means we need disguises," said the Queen. "Murgott, keep your cap down over your eyes. Hodie—you don't have a cap—not a soul will know you anyway with all those curls."

"You did," Hodie said. "In the end."

The Queen pressed her lips together and looked annoyed.

"The thing is, Ma'am and sirs," Rufkin said, "it needs variety. When we start sneaking past other ships, we each need a role to play. Like the seven dwarfs in the *Dwarfly Brothers*."

"This isn't one of your father's productions," boomed Murgott. "You'd be wise to keep your background in the background."

"Hush," said the Queen. "Rufkin, go on."

His throat fluttered with nerves. "If we all look excited and daring, everyone will know we're up to something. We have to look normal. Right now that means confused and afraid…"

"I refuse to look confused," Murgott said in a dangerous voice.

But Rufkin couldn't stop. "No, everyone reacts to disaster

in their own way. They're confused and afraid underneath, but some pretend they don't care. Some go nuts. Some pretend to be coping but they're actually not."

Swan smiled. "I'm getting the point. Variable secondary reactions to the same stimuli."

Rufkin stood straighter. "We each need an attitude to act when we're on deck or visible in the wheelhouse. Captain Murgott, I admit you'd be brilliant at the Attitude-brave." He could almost feel the heat of Murgott's blush. "Your Majesty could do the Attitude-angry. With perhaps a pirate's bandana around your hair." The Queen's eyes gleamed. "Lord Hodie—the Attitude-staunch." Hodie looked slightly suspicious.

Rufkin turned to Nissy. "Could you bear trying the Attitude-tantrum?"

She rubbed her hands. "Just watch me."

"I'd like to be Desolate," suggested Swan. "I can pretend someone has ruined my life's research."

Rufkin grinned. "Do you need a rehearsal?"

Swan's teeth gleamed through his straggly beard.

It was a challenge finding a way to tell Littlewink how excellent he'd be at Uptight and Panicked. Um...

"Imagine no stars ever again," Rufkin said. "Imagine you'd never again sit on a hilltop and think about the beauty of the night."

Tears filled the ogre's eyes. Choking sounds emerged from his chest like a motor with hiccups.

Rufkin reached up and clapped him on the back. "Perfect."

Delilah O'Lilah was much easier. She was happy with the Attitude-sweaty down in the engine room, she said. If she had to come on deck, she'd try her best to do Attitude-doddery.

Rufkin gave himself the Attitude-feeble. It had the least acting to do.

~

The *Chalice* sailed up into the last of the flotilla—with luck the wash and slosh of waves would smother the hum of her engine. Slumped at the rail, Rufkin was doing what he'd always wanted, acting on his vacation. He spluttered a laugh so like tears it was perfect for Feeble.

Murgott called from the wheel. "Shipping's come to a halt ahead. It's milling around. We're a nautical mile from the middle of the rose."

Nissy darted from the cabin. Rufkin followed as Feebly as possible. She clambered up the short mast further than she usually dared.

"The *Sea Honey*! I see her!" Her smile disappeared. She adopted her Attitude-tantrum. "I hate this, I want to go home!"

Rufkin gave her a Feeble thumbs-up. Then he managed a Feeble scramble up the rat-lines to the crow's nest. He'd left the binoculars in the cabin but that didn't matter.

Bows pointing in, too many ships to count were drawing into a wide circle from all directions, somehow tied together by the unknown force. Barges, freighters, warships, fishing boats—a scruffy red tug, a beaten-up police launch. He even saw the curved top of a naval barrel-boat, the conning tower open. The captain was lying half out as if he was seasick.

Rufkin held the rim of the nest, expecting some sort of commotion from the magnetic power. When it happened, it wasn't in the way he had thought. A warship jerked sideways. A barge next to it smashed in the opposite direction. All around the wide circle, metal crunched and screamed. Sailors used poles to try to fend other vessels away and avoid being crushed. Four ships ahead of the *Chalice*, a gangway leapt into the air by itself, twisted sideways, and crashed down, binding two vessels together.

The middle of the circle, like a wave-covered lake, remained empty. If there was a magnetic force, it was an odd one. And magic—science—hadn't affected the *Chalice*. Unless of course it was magic that helped keep the *Chalice* free.

Rufkin looked again at the empty circle. The *Sea Honey* nosed into it a little but went no further.

For a moment his spirits felt truly weak. The disguise of the *Chalice*, a flutter of rags, was so flimsy. Couldn't they just wait here till it was over, whatever it was?

Of course not. He slid down to the deck as fast as he could. "Sir," he cried to Murgott. "We have to move up before we're stuck. The channels are closing."

"I'm onto it, boy. And I'll keep up my Attitude."

Murgott's old skills, learned as a pirate, still lived in his hands. Waves curled away from the sides of the *Chalice*, foamed and glistened in light and in shadow.

Rufkin drooped back at the rail. His heart kept up a steady boom like a muffled drum. *Vosco, hold on*, he breathed. *Vosco, hold on.*

—

SISTER BESIDE

The *Chalice* coasted so sneakily, it seemed only the swish of waves kept her moving. A cry came to Rufkin's ears, a lonely gull. The cry came again—his own name? He glanced to the wheelhouse—along the deck—nobody was there.

The cry came again. "Rufkin!"

The *Chalice* had edged up beside a battered yacht. At the rail was his sister in cabin-boy costume—this was the *Lordly Sword?* She stared at him in a genuine Attitude-horrified.

At once, he put a finger to his lips: *Shut up.*

She made quick gestures back in their family signals: *What the blast are you doing here?*

He felt sick, angry, betrayed: *I'm trying to be some use this summer.*

We thought you were safe, Ahria gestured. She'd started to sob.

"Rufkin, are you all right?" called Queen Sibilla's soft voice from the cabin. Ahria blinked at her over his shoulder.

"Please, Ma'am, go inside," he whispered.

The Queen did a good Attitude-angry—beat her fist on the red bandana round her forehead and flounced off.

Ahria started to point, but Rufkin drew the flat of his hand over his throat. *Stop at once. Don't draw attention.*

His sister's hand dropped. She turned her head away for a moment. Then her fingers appeared on the rail and carefully sent: *Good luck*.

The *Chalice* was passing the *Lordly Sword* more quickly now. He wanted to ask Ahria something.

Watch me. He hurried to swathe an imaginary fox-fur collar around his neck. He minced a few steps, widened his eyes—tried to widen his cheekbones as well, and gave the warmest smile his face could manage. Then he raised his own true hands in a question.

Ahria made a terrible face and stuck her finger down her throat.

Our parents think so too? he signed.

Ahria nodded and pretended to throw up in the worst possible way.

Oscar, looking drawn and worried, appeared next to Ahria. She jerked her head towards the *Chalice* and whispered in his ear. Oscar turned. The expressions crossing his face almost made Rufkin laugh.

Ahria sketched a quick bow to where the Queen had disappeared. He had a glimpse of his parents coming up on the deck, saw their shock and their fear for him. His mother reached out her hands. Oscar gave Rufkin a Salute-respectful. Then the *Lordly Sword* had fallen astern.

The *Chalice* snuck up into a narrowing channel. It was even easier now to act Feeble. They had to save Rufkin's own family as well as Vosco. And there was still no real clue what lay ahead.

—

DANGEROUS
GOODS

Slowly Murgott steered their stealthy path through the circle of ships. Some of the tablecloths ripped off their nails and blew into the sea. Nissy, pretending Tantrum as if she was born to it, hammered in the remaining rags so that they still disguised the bow. Ahead by three ships—then two—was the *Sea Honey*.

Though Rufkin felt heartsick, he whisked around with words of praise to help everyone maintain their Attitudes. He'd always done better if someone said, *Good, now how about that?* instead of *Oh for heaven's sake, you're useless, improve your game.*

Swan, as Desolate as a bird shedding feathers, handed out pistols. Lord Hodie stowed a bunch of handcuffs in pouches on his combat jacket. One set was big enough for Goodabod if they were so lucky.

Rufkin had only the dinky knife he'd stolen from the *Sea Honey*. Besides, he'd been told to stay put on the *Chalice* with Nissy. Thank goodness.

By now even from the deck he glimpsed the far side of the circle of ships. There must be hundreds of them, and thousands of people—maybe twenty or thirty thousand or even more. Another three warships, fishing trawlers with massive pulleys for hauling nets, and several ferries were stuck in the crush. A puff of smoke burst from somewhere—someone's funnel might have exploded. The pulleys on a trawler buckled and crashed on the ship next to it. The turrets of one of the warships juddered and screeched as they started to turn.

All of a sudden, explosions and shots rang out around the circle.

"It's random firing again. This is our chance," yelled Hodie. "Go! Go! Go!"

Gunshot and cannon fire filled the air. Lord Hodie (Staunch) adjusted the davits supporting a lifeboat. Littlewink (Uptight and Panicked) pretended to knock the lifeboat by accident so it dropped into the sea. Down by the stern, Delilah O'Lilah (Sweaty) dealt with Nissy (Tantrum) to draw any attention away. Murgott (Brave) stormed from the wheelhouse with the Queen (Angry). Desolate Swan took charge of the wheelhouse.

Within moments, Hodie, Littlewink, and Murgott were all down in the lifeboat.

Rufkin remained staunchly Feeble at the rail. Now it was up to them, three men, all strong ones. Against Madam Butterly and her thugs—nine, because he counted Calleena. This time he would think things through. He would absolutely not rush into trouble, especially while random war raged overhead.

He thought for at least half a second.

~

Rufkin whisked onto the rope ladder, slid easily down the side of the *Chalice* and rolled into the bow of the lifeboat. A boom from a warship...

Nissy in her flailing Tantrum put both hands over her heart and sent a thumbs-up. He signed: *Thanks, get inside where you'll be safer.*

Then Murgott had spotted him. His chest and shoulders began to expand. Like the build-up of pressure before an explosion, Lord Hodie glared. Littlewink's eyes were black with fury.

But Rufkin was ready. He signed: *Hush.* "One sentence," he said softly. "I'm the only one who knows the layout of the *Sea Honey.*"

"You're not," said Hodie. "I was on her for a week myself when I was Harry."

Oh. "But I snuck down here without you noticing," said Rufkin. "That's a plus for me."

A flash and explosion—sparks rained down, a plume of black stung Rufkin's eyes.

"You've had three sentences," said Murgott. "I'm a Special Major and captain of the *Chalice*. You're crew. No more mister smarty-pants. No more sentences at all."

The lifeboat joggled. Someone else had landed beside Rufkin.

"No argument," said Queen Sibilla, hand on the scabbard of her leather belt. "Get going while they're all distracted."

~

Amid the crash of random cannon, Littlewink's ogre-sized muscles guided the lifeboat through the inner ring of shipping. At first there was no view of the *Sea Honey*, but soon her hull was visible again between a freighter and a paddle steamer that should have been plying a river. Lord Hodie held up four fingers, then added one more for Rufkin. Rufkin wasn't sure how he felt about being counted. Murgott pointed ahead at the *Sea Honey*, held up four fingers for Madam Butterly, Calleena, Thunderhead, Goodabod, and five more for the rest of her crew. So five against nine.

Erratic cannon continued to boom. Gunfire rattled.

"Nobody knows who's enemy and who isn't," said Littlewink. "The damage Madam Butterly has caused must run into the billions."

"If she's caught, she'll have to pay for it," said the Queen. "She will be ruined."

A new sort of roar sounded ahead. On the *Sea Honey*'s top deck, a turret rose up and started to turn.

"Her swivel gun too?" said Hodie. "I thought she was protected from the magnetic whatever-it-is."

But the yacht's gun emerged smoothly from the turret and tilted up. It fired three cannon shots eastward right over the ring of ships. The turret turned in a slow quarter-circle to the north and fired three times again. Another precise quarter-turn to the south and three shots…

"She's showing everyone she has control." Murgott was tense.

"It's what you had us do in the War of the Blue Key," said Hodie. "Wait for it."

The experts were right. All the firing from the other vessels, random or otherwise, died away.

The *Sea Honey* finished quartering the water with her swivel gun. The last echoes faded. The ocean lake rose and fell as if it breathed.

A series of flags was run up her mast. With no wind it was hard to read what they said. Rufkin squinted. One was red, like an angular B. The other was a blue plus sign on white.

"The B and the X?" murmured the Queen.

They called the plus sign an X? Rufkin supposed the Queen might know.

"X—'Stop carrying out your intention and watch for my signals,'" said Murgott. "The B—'I am taking in—or discharging—or carrying dangerous goods.'"

"They're carrying Vosco," said Rufkin. "He's not dangerous, he's only four."

"Pipe down, small-change," muttered Murgott. "She's warning other vessels to keep their distance. Don't know what else they can do anyway. But at least she has the grace to give us a warning."

Madam Butterly had also shown the thousands watching that she knew more than any of them. Rufkin saw how the Queen's hand had moved close to the royal dagger. Chills ran down his spine.

"Surprise must be our friend," murmured Littlewink. "But the faintest sound might be heard."

"Light air." Murgott glanced at Rufkin. "That means no breeze but not dead calm. It's unusual for early summer."

A strange stillness fell over the waiting vessels. Mist coming off the waves chilled Rufkin again. He glanced back at the *Chalice*. For a moment he saw part of the wheelhouse window through a hazy drift. Then the mist made it difficult to see any ships properly. They were ghost ships, flickers and shadows.

"This is our chance," Hodie whispered.

A creak of oars, soft as a slow turning of a single page, and Littlewink had the dinghy against the platform at the *Sea Honey*'s stern.

Murgott took the oars. Littlewink braced a hand on a rung attached to the platform. Hodie sprang onto the ogre's shoulders and slipped a grappling iron around a higher rung. For a moment he waited and listened—in a quick twist he was up on the platform.

"Stay here," Murgott said to the Queen.

"You must be joking." She sprang after Hodie.

Murgott's teeth clenched at Rufkin. "You stay or I'll have your guts for my dental floss." He shipped the oars, then was up the rungs behind her.

Littlewink lashed the grappling-iron rope tight to the dinghy and scuttled up after Murgott.

Rufkin flexed his hands and set them on the ladder. The others had climbed the steps to the main deck. He climbed too, soft as a cat…

Ah—he'd forgotten the cat. There it was, peering down from a deck above, its fur like a puffball. The lime-green eyes turned from watching Hodie to watching Rufkin. He mimed *Hush* before he crept on.

~

THE KNOT IMPOSSIBLE

GLINTY BLACK
BUTTONS

Hodie led the way along the main deck, crouching, watching, then easing ahead. Rufkin stopped for a moment. The air felt hotter but it was probably just his nerves. Between feathers of mist the surface of the sea reflected the hull of the *Sea Honey*.

The ogre, Lord Hodie, Murgott, and the Queen were out of his sight for only a second when someone shouted. A pistol fired.

Rufkin flung himself forward, elbowed past Murgott—who was throttling the butler—on past an enemy sailor, and found a door into the cabin lounge. He leapt through and made for the door into the corridor, but Goodabod came roaring and had hold of him. Rufkin kicked the ogre's wrist—Goodabod swung him around—then Lord Hodie leapt straight for Goodabod.

Rufkin was free.

He flung himself at the door again—it had jammed shut. Thunderhead appeared from somewhere and punched at Hodie's stomach. But Hodie wheeled and knocked his own fist at Thunderhead's ear. The wall of mirrors reflected the struggle, thrashing bodies, movement—a crewman came straight for Rufkin. He dropped to the carpet and rolled. The man fell over him.

Rufkin leapt up. The Queen had an arm round Calleena's throat—where was Madam Butterly? Her fur coat hung on a hook—it hadn't been there a moment ago.

The fighting stopped. Murgott had his pistol trained on one crewman and Thunderhead. Hodie had his on two crew members and the butler. Littlewink had Goodabod in an arm lock, and the Queen—now she had Calleena and the last man of the crew in her pistol's sights.

"And the boy Robiasson as well," came Madam Butterly's voice.

The coat hadn't been on a hook at all—it was on Madam Butterly. Her smile was narrow. So were her eyes. Her face was the face of Lady Gall drawn by a bigger and slightly clumsy hand. Well, Rufkin supposed her elastic surgeon was the large-handed Goodabod.

Murgott motioned with his pistol. "Sit down."

Madam Butterly didn't seem terribly worried. All she did was show her empty hands and stayed where she was. Hodie whisked manacles from his combat jacket and began snapping them on the crew.

"Where's Vosco!" The Queen still had her pistol aimed at Calleena.

Calleena turned her eyes to Madam Butterly, who glanced at the double-faced clock. Both women stayed expressionless.

Rufkin flew to the inner door again. It still didn't budge. He tried with his shoulder, hard as he could, but only rebounded. Littlewink waited for Hodie to handcuff Goodabod, then took a giant step and thumped once on the door. It popped open.

At once Rufkin was into the innards of the yacht. He slithered on the floor, throwing each door open as he came to it. "Vosco!" Was he on this deck or the one above? "It's Rufkin! Vosco, say *help!*"

He refused to think of the deep-dragon. But how much time did they have left? Why did Madam Butterly want Vosco here, at the compass rose?

He came to a door marked engine room. His hand was on it when further along he spotted the cat at another door, a tilt to its ears. Rufkin sprang and slid the latch. "Vosco?"

There Vosco stood in the middle of a small cabin, hair so sleek it could have been paint. His face had been properly washed. So had all of him, very likely. He gave that look of his that was not a smile but meant he was interested. He patted his own chest.

"That is some shirt," said Rufkin. It was far too big for a four-year-old though not big enough for a grown-up. The buttons were glinty and black. It had a stand-up collar and gold edging. The cuffs had gold edges too. Embroidered green and blue flame reached up the sleeves. Vosco turned around to show the back. Across his sharp shoulderblades lay an embroidered dragon in green and blue.

There were many pieces still missing in this puzzle of the knots of shipping, the failure of machinery, the plague of lizards, the flooding loneliness Rufkin had felt out on the sea. But something cold clutched his insides.

~

Rufkin grabbed Vosco's hands and ran with him into the lounge. "Quick! Back to the *Chalice!*"

Queen Sibilla still had a pistol trained on Calleena. "Rufkin, keep him out of the way."

Madam Butterly, not yet manacled, glanced at Queen Sibilla with the tiniest grin. Thunderhead and Goodabod exchanged sly winks. Calleena merely smiled as Lord Hodie fixed her handcuffs. He fished in his pockets for another set.

The Queen lowered the pistol and dropped to her knees next to Vosco. "He's paler and thinner than any little boy should ever be." She hugged him, then leaned back. "Such a shirt—where did you get it?"

Vosco flashed a sour look at Madam Butterly.

Madam Butterly spoke. "We don't have much time for a welcome. But you've seen the young duke to say goodbye."

"You don't seem aware that you and your crew are under arrest," Murgott growled. "Hodie, get some cuffs on her."

"Please let me have two more minutes." Madam Butterly's elastic smile moved not another muscle on her face. "Thunderhead, you checked the speaker system?"

Thunderhead nodded.

"What's this about?" asked the Queen.

Though the air seemed suddenly hotter and more humid, Madam Butterly nestled into her coat. "The royal family believes it is the only group of people with a form of magic in touch with nature."

"It isn't," said the Queen. "Only mostly."

At last Lord Hodie took a pace towards Madam Butterly

with a pair of handcuffs. She turned to the window, the outside of its pane moist from the mist. Then she touched a magazine on a pile beside her. "At moments of crisis, it is said you talk to your brother through using a picture. Would you like to try now?"

Lord Hodie put an arm out to stop Queen Sibilla, but she picked up the magazine. On the cover was a picture of King Jasper in vacation gear in the City of Canals. The air around it quivered. Rufkin stepped closer to see. The image of the King shimmered, then instead of a check shirt and fishing hat, he wore an army tunic. The image moved; the King passed a hand over his eyes and stared straight out as if he saw—well, his sister the Queen, Rufkin supposed. Would he also see the boy just to her side? Would he see Hodie, Murgott, Madam Butterly, the *Sea Honey*'s cabin?

"It's all right, Jasper," said the Queen. "There's no need to hurry home. Madam Butterly seems to have engineered the disaster somehow. We've just caught her."

"But where are you?" asked the King. "Who's with you? Sibilla, I'm on my way. I'm in a Royal Fontanian air-car. It's one of the first we made. No repairs with zirbonium, so it's safe. We figured out that much. Quick. Tell me exactly…oh, is that Vosco? What—"

A chime came from the two-faced clock.

At the same moment a low rumble began outside. It increased to a roaring, louder and louder. Calleena let out a scream but bit it short. Madam Butterly's face was frightened too but her cheekbones had turned bright with satisfaction.

Through the window Rufkin saw a quiver in the silvery

ocean. The trembling intensified and he braced his feet. Then it stilled again, like the glass of a mirror framed by the vast loop of ships.

The *Sea Honey* rocked again, the Queen tipped sideways against Hodie, and the magazine dropped to the floor. Rufkin snatched it up. King Jasper's eyes stared directly at his.

"Who are you?" demanded the King.

"I'm Rufkin. Nobody," said Rufkin. "An ordinary boy."

Something like relief flickered in the King's face.

But out at sea, waves started to simmer hard at the circle's mid-point. Under the skin of the sea were flashes of luminous green, surges of movement. At first Rufkin thought it must be a massive sea animal, but it seemed to break up—it re-formed, broke up again with bursts of green and bright blue swirling with sediment. Waves grew wilder, bubbling as the shape expanded and grew.

Rufkin still held the magazine. It looked as if the magical image of King Jasper saw past his sister through the cabin window to the mist and sea. His expression had changed to one of shock. Rufkin glanced up to see rocks bursting through the waves. The magazine fell from his hands.

"An island," Queen Sibilla cried. "It's an island!"

Rock continued to heave out of the sea, blue and green steam fountaining from it.

"Volcano," Rufkin breathed.

"Not quite," said Lord Hodie.

"Worse," whispered the Queen.

—

ROSE ISLAND
AHEAD

Mud and gravel rained on the deck of the *Sea Honey*, steamed and fizzed amidst the thrashing of water, the rumble of rocks groaning like a huge machine. The super-yacht trembled.

Now the island began to settle in the form of a cone. The flares of green and blue lessened, but the whole place was surrounded by an unearthly glow.

A clatter or two on the deck must be a last fall of pumice. Vosco's hand gripped the side of Rufkin's pants. The Queen had grabbed the little boy's other hand. The *Sea Honey* steadied again. The roaring was just a low rumble.

But a great ogre bellow sounded behind Rufkin. Under cover of the eruption, Goodabod had burst his manacles. He yanked apart Thunderhead's cuffs and in the same movement knocked Hodie down.

Murgott wheeled around. The butler, in handcuffs, lunged into him sideways. Littlewink threw his huge self at Goodabod, and the two mighty bodies began wrestling around the cabin. The Queen dived to snatch up Hodie's pistol, but Hodie was on his feet again.

Murgott grabbed the butler and heaved him behind a

sofa. He aimed his gun at Thunderhead, but the man had grabbed the back of the Queen's belt. He snatched her pistol and threw her aside. He set his shoulders into a corner and trained both guns on her. "Drop your pistol, Murgott!"

Murgott's weapon fell to the floor. Hodie was completely still. But the ogres still tumbled and roared, kicking and gouging. Goodabod struck the final blow. "I do harm at last to save myself!"

Littlewink lay and looked at the cabin ceiling, maybe seeing stars.

Thunderhead jerked one of the pistols at Rufkin. "Get the keys. Release the butler. Then get out of the way."

Rufkin hesitated. Thunderhead aimed his pistol at the floor near Rufkin's feet, and fired.

Murgott spoke in a hoarse voice. "Just do it, boy."

The butler struggled out from behind the sofa while Rufkin fished in Hodie's combat jacket for the keys. As soon as he was freed, the butler released Calleena and the rest of the crew. In one more minute the cuffs were on Queen Sibilla, Murgott, and Hodie. Goodabod and the crew put all the spare sets on Littlewink, who was sitting up now.

Rufkin—well, he just crouched with Vosco.

By now the tip of the island had formed a glowing blue pit. Blue-black with licks of green flowed out like lava.

Madam Butterly was pale. Even the ogres had turned a light blue. She took a step—she was tottery. She took another step to the door of the bow deck.

"Don't open it!" Lord Hodie cried. "The air will be poisonous."

"You think it's a real volcano?" Calleena tried to laugh. Rufkin thought it more of a frightened gulp.

Thunderhead ordered two crew to the engine room, one to the bridge. The others stayed, weapons ready. After a moment Thunderhead pressed a button by the door and spoke into an intercom. "Slow ahead."

The engine started again, and the *Sea Honey* made for the new island. Madam Butterfly kept a hand on the door. The ships in the circle—all they could do was watch and wait, Rufkin supposed. Particles of shiny ash made it hard to focus, but the surface of the sea was unruffled now.

The *Sea Honey* reached the new shore. Her bow eased into the shingle and the stones rose around to cradle her. In one stride even Rufkin could be standing on the new land itself.

At last Madam Butterfly slid the door wide.

An eerie call cut through the air. Rufkin could almost see the sound caress the side of the island. He shook his head to clear his eyes, his ears. The call held huge loneliness but something more—a sort of triumph. As the cry echoed, the sides of the pit drew open.

There lay a cavern where blue and green flickered and sparked. Deep in the fire, something started to shoulder into the ash of day.

—

ROYAL BLOOD

It was bigger by far than the shape Rufkin had seen in the ocean—that was a sprat compared to what emerged from the cavern. No King Jasper or dragon-eagle could battle a creature so massive. He could hardly tell it apart from the rocks themselves—it seemed to meld into them. Its head, only half-seen, had something that looked like a crown glowing a strange fiery green. What might be a tail seemed to have spines of green-black. This was the deep-dragon.

Again the call came. Queen Sibilla let out a slow sigh. Rufkin stole a moment to look at her. Her eyes brimmed but her chin was high. The bandana was gone and her hair was spectacular crinkles. Even in handcuffs she had leaned as far towards Vosco as she could. And Lord Hodie stood close to her.

Rufkin looked back towards the cavern.

Madam Butterly was trembling so much she had to hold the side of the door. She beckoned Calleena.

With shaky hands, Calleena straightened Vosco's shirt. She led him near Madam Butterly.

"No," cried Queen Sibilla. "What are you doing…" Her voice choked up.

Madam Butterly didn't turn.

None of the grown-ups looked able to speak, not even Murgott—not even Lord Hodie.

It was up to Rufkin? "Stop!" he tried to cry, but his voice too was a useless husk.

Madam Butterly folded her hands into the sleeves of her fur coat and glanced back at last. "It is a deal. When it comes to business, one must keep one's word."

"What deal?" said Lord Hodie.

"Mistakes can be made." Madam Butterly moistened her lips before she continued. "Then one does one's best to put them right. We can't afford another mistake. You'll soon be released. And you will thank me. All Fontania will thank me. Keep quiet. Wait."

For a moment the shape of the deep-dragon melded back into the rock.

"The deep-dragon..." Madam Butterly's voice stumbled. "I didn't believe an old story about the reason magic resides in Fontania." She gave a short laugh. "If *reason* is a word that can apply to magic."

Vosco shrugged away from Calleena and flopped on the floor. Only Rufkin seemed to notice him shove a hand under a chair. He dragged out the trumpet and stuck his hand back. For a moment there was a tickling game, Vosco's fingers with the nose and whiskers of cat. Then the cat pushed out something purple with its front paws and they had a tussle game with the cat's claws hooked into the pom-pom.

Madam Butterly looked up the island at the vast shape only half-visible. "I broke through the lowest part of the mine and found a network of caverns—lazulite in brightest blue, great sculptures of crystal as if they'd been formed by an expert hand. Such riches—but there was a price. The deep-dragon lived there—it gave me three years. Three exact years." She glanced at the clock with two faces. "I had to work fast. This was for everyone's benefit."

Murgott growled with disgust. "That's what Lady Gall said when she took charge of Fontania thirty years ago. Everyone's benefit? Her own greed and wickedness."

Madam Butterly's vain smile could have shattered glass. "A leader as commanding as Lady Gall deserved a disciple who surpassed her and reached new heights. A disciple who found she could control the greatest power in all of nature. You see her now." She moved to smile across the lounge into the carved frame. VIDA BUTTERLY. FOREVER VICTORIOUS. "Wealth is beautiful. Wealth rules. Wealth is Queen and King and Parliament," said Madam Butterly.

The hilt of the dagger showed at Queen Sibilla's waist. The royal dagger. Her hands had been tied in front of her—she could reach it. Wouldn't she use it at last? Surely she would be justified.

Her eyes burned with anger. "But why take Vosco?"

For a moment Madam Butterly looked the slightest bit sorry. "The deep-dragon's youngling escaped through the mine. I promised a child in return if the youngling wasn't found within the three years. Now, it has come down to one child in exchange for the safety of all of us. Or it truly is the end-of-days."

"No," Rufkin tried to whisper but there was only silence.

"His family. His parents," breathed Queen Sibilla.

"That's why at first I wanted an orphan," said Madam Butterly. "But his parents are busy with important issues and they have six other children. They won't miss this last one." She looked eager again. "And he's of royal blood. That raises the stakes."

Calleena spoke again, her voice hard. "It is only one child. One little boy just doesn't matter."

Madam Butterly wanted a child nobody cared about. But that was the thing, Rufkin understood at last—every child was a necessary child.

~

The deep-dragon took shape again, dark green, darkest gray, and midnight indigo. The eerie call sounded a third time.

"Enough," said Madam Butterly. "Now the little boy goes up the island on his own."

A four-year-old. All by himself. "No," gasped Rufkin.

"Thunderhead, follow my orders," said Madam Butterly. "Thirty thousand people are watching. They don't know what they're waiting for yet. They're about to see." She held out a hand.

Thunderhead passed her some sort of device.

"The speaker system," muttered Lord Hodie.

"Vosco, stop playing," said Madam Butterly. "Come out here. I'm getting angry."

Vosco shot her one of his dark looks. He stood up, slung the trumpet over his shoulder and pulled on the beanie.

There was no question what Rufkin must do. He squared his shoulders, glanced at Murgott, and gave the merest salute.

Murgott looked as sick as Rufkin felt. But he muttered. "Boy, an ounce of luck can do more than a ton of experience."

Rufkin took a step and began reaching for Vosco's hand.

"Rufkin, wait," whispered the Queen. "Don't look, but ease back to me."

In a couple of seconds he sensed the Queen right behind him.

"You've really chosen to go with him?" she murmured.

His shoulders stayed straight. He nodded.

"Then take this." She slid something into his belt at the side. A shock went through him. The royal dagger.

"I can't," he whispered. "I'm way too ordinary. It's not allowed."

Her breath moved his hair. "Many kings and queens have been far less than you."

"Thunderhead," snapped Madam Butterly. "Get the child out here."

Captain Thunderhead wrenched Vosco up by one arm and slung him down on the bow deck.

Rufkin strode through the door and stood beside him.

—

THE YOUNGLING

The deep-dragon gave its call yet again. It was the most beautiful sound Rufkin had ever heard. He was going to die, he was pretty much sure of it. His soul hurt because he would not have years more in which to remember such music, born as it was from underground and undersea.

Blue and dark green flared in the cavern. The creature seemed to lower its head.

Glints and flashes from the vast ring of ships caught Rufkin's eye. All those people watching through telescopes and binoculars, and none could help.

~ Where is the youngling? ~ said a voice as strong as a furnace, so strong it rippled the water of the mirror-lake.

Madam Butterly stayed on the deck and raised the speaker-device. "Greetings," she cried. The words floated over the water in every direction. "Greetings," she repeated, "to my audience in ships from all over Fontania. You fear that we are living in the end-of-days. You fear the breakdown in nature and machinery. But you are witnessing my great accomplishment. I have brought you the greatest creature, the wonder of underground and undersea. Watch and listen."

Now she turned, raised her hand and pointed to the top of the island. "Welcome, deep-dragon. I have for you what I promised. The child is here."

~ Show me ~ the voice called down the island.

"I've kept my side of the deal," Madam Butterfly said into the speaker. "You lost your own youngling, I've brought you another. But this is a royal child. He has the potential for magic."

~ I have magic already ~ said the deep-dragon.

"That is true." Madam Butterfly lifted her chin. "Still, a royal child is more than you asked for, and so I want more for him. A new deal. None could be better for you or for me. In return for my bringing you the royal child, I want ten years' control of the mines of underground and undersea."

Rufkin felt Vosco's hand slip into his.

~ Set the youngling on the shore ~ said the voice from the blue-green furnace.

Madam Butterfly bent down to Vosco.

"Don't you touch him!" Rufkin let Vosco go for a moment, and stepped from the bow of the yacht onto the cradle of stones.

He stretched up his arms and Vosco jumped. *Ouch*— the darn trumpet gave Rufkin a knock. Then he put Vosco down.

Hand in hand, they set off.

~

It looked like a long trek to the top. One step at a time, that's how they'd manage. Gravel and blue-tinged pumice crunched under their feet. It didn't feel hot, just smelled rather ashy. The stuff like lava had stopped flowing.

Rufkin hardly dared glance ahead. He smiled at Vosco. The knitted beanie was pretty funny.

"You look like an acorn," he said.

"Nut," said Vosco.

They crunched some more steps.

"Trumpet." Vosco held it up.

"True," said Rufkin.

"Cat," said Vosco.

What? Rufkin looked back. The cat, slinking after them, stopped and looked the other way. "Yes, you spotted it."

"Rufkin," said Vosco. "Big."

"Bigger than you. Why didn't you talk more before?" Rufkin asked.

Vosco stared as if it should have been obvious. "Becoss," he said.

—

BECOSS

The deep-dragon wasn't as scary once they were close to it. Rufkin knew that was only because he'd had all those steps one after the other to get used to it. He still couldn't tell where the deep-dragon began and the rocks ended. His nerves thrummed.

~ Two younglings ~ said the deep-dragon.

Rufkin didn't see its mouth move. Maybe the voice simply rang in his head. "The little one needed company. Hope that's all right."

Part of the rock seemed to loom closer. ~ Why did you choose to come? ~

Rufkin didn't know how to put it into words.

"Becoss," said Vosco.

Words wanted to rush from Rufkin now. "Yes, because he's not a great one for talking himself. Because it didn't seem right that someone just chose him, someone not even his parent. Because Vosco doesn't have any idea what this is about. Madam Butterfly's a user."

The deep-dragon's head came almost into view as it swayed in front of him. That crown was its scales, holding in what looked like molten green metal.

"You don't understand," said Rufkin. "May I explain?" After all he'd nearly made it into the debating team. He took in a breath but coughed. "Sorry, that was the ash."

~ Pardoned ~ said the deep-dragon, or the voice, however it worked.

So Rufkin did his best to make clear that just because somebody—or something—had lost its own youngling, it didn't mean it could grab somebody else's. "And I don't mean you, necessarily," he said. "I mean, Madam Butterly has no right to do this."

The rocks shifted as if the deep-dragon still hadn't understood. Rufkin held up his hands like little plates. Vosco copied as he'd done way back on the riverboat. "And if she'd done proper research she would have known she had no right to get into your crystal caverns either, if they belong to you."

The deep-dragon seemed even more puzzled. ~ Belong? ~

"And also," said Rufkin, "what about sharing?"

The deep-dragon made a sound as if the inside of its head was tied in a knot by now.

"Let's start again." Rufkin tested the rocks with his hand—just warm from the sun—and sat on the lip of the cave. Vosco sat with him, and the cat slunk up.

~ What is that? ~ the deep-dragon asked.

"It's a cat. This one's a pet," said Rufkin. "Do you know what a pet is? It's—um—it's not like a child or youngling but it keeps you company. You have to look after it. But usually and actually you have to look after a child far better."

"Becoss." Vosco tipped a handful of pumice into the trumpet and out again.

~ The child brought a toy ~ said the deep-dragon after a moment. ~ What did you bring? ~

Rufkin fished in his pocket. His wrist brushed against the royal dagger that the Queen had given him. He brought out the hero figurine. "It's a toy but it's of a real guy." He pointed to the *Sea Honey*. "He's there. He's a great hero."

~ But you are the one who came up the hill ~ said the deep-dragon.

"True," said Vosco.

"Oh, no, I've explained that," said Rufkin. He brought out the tiny knife too and laid it down with the figurine.

Vosco picked up the knife, fiddled with the safety sleeve and scratched HELP on a stone.

"That's playing," said Rufkin. "It shows he's learning." He flipped up the safely sleeve and put the knife back in his pocket in case Vosco cut himself.

Vosco tapped the dagger in Rufkin's belt.

Rufkin was pretty certain now that he wasn't meant to fight the deep-dragon with it. He drew it out. "And the Queen let me bring this." He held it up on palms that tingled.

The deep-dragon let out a long breath. Rufkin raised the dagger higher. The nearer it was to the deep-dragon's scales, the more the shade of its metal darkened to darkest green.

"It's the sign of the monarch," Rufkin said in a shaky voice. "It shows the dragon-eagles who can be trusted."

~ A sign of a fair heart ~ said the deep-dragon. ~ Fair means beautiful and fair means honest. A sign of friendship. I know, for I made it myself long ago ~

"It's from one of your scales, isn't it?" Now Rufkin's hands really trembled. "The stories say, 'The greatest monarch has affinity with the greatest creature.' Affinity means fellow-feeling." And he, an everyday boy, was holding the sign.

Beside him the creature seemed a vast shadow of sadness. But Rufkin felt somehow that it trusted him now.

"Excuse me," he began again. "I know Madam Butterly opened the cavern. But what actually happened to your youngling?"

The deep-dragon made a rippling movement. Rufkin thought it might be the way it shrugged.

"It simply disappeared?" he asked. "Got out through the mine and didn't come back?"

The rippling movement happened again like shadows inside the rocks.

"Well…" Rufkin frowned. He was aware the deep-dragon watched closely. "Maybe your youngling got lost and can't find its way home. Maybe it was old enough to leave but you hadn't noticed. Maybe…it needed more attention. Or it wanted a friend. Maybe there was only a misunderstanding between you that can be forgiven. Have you thought of all that? Like—did you get over-occupied with something?"

The vast sense of loneliness spilled over him. It was hard to think under such sorrow. But the deep-dragon's eyes darkened. In the crown of metal scales, the molten green flared.

"None of it might be your fault," Rufkin hurried to say. "And in the end it doesn't matter, it's just important to find your youngling, if that's still possible. Like, it's important to get Vosco back to his parents if that's possible. So Lady Polly and Lord Trump can do better with him."

~ What did they do wrong? ~ the deep-dragon asked.

"Nothing, apparently," said Rufkin. "It's the 'nothing' that was the problem. They were too busy to talk to him, play with him, that sort of thing."

The deep-dragon gave a rumble, like people do when they finally get an idea. That infinite loneliness Rufkin had felt out in the ocean was like the sadness he sensed now, many times greater, in the deep-dragon.

"You haven't been out of your caverns for years, right? Hundreds? Thousands? More years than you could count?"

~ I can count past infinity ~ The deep-dragon's eyes looked amused for a moment. However, it nodded.

"For what it's worth, and it's just my feeling, your youngling is out there somewhere. Queen Sibilla felt something too. She can talk to the dragon-eagles, so I reckon she'd know."

The shape of the deep-dragon reared up as if it stared at the ocean, the circle of ships with its thousands of people, the gleams of telescopes trained on the island.

With a sigh like stone sliding, the shape dropped back. ~ Dragon-eagles. Yes. An old one and a young one ~

A shout from the speaker-device came up the slope from the *Sea Honey*. "Let us continue!" Madam Butterly took a tentative pace from the yacht onto the shingle. "You have had time to inspect the child. Both of them. That is, if you wish perhaps to keep the older one too."

She turned and beckoned. Thunderhead, Goodabod, and the crew led their prisoners onto the deck.

Madam Butterly looked back up the island and used the speaker again. "Let us close the new deal."

The deep-dragon, half-visible, lowered its head to peer at faraway Madam Butterly.

"You agree that I've brought more than you asked for," she called.

The deep-dragon gave a slow nod.

"And in exchange I have ten more years of the use of underground and undersea." She raised her arms like a queen in triumph.

The deep-dragon's voice shook the pit of Rufkin's stomach. ~ Our first deal is ended. I understand now you had no right to make it at all ~

"But it was made and it was kept," cried Madam Butterly. "It was more than kept, it was increased. Now—"

~ Be silent ~ This time the island quaked with the depth of its voice. The mirror-lake rippled. On all the ships Rufkin could see, people crowded the rails.

The great shape seemed to examine the group on the bow of the *Sea Honey*.

~ Why are some of them in chains? ~ it asked Rufkin in almost a whisper.

"Short story," he said, "they were trying to stop her. I'm actually one of them. So is Vosco."

The deep-dragon seemed to shoot just a glance at the *Sea Honey*, but there was a burst of green. The manacles fell from the wrists of the Queen, Hodie, Murgott, and Littlewink.

~ There will be no second deal ~ said the voice, roaring like flames ~ And you will pay for any damage you have caused because of the first one. You will pay for any unhappiness ~

Madam Butterly lifted an arm again. "I have worked for the good of everyone. It is my victory."

~ You are responsible for using precious lazulite in a way that has caused distress and misery ~ said the voice strong as fire.

"I had no time to—" began Madam Butterly.

~ You are responsible for the natural world losing its balance ~ continued the voice. ~ More distress and misery ~

She tried to protest again. "I had no idea…"

~ Third and last… ~ The deep-dragon's voice made the ocean lake quiver. By now Rufkin could tell that everyone was listening harder than ever, all thirty-odd thousand. ~ Third and last. You are responsible for losing a youngling and stealing another. Victory? I say it is villainy! ~

A scattered shouting began in the circle of ships. It grew to a rage, an enormous booing from thousands of throats, all jeering at Madam Butterly.

For a beat or two her arm stayed up. Then she lowered it, slowly, in little jerks. She understood at last. In front of the world she had been beaten.

There she stood, in her fox-fur coat. The richest woman? All those witnesses behind the telescopes and binoculars knew she had caused the end-of-days for her own selfish reasons. What was more, she'd tried to bargain using a child. She'd have to pay for it all.

There was nothing she could do. She hunched into her coat in the Attitude-insignificant, Attitude-crushed, more worthless and hopeless than the most hopeless beggar Rufkin had ever seen.

"I reckon she is completely puckerooed," he said, using Littlewink's wonderful word.

The deep-dragon blinked at the circle of ships. ~ So many of them ~

"Madam Butterly knew everyone would have to watch," said Rufkin. "I think it's your magnetic power, or whatever you call it."

~ I can do something about that if it's troublesome ~ There was a sort of change in the air.

A few engines choked into life. But most of them cut off again, apart from three naval launches, heading for the *Sea Honey* from different directions. Good. The Royal Navy of Fontania was on the job.

The Queen started to jump off the yacht, but Hodie took her hand and seemed to warn her. Poor guy—he was still so worried.

Murgott stepped down, though. He glanced up at the deep-dragon and gave a small bow just a little bit trembly. Then he strode to Madam Butterly and snapped handcuffs on her. She knelt, huddled in her fox-fur collar.

Queen Sibilla and Hodie moved onto the stony shore together. Lord Hodie started up the island, but now the Queen held him back. Rufkin saw her touch his shoulder in a reassuring way.

Rufkin waved to let them know that Vosco was okay and Hodie could just stay and help the navy when it arrived.

Hodie and Murgott both gave Rufkin a little salute. But they were standing in Attitude-jittery.

—

AND SO...

The deep-dragon must have thought Hodie and Murgott looked decent sorts. It called to them gently ~ Let me take a little more time to understand this pair of younglings ~

But Vosco bounced his stone saying HELP down the island and waved the trumpet at Queen Sibilla. She took a step up the slope by herself. The men looked even more nervous.

"That's the Queen," said Rufkin.

The deep-dragon watched her come further. Halfway, she stopped.

~ She let you carry the sign ~ murmured the deep-dragon. ~ Hold it high and let me see ~

Rufkin held the royal dagger up in his right hand. The Queen bowed to the deep-dragon. The shape in the rocks seemed to bow back. She raised her hands in a gesture of true and warm welcome.

There was a kind of long moment where Rufkin didn't really see what happened. Then the dagger was gone from his hand. The Queen had it, holding it high. It glowed like a flame of blue and silver, and she shone in its light.

The great shape in the rocks seemed to nod. Vosco raised the trumpet and blew a rumptipaze.

The cat shrank down with its ears back. The deep-dragon winced too, but once again it seemed amused.

"Sorry," said Vosco. He stroked the cat, then put a hand up to stroke the stones that might be the deep-dragon. He could pretty much reach a possible ankle.

The necessary child. A magical boy. That was Vosco, wasn't it? Of course it was, just look how unafraid he was. It didn't feel right to be proud of someone else's kid, but Rufkin felt proud anyway.

The stones rippled again as if the deep-dragon was shaking its ears. ~ Does that thing make a more enjoyable sound? ~

"Even I can do better with a trumpet than Vosco," Rufkin said. "And I'm wishing I hadn't said that."

But the deep-dragon's eye dark as a window at night seemed to turn to him.

Vosco passed Rufkin the trumpet. He put it to his lips and rippled some phrases of a nursery rhyme—"The Egg on the Wall." "For instance," he said.

The huge head swayed down and examined the trumpet more closely. Its breath smelled like vast amounts of charred toast. The cat licked its paws.

"Your own music is wonderful," Rufkin dared say. "I heard you before. Do you know anything...well, happier?"

For a moment the deep-dragon's eye flashed the green of sorrow. The crown on its head turned a green so deep it was close to black. Rufkin flinched.

But he remembered the story of the silver-feathered dragon-eagle imprisoned for years while it healed after the

Great Accident. Its crown of glowing green contained the weight of its sadness and pain. The King, who thought then that he wasn't the King, had bowed to the dragon-eagle. When it had to bow back, its burden of anger and grief began trickling away.

So Rufkin just had to start. He glanced down the slope at the Queen and saw her smile. He raised the trumpet again.

It wasn't like performing to an audience. The circle of ships, the Queen and Lord Hodie, Madam Butterly and her thugs, even his parents and Oscar and Ahria were watching, listening. But all Rufkin was trying to do was console a sorrowing creature as huge as a castle, and keep a clever but lonely four-year-old content till he could be on his way back to people who loved him.

The music began softly. He wasn't sure where it came from—somewhere in his memory. Then from sadness it changed into hope. It became a march, and then after a few more bars Rufkin made it a dance-tune. The deep-dragon's voice joined in by the third verse. Vosco beat his hands in time and sang all the words he knew, which turned out to be hundreds. The cat put its ears flat back but kept sitting there.

Then somehow, probably because of magic, the tune of hope and happiness turned into pure joy. Because above the new-formed island great wings beat in the air. The dragon-eagles, feathers of silver light as thistledown, were circling, dipping their wings to the royal dagger and Queen Sibilla.

The shape in the stones lifted its head and called to them. For the first time in thousands of years, the deep-dragon was meeting its ancient friends. And they landed beside Rufkin and added their song.

By now, banners had been broken out on many ships. Rufkin saw what must be tablecloths flapping as Nissy and the others danced and waved on the deck of the *Chalice*. All around the sea-lake there were drums and guitars and harmonicas, and more trumpets, and piccolos and flutes, and glorious voices, in tune or out of it. He bet even the Mucclacks, if they could be here, would be roaring full-throated.

Rufkin didn't want to stop playing, but kicked up his knees to show his family he was fine, more than fine. Oscar and Ahria would be singing and playing too, he was sure of it. So would his parents. Vosco kicked about too in his own stamping shuffle.

Then Rufkin took the music up a scale to try his best to meet the promise he felt in the world. And beyond the great ring of ships he saw a shadow. For a while it circled out there, half-seen but drawing closer. Then it vanished, but just for a moment. In the mirror lake, a shimmer appeared. And the deep-dragon's voice lifted with heart-bursting happiness. There was an eddy, a swirl, a surge. The pattern showed that something that used to be lost, alone, and afraid was playful again.

Here was the youngling, arrowing home.

∗ CURTAIN ∗

Brilliant Academy
⇀ City of Spires ↽

Rufkin Robiasson, school project, Year Nine

Write a document for publication. This will be 30% of your final mark for research and communication.

A LORD HODIE FANZINE

Lord Hodie, Personal Details

Age	23
Height	6 foot 3 inches
Weight	pretty heavy but most of it's muscle. Bones as well of course.
Shoe size	looks like a 12 maybe 13 Fontanian, the number was a bit rubbed off
Hair	straight brown
Eyes	straight brown

Don't be too smart, Rufkin, and be far more precise.

Are you trying to be smart again, Rufkin?

Training and Education

Grounds of Grand Palace
On-the-job with <u>Corpral</u> Murgott
Military Academy, City of Spires.
Graduated top of his class.

Rufkin, you must watch your spelling

Present Job

Rufkin, there is an official term for the position. Find it and use it.

Protector of Queen Sibilla and various royal children depending on who needs the babysitting.

Preferred Weapon

Pistol, sword, rifle. Actually he likes driving military vehicles best.

Main Adventures and Exploits

Trip to Um'Binnia
The Pastry Riot on Battle Island
The _mustery_ about the cats of Much Glass
The Battle of Eagle Hall
The search of Lake Riversea with Metalboy II
The Ghosts of the Isle of Bones
Coping with Special Major Murgott   *Do not be smart*
A few more

repeat — watch your spelling AND proofreading

Rufkin, this is not adequate research

Further Ambitions

To win a barrel-boat race

Most Desired Food

Um'Binnian Cabbage Cream (he says it grows on you)
Herbed Spotty Plumpoe (but any fish will be okay)
Anything cooked by Lady Polly
Murgott's apple pie

Famous Sayings

"Maybe magic is simply science that is still to be explained."
"It's more important to have a packed lunch than a fresh pair of socks."

The question most people want ask about Lord Hodie

Will he ever marry Queen Sibilla?

Lord Hodie's answer

I'd never daire ask him.

Fair enough. Nor would I.
Do watch your spelling.

A little-known fact about Lord Hodie

He has never learnt to ride a bicycle.
Another one: he is USELESS at playing the trumpet.

Would you like the opportunity to present your project at the grand school assembly?

Yes ☑   No ☐

YES! I CAN INTRODUCE IT BY
PLAYING THE TRUMPET.

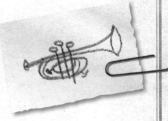

ACKNOWLEDGEMENTS

When I started the first Tale of Fontania I had no idea I'd spend the next five and a half years writing about magic, heroic children, wise and foolish grown-ups, and plenty of villains. It has been great fun working on the quartet. But I have many people to thank for their help.

First, very special thanks to Gecko Press for their determination to make each Gecko book a "curiously good" one, and for choosing the very best people for the publishing process. That starts with Julia Marshall herself and Jane Arthur and includes Rachel Lawson, who is a paragon of editors.

Thanks to Sam Broad for the amazing artwork, the detail in the covers and interior, and especially the quirky maps. And thanks to Luke Kelly for his brilliance with design.

I have been so lucky to have Jane Parkin edit each one of the Tales. It is a pleasure to work with a Queen of Editors who cares about the characters and even asks me to write just a bit more about, for example, the Ocean Toads.

I've been blessed with the readers who looked at drafts of the novels and gave useful comments and encouragement. Barbara Murison has long been called a national treasure. Her knowledge of children's writing has helped enormously.

Emma Neale's ear for a phrase and skill with words has helped too. If she scribbled a wise academic remark in the margin as well as a *ha! ha! ha!* I knew I had hit the right note.

Abe Baillie's feedback on a draft of *The Volume of Possible Endings* was very encouraging. And I thank him very much indeed for the word *rumptipaze*, which became important in *The Knot Impossible*.

I also thank Olive Easton Neale, early inspiration for the character of baby Sibilla in the first Tale.

Nor can I leave out Zac Baillie, who was so much Help. Help! Help! with the character of Vosco, that remarkable four-year-old.

Thank you, Lesley Graham and Jane Arthur, for so much help and fun working on the music for "The Anarchists' Marching Song" in *The Volume of Possible Endings*. (Yah-ha! to any rules!)

Joan Druett's tips about sea-faring matters were inspiring and practical. And I'm very grateful to other friends and family who have been patient and encouraging during my long exploration of the land of Fontania.

I have a huge tribute to give Creative New Zealand for a generous writing grant that made it possible for me to write the third and fourth Tales in record time. I am indebted to their belief in the importance of writing for children that encourages the development of imagination.

I'd hoped that when I reached the end of this list I would have found the best words to thank Chris Else. He read many drafts of each Tale. He was always encouraging, but also tough—exactly what I needed and wanted. He rejoiced with me when the novels won prizes, and listened to my grizzles when the writing was difficult. I am still searching for the glittering words to thank him properly.

To every one of these kind, generous, wise, and clever people, I give a heartfelt Salute-respectful.

Barbara Else

THE TRAVELLING RESTAURANT

★ New Zealand IBBY Honour Award for Writing 2012

★ White Raven Award 2012

★ NZ Post Children's Book Awards 2012, Honour Award

★ LIANZA Children's Book Awards 2012, Junior Fiction Award

★ Storylines Notable Book 2012

A heaping plateful of adventure, spiced to perfection with dangers, deft humor and silly bits. —Starred review, *Kirkus Reviews* (US)

This is one of the most enchanting books that I've read for a long time…It's got everything you've ever wanted from a fantastical children's tale; very well written, funny, and at the heart of it is this beautiful relationship…I can't recommend it more highly. Fantastic. —*Kate De Goldi* (author)

Constant action, lively language, and a Mahy-esque sense of whimsy carry the narrative as the mysteries unfold. —*Horn Book Review* (US)

I love the quirkiness of the storytelling…I also loved the music, the food, the wit, the warmth, well, all of it really…This is a very special book. —*Story Time Books for Kids* (NZ)

A rich tapestry of a tale, wonderfully inventive, full of flawed but likeable characters with a plot that gets you by the throat. —*Readings* (Australia)

THE QUEEN AND THE NOBODY BOY

★ NZ Post Children's Book Awards 2013, Honour Award

★ LIANZA Children's Book Awards 2013, finalist

★ Storylines Notable Book 2013

Hope, fear, friendship, loyalty, humour and imagination all packaged between stunning covers make a recipe for an excellent read. —*Bookrapt* (NZ)

It's as good as the first book if not better...this is a classic fantasy adventure story. —*Kate de Goldi* (author)

It's an exciting, funny and original fantasy that is grounded in everyday life....*The Queen and the Nobody Boy* is destined to be a classic. —*Judges Report, New Zealand Post Children's Book Awards 2013*

This is a quirky, zany and thoroughly entertaining read that should appeal to lovers of magic, fantasy and adventure. —*Kids Book Review* (Australia)

THE VOLUME OF POSSIBLE ENDINGS

★ LIANZA Children's Book Awards 2015, finalist
★ Storylines Notable Book 2015

Another magical mystery from the land of Fontania. This enthralling tale can be read as a stand-alone novel or as part of the award-winning Fontania series. All three books in the series will appeal to pre-teens who enjoy well-written stories with a touch of magic, humour, and plenty of action. —*Bookrapt* (NZ)

Else contrives a plot that leaves neither characters nor readers much chance to catch their breaths. Many chases and narrow squeaks later (highlighted by a nerve-wracking ride in a small homemade submarine...with a bear), a tumultuous face-off brings just deserts...An entertaining romp, more comical than scary and with a poignant but hopeful close. —*Kirkus Reviews* (US)

It is an excellent tale of magic, adventure, invention, humour and silliness...The crazy motorbike riding anarchists are a highlight but the true strength of the novel is the snappy, witty dialogue between the characters. —*Your Weekend* (NZ)

The detail is magnificent. The sentences marvellous. The characters magical. The story mesmerising...This book comes with a tiptop recommendation from me and is one of my favourite reads of the year. —*Poetry Box* (NZ)

It's exciting and fun and full of action, with a wonderful feisty heroine. —*Create a Kids Book* (Australia)